WARBLER COTTAGE ROMANCES

Meet the endearing Van Herewaarden family in this compelling romance series set in the Netherlands from the 1930s to the 1960s. Bask in the warm, nurturing love and be inspired by the deep-rooted faith that permeates their home, the Warbler Cottage, and unites them together through times of sorrow and joy, tragedy and triumph.

Follow the continuing saga of the Van Herewaarden family in the next two volumes of the Warbler Cottage Romances.

A Longing Fulfilled follows sixteen years after *The Discerning Heart*. Inge's childhood friend, Bram Dubois, loves her and wants to marry her. But she's afraid to follow Bram into the jungles of Suriname where he is called to serve as a missionary doctor. Can Inge's love for God — and for Bram — overcome her fears of the unknown?

A Gleam of Dawn takes place twelve years later and focuses on Inge's half-brother Harro as he pursues the lovely, enigmatic Judith. Although he wins her love, she harbors a painful secret that threatens to destroy their marriage.

THE WARBLER COTTAGE series, with its vivid, memorable characters and intriguing locales, offers an unforgettable reading experience.

By Jos van Manen Pieters:

Warbler Cottage Romances

THE DISCERNING HEART

Jos van Manen Pieters

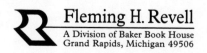

Fleming H. Revell
A Division of Baker Book House
Grand Rapids, Michigan 49506

The Warbler Cottage trilogy was originally published in the Dutch language as *Tuinfluiter Trilogie*. This volume appeared under the name *En de Tuinfluiter Zingt*. Original editions Copyright © 1967 Uitgeversmij J. H. Kok B. V. Kampen, The Netherlands.

Translation into English by J. W. Medendorp.

Library of Congress Cataloging-in-Publication Data

Manen-Pieters, Jos van.
    [En de tuinfluiter zingt. English]
    The discerning heart / Jos van Manen Pieters : [translation into English by J.W. Medendorp].
        p. cm.
    Translation of: En de tuinfluiter zingt.
    "The Warbler Cottage trilogy was originally published in the Dutch language as Tuinfluiter trilogie"—T.p. verso.
    ISBN 0-8007-5435-2
    I. Title.
PT5881.23.A5T813   1992
839.3'1364—dc20   91-34761
                                                              CIP

Copyright © 1988 by Uitgeversmij J. H. Kok B. V. Kampen, The Netherlands.

Published by Fleming H. Revell
a division of Baker Book House Company
P.O. Box 6287, Grand Rapids, MI 49516-6287

ISBN: 0-8007-5435-2

Third printing, December 1994

Printed in the United States of America

Warbler Cottage Romances

THE DISCERNING HEART

⋖ Chapter 1 ⋗

The canal house in Amsterdam had a certain arrogance about it as it stood there with its high windows, tightly shut lace curtains, and hard granite steps. It carefully hid the lives being played out behind its walls.

An observant passerby would have noticed how, at that moment, the broad front door opened slightly. What would the house divulge—a stately matron with rustling skirts, a grand señor with wide-brimmed hat?

Alas, the glory days of the canal house were long past.

Who lived behind this green door with the antique copper bell? For the moment, the passerby remained in uncertainty, for, in the hall behind the green door, a rather remarkable conversation was unraveling which, from the perspective of the frightened young blond woman who held the doorknob in her hand, had taken a rather unsettling turn.

"This cannot go on any longer," bellowed Doctor Franken

as he grasped the shoulders of the girl with his enormous hands.

"Marion," he continued more gently, "you must get out of here. Completely out. Yes, I know I'm here for your mother, but frankly, I'm more concerned about you. I can assure you that there is not that much wrong with your mother."

He made an expressive gesture. "She's all nerves. She has to work, she has to be busy so she doesn't have the time to imagine all kinds of ailments. Your taking everything off her hands must come to an end."

He was gone; the door slammed shut behind him. Marion massaged her shoulder with a pained expression on her face. She sat down on the stairs and thought hard about the advice that Doctor Franken had given her in his own boisterous way: "Get away! Out the door. Into the world."

Away from Mother, with all her imagined maladies; Mother, who always had to be looked after; Mother, upon whom Marion had waited for the four years since she had finished high school—day in, day out.

Away from Father, who shut himself up in his office, absently listened to Mother's litany of complaints, could bury himself for hours in his newspapers; Father, who would spontaneously slip her a ten-dollar bill: "Buy yourself another nice book, my child. There's not much here for you with us old folks."

Life immediately flashed into her blue eyes, eyes which otherwise were so quiet in her round, still somewhat childlike face. Her books! Shelves full of them—novels, poems, textbooks—many, many pages full of spiritual and intellectual treasures.

" 'I love a story; it attracts me like a man . . . ,' " she quoted softly to herself.

This was the Marion whom hardly anyone knew. If only the mirror could speak. How often she had stood there, appraising herself with a critical glance. She was so ordinary, so terribly ordinary.

Edith always loomed in the background. Edith, her sister, two years her elder, in whose shadow she had always lived. Edith never wanted to learn; books didn't interest her. She was pretty and bold—always game. She had long ago escaped the dreary treadmill of life with Father and Mother.

Marion had often angrily turned Edith's picture around on her dresser and thought, *It isn't fair. Edith has nothing to offer except her pretty face and her flair. But has Edith ever given anything of herself? She can't, because she has no inner well from which she can draw day after day. She has never taken the trouble to develop herself mentally or spiritually.*

My capital, thought Marion fervently, *grows continually.*

In her mind lived the enchanting phrases from the books she had devoured after Mother was in bed and Father was busy rustling his newspapers.

The rapid, tumbling flood of words of a compelling novel, the lilting, melodious words of a short poem, the searing scream of defiance, the short, pulsating phrases full of music and meaning. And there, in the midst of them all, like sparks shooting from the unbroken gray of the daily routine of the old house, the caressing words of comfort from the Holy Book: "Be not anxious in anything . . . Cast all your cares on Him . . . Blessed are the peacemakers, for they shall be called children of God."

Edith's picture was always returned to its place of honor by Marion. The angry fire in her eyes never stayed long. Blessed are the peacemakers, for they shall be called children of God. How devoutly Marion struggled daily to be a child of God! Yet how her heart yearned for the sparkling life that Edith enjoyed. The conflict in her life was intensifying. She was ready for a new beginning.

Dr. Franken had suddenly realized something there in the

hallway. *This girl will never blossom here. She will become such a loner, with her old father and whining mother, that she won't dare look at a man. It's a sin to do that to such a beautiful thing. Those big innocent eyes can seem so afraid.*

Unaware of the doctor's reflections, Marion sat humbly on the steps. Thoughts can wander far, but now they returned to their point of departure: *Out the door!*

But to where? What should she do? An office job didn't appeal to her. Children? A longing welled up in her and began to grow. Children were so warm, so alive. Dr. Franken's suggestion began to appeal to her.

Slowly, she stood up, stretched and began to sing.

Her desire began to take form. She imagined herself standing by the little bed of a child; a child who needed her, who cried for her, Marion Verkerk. The craving for a new life had been fed.

Out of the sitting room clattered the voice of Mrs. Verkerk. "What's taking you so long?"

Marion combed her hair back out of her eyes with her fingers and stepped into the room. "Here I am, Mother."

"That will not happen here again," vowed Reinier Van Herewaarden as he tucked the covers around his little girl. She slept so peacefully, so completely relaxed, as only a child can sleep.

Some housekeeper! he thought angrily. *Every night, out the door, and a not a speck of love for this child.*

"Oh, Ingeborg, my little girl, if only you had a mother who could care for you! A mother who would work for you and play with you, who would make your life a celebration!"

He thought about Magda, astonished that she was the mother of this warm, lively creature. Magda, who for years now lay sick, dying of the cancer which ravaged her body.

Every day he made the trip to the hospital, and every day the distance between them seemed to grow. She had always been self-centered, but now her thoughts circled ever more closely around herself, and Reinier was painfully aware of it. *There is scarcely any room in her life for us anymore.*

She seldom saw the child anymore, who had grown from a cuddly, rosy baby to a spicy little four-year-old, always in the care of strangers, a bit neglected, a bit lonely, unendingly devoted to the big, strong man who was her father.

Reinier Van Herewaarden left his daughter's room, careful not to wake her. Frowning, he surveyed the confusion that ruled the house. What would ever become of his daughter with such an upbringing?

Later, as he sat downstairs with his head propped up on his hand, he pulled the paper to himself. Maybe a nanny was the solution? He sighed. Two strange women in his house—as though one were not already enough.

Yet it can't go on the way it is.

A small ad attracted his attention. Unassuming, originally worded: "Who is willing to entrust their children to my care? Twenty-one years old. No experience with children, but lots of goodwill. Marion Verkerk, General Delivery, Amsterdam."

It was so disarming, so straightforward. It was as though the little ad said to him, "What are you worried about, Reinier Van Herewaarden? There is someone who wants to care for your little girl."

He gave in to the sudden impulse and wrote a letter. Sitting down again, he buried himself deep in the chair, letting the thirty years of his life pass in review. The angry lines of his mouth set deeper.

There were his years of youth at the House of Herewaarden with his genteel mother, born to nobility, so devoted to convention and tradition; his unfortunate brother Diederick; his father, the baron, who died altogether too soon.

He recalled his struggle as a growing boy for a life of his own, his flight from the petty world of "class marries class" and the oft-repeated, "But you should have nothing to do with such people, Reinier."

He had been disgusted by the whole thing. His interest lay in business. In spite of much opposition, he invested in a factory and took over the management himself. If Magda had not come along then . . .

How beautiful she was, how innocent!

He laughed a short, sneering laugh. *Innocent! Ha!*

He saw it all now, so mercilessly clear. Riches and honor—that's what Magda wanted; to climb the social ladder, to parade around the glorious old estate, the House of Herewaarden.

His mother was rather fond of this girl, the daughter of old but poor nobility, yet beautiful and prudent. If they were only married, his mother had thought, she would know how to rid Reinier of those silly commoner ideas about having one's own work and earning one's bread with one's own hands.

Reinier had heard rumors about Magda. Friends had warned him, "Watch out, old boy. Once she has her hooks in you . . . !"

But he had turned a deaf ear on it all. "I'll have you know that Magda is simply marrying me for who I am."

He had made his preparations and bought a small villa in a town several kilometers from his parental home. This was where he wanted to live, in a place where he would no longer be "the young baron," but a man whose worth would be measured by what he himself had achieved.

He traded in his long, gleaming sedan for a simpler, more practical model, and dreamed of himself being very happy with his beautiful little wife in a world all their own, a world where they could be themselves and could build the perfect family, free from the burden that had weighed so heavily on him in his youth.

How differently it had turned out.

Magda had made one scene after another when he slowly began to reveal his plans. But he had gone through with them, stubbornly and obstinately. He should have listened to good advice and cut all ties, but his enamored heart wouldn't listen, in spite of the fact that his shimmering illusions were being dismantled piece by piece.

They spent a short time together here, both of them with their own disappointments. A few hours of happiness and many hours of misunderstanding had followed their dazzling wedding.

When Inge announced herself, a ray of hope fell into his life. A child would make Magda gentler, more homey. Such a thrashing bundle of life would certainly take away Magda's burning desire for the great big world.

He had done everything he could to help her enjoy their life together. He let her redecorate the entire villa according to her own taste. He had a beautiful garden planted. He brought her lovely little presents time and again. Their relationship didn't improve. When she she couldn't go out anymore because of the child growing within her, she sat in silence for hours on end in her boudoir and retreated farther and farther within herself.

Their daughter was born: Ingeborg Louise.

Those were days of great joy for Reinier. Would everything be better now? With renewed vigor, he threw himself into his work at the fledgling factory. Business was good. A warm gratitude filled him. He had a job that brought him contentment; he had a healthy, well-formed child; he had the wife of his choice. Didn't he have everything a man could possibly wish for?

Yet the old conflicts between them came up, were settled,

and came up again. No rest prevailed in the warm, tastefully decorated rooms of the house Reinier had chosen for celebrating his happiness.

And in the eye of this storm between the two adults, who each day tried to win the other to their own point of view, grew Ingeborg Louise, their child!

Then someone else slipped into their lives, silently, treacherously, like a thief.

From Reinier, he took the final hope of the happy fulfillment of his dream.

From Magda, he took everything—her future, her lovely body, her health—everything but her proud heart.

Cancer.

She had shrieked, sobbed, sulked. Before long, she was brought to the hospital, and there she now lay, the sad figure of faded glory.

Reinier had not known much joy in the years that had passed since their marriage. It was Inge who cast sunlight into his life. He barely maintained sporadic contact with his mother, estranged as they were since he had arranged his life to his own liking.

The lost son, he thought wearily.

If only he had it in him to return to the manor, perhaps everything would be smoothed over again. But he couldn't. He couldn't abandon the business that he had built up with his own hands.

Go back to that confining way of life? Never!

Leave the situation as it is now? Thoughts can wander far, but now they returned to their point of departure. What would become of Ingeborg with such an upbringing?

As night overtook evening, Reinier Van Herewaarden sat lost in his thoughts. Almost within reach stood the old, venerable family Bible. Many who had borne his name before him had, with rejoicing, therein inscribed the names of their children. Many who had borne his name before him had, with grief, registered the date of death of their loved ones. Many generations had drawn comfort from this old book.

Reinier did not think about it any further. The book's heavy clasps had not been opened in years. With his slightly graying head propped up in his hand, he drifted off dreaming of a happy future for Ingeborg, his child.

And so he passed the evening.

Mrs. Everdings, the housekeeper, had not yet returned home.

❧ Chapter 2 ❧

And so it was that Marion Verkerk, on the morning of a late summer day in September, paced up and down the platform waiting for the train that would bring her to Brabant—to Inge Van Herewaarden, the child who had been entrusted to her care.

Marion's departure from her parents' home had not been without difficulty. She sighed slightly as she remembered the many objections she had had to overcome. But as the train pulled in, she felt a jubilation come over her. The anxious lines fell from her face, the excitement of the new gripped her.

She didn't look so bad, this Marion Verkerk, as she sat there with a faint smile on her slightly opened lips. Her blond hair, parted in the middle, fell with a natural wave to her shoulders. Her blue-gray suit mirrored the color of her eyes. Those eyes, those eyes of Marion Verkerk. Had a portion of the spirit of Edith descended on her—a barely suppressed levity?

The morning was not yet half over when she laid her hand to the gate of the Warbler, idyllically nestled between shrubs and flowers. She held her breath for a moment. What a house! This was something altogether different from the old shed in which she had lived her whole life. A canal house may have its own charm, but you could smell the forest here!

An old curved pine bent protectively over the dark, thatched roof; multicolored dahlias bordered the gravel paths. The scent of pine and flowers wafted over her.

Behind the curtains, everything was still. The house appeared deserted. She resolutely pushed open the garden gate and gave a start when it fell shut behind her with a clap.

No one responded to her timid ring. Again and again she heard the sound of the bell die away in the house. Was no one there?

Bewildered and disappointed, she turned from the low front door, which was girded with intertwining vines, and walked around the house. There she found the most beautiful child's paradise anyone could imagine.

In the middle of the lawn stood a swing. Little feet had trampled the grass underneath. A sandy strip marked the spot where a child slowed her flight to a stop.

There was also a sandbox full of lovely white sand. In a little patch of soil lining one side of the grassy yard lay a miniature rake, casually discarded.

But where was the princess who belonged in this little kingdom? Marion pressed her nose against the window of the back room and ventured a glance into the kitchen next to it.

What she saw made her shudder. Such an endless shambles! Had the housekeeper, whom Mr. Van Herewaarden had written her about, run out on him? If so, not much was lost. What a slob!

Marion stood in the fragrant morning. What should she do? She looked at her watch—only ten o'clock!

17

Making a bold decision, she lifted the latch on the kitchen door. It was open. A quick inspection of the rooms told her that no one was home, as she had suspected.

When she returned to her starting point at the back door, she suddenly heard a clear, firm little voice ask, "Who are you?"

She beheld a little girl with a head full of dark curls and jet-black eyes in a dirty little face. This had to be Ingeborg! The child repeated her question.

Marion knelt down by her and replied, "I'm Miss Marion, Inge. Didn't Papa tell you that I would be staying with you to take care of you?"

She took out her handkerchief and wiped some of the dirt from Inge's face. The child gazed at her curiously.

"Can you tell stowies?" she asked.

"I sure can," answered Marion sincerely. "At least a hundred of them."

"Then I think I wike you," decided Inge. Obviously she hadn't quite mastered certain letters of the alphabet.

Marion, although unaccustomed to children, found her charge adorable.

After talking with Inge for a while, the situation in the Warbler became somewhat clearer. From the child's chatter, Marion determined that Inge's father had had a falling-out with Mrs. Everdings, the housekeeper.

"She was such a wying witch!" said Inge confidentially. "She scwatched me aw the time."

"Inge!" reacted Marion. She did her best not to laugh. Inge must have learned a few new words in the street.

As Marion investigated the whereabouts of Mrs. Everdings, Inge explained that once Papa had gone, Mrs. Everdings and her big suitcase got into a car. She had told Inge that she should stay outside and play until Papa came home.

"And I hope that she nevew comes back," concluded Inge with satisfaction.

Marion then went on the attack. Her experienced eyes spotted the long, gray spiderwebs connecting the furniture to the floor. In the kitchen hung the stale odor of burned food and dirty dishes. Within fifteen minutes, a large kettle of water sat singing on the stove. The doors to the garden stood wide open. *With a quick once-over,* thought Marion lightheartedly, *I'll see to it that this place is livable by the time the boss gets home.*

After half an hour, she and Inge had become best chums. The child crawled along the baseboards with a dustcloth in her little fists, while Marion tidied up the neglected dishes.

She did the work with pleasure—work for which she had not been hired—the same duties she had discharged at home, year in and year out.

She peeled a few potatoes, opened a can of vegetables, and was able to flag down a passing milkman for a bit of pudding. And so, with all haste, a simple meal was soon created. Meanwhile, Inge, now occupied with a brush and proud that she could "help," learned an old song about the three tiny tots and the lovely warm day in September.

At noon, Marion viewed the results of her labor with pride. The beautiful old furniture, rid of its coat of dust, gleamed with distinction in the afternoon sun that streamed in through the windows. The table was festively set for three. A vase with flaming orange dahlias against dark leaves stood like a live painting before the hearth.

The kitchen was clean and shining; the spiced scent of fried potatoes filled the air. No one would notice the bit of dust and dirt under the mat. Marion could not do magic, but what she had been able to accomplish in a few hours could have been called a miracle. The rest could wait until tomorrow.

Marion looked at herself in the polished hall mirror. The

warm color in her cheeks was far beyond any cosmetic. She still glowed from her haste. A quick comb through her blond hair, and *voila!* Let Mr. Van Herewaarden come; everything was ready.

When Reinier rode through the gate and the engine of the little car was still, he heard two voices, singing about a lovely warm day in September, drift through the open kitchen doors.

Since he had already prepared himself for another dubious meal in a messy house opposite an angry, tight-lipped woman whose humor, after the morning's climactic outburst, had undoubtedly reached an immeasurable low, he had to stand for a moment to digest all this.

Suddenly he recalled Miss Verkerk was due to arrive that day. How could he have forgotten? He walked around to the back of the house. Suddenly he stood in the open door, a tall young man with eyes that seldom betrayed anything that was going on behind his high forehead. "Good afternoon, ladies," said Reinier.

Inge, who was in the middle of a quick washing up, flew into his outstretched arms, soapsuds and all.

"Marion Verkerk," said Marion, extending her hand to him.

Reinier lifted the child onto his shoulder and stepped into the room. He looked over the situation, taking it all in, and turned. Carefully he set Inge down, and his hand came down heavily on Marion's shoulder.

"My child," he said with difficulty, "have you. . . ?" He paused for a moment. "It has never been like this here before," he continued. "So festive, so full of atmosphere."

Again he extended his hand to her. "I thank you," he said somewhat more formally, but still sincerely. "I must say that I do not yet understand the situation, but things haven't turned out worse for me, in any case. Where is Mrs. Ever-dings?"

Marion wasn't certain how to react to his inquiry.

"Would you care to sit down for lunch?" she asked, at something of a loss for words. "Then I will try to explain to you what I know about what happened here after you left."

He listened attentively to her tale. Slowly her bashfulness faded.

Reinier savored his meal. He would hear nothing of her apologies for the simple table setting. "What you have achieved in just a couple of hours is already something wonderful," he said with a sweeping gesture. "Maybe you won't believe it, but I have not eaten this well in weeks."

Marion blushed at the compliment. A warm feeling of fulfillment radiated through her. She had seen the glance he had cast at the newspapers and letters that were neatly stacked on the low table next to his heavy armchair and at the flowers that she had so tastefully arranged. To her, these were all things that went without saying in her daily routine. At home she had grown accustomed to insuring that nothing was out of place.

Now she realized, with amazement, that here these things were noticed and appreciated as something out of the ordinary.

She stood up to remove Inge's bib. Reinier observed her as she stood there, bent over his child. It was certainly fine with him if his house now became—for the first time—a home.

With a sudden burst, he slid his chair back from the table, caressed Inge's hair, and said curtly, "Miss Verkerk, I wish you a fine afternoon. I must go now."

And to Inge, "Be good for Miss Marion, now, doll. I'll see you tonight."

Then he disappeared. Marion frowned a little at this hasty leave-taking. He didn't even look at the mail. In the long run, she would get to know her boss's ways. "Every chief comes with instructions," Edith always said, and she would know. Marion set her shoulder to the next part of her task.

Reinier started his car and drove automatically to the factory. Thoughts swirled through his brain, unrelentingly. It was miraculous how much such a girl could alter the same old, everyday grind. Yet she had entered the picture so quietly, without fanfare, and practically without words. She was one in a million, at first appearance. Not refined, not beautiful, just a simple girl.

Why was it, then, that through her, the image of Magda as she had been three years before loomed so large before him? Why was it that he now saw the empty place in his life more sharply than ever?

If Magda had only had a little of this pure femininity—a few of those loving, caring gestures—perhaps his recollections of her would lose some of their bitterness.

He had had three housekeepers, yet none of them gave him this experience. And today, Marion Verkerk came.

"Fifty guilders a month," they had agreed, but with such informality that it shocked him, raised as he had been in an atmosphere of rock-solid accounting. She took the helm of his ramshackle house in her slender hands without a single word about extra help or overtime—with the same simple quietness with which she had folded her hands in prayer before and after she ate.

He cursed under his breath. Was he now seeing Magda's poverty more sharply through her? And his own? He threw himself into his work to silence the tumbling thoughts.

But as the afternoon passed, he caught himself longing to go home. There was someone waiting for him, a woman who was friendly and polite, with whom he could carry on a conversation.

What a hermit he had become! His life had run in one

continuous circle these last few years—the visits to Magda, his work, and the child. He had no friends here. His former friends had dropped out of sight. The Warbler had become an island on which he lived for months at a time, alone with his worries.

It was barely five o'clock when he stood up and made his way to the car. Work had not gone well.

Meanwhile, Marion had been exploring. She found the upstairs in the same state of disrepair as the rooms below. The afternoon was flying by, but now the beds were clean, the dirty wash had been collected, and the sinks had been given a good going over.

Inge played sweetly behind her. Marion could tell that the child was not accustomed to having much attention, and she was not in the least bit spoiled.

Before they knew it, the afternoon was over. Marion heard the car drive up and looked at her watch. It was not yet 5:30.

As Reinier entered, he found the room empty. He stretched out on the couch and listened closely to the sounds coming from above him.

Inge was just about dressed. Now that evening was falling, it was getting somewhat cooler. Marion had replaced the child's cotton playsuit with a red velvet dress and a little lace collar. Above the dark curls, still damp from their washing, danced a large white bow.

"There," she said, satisfied with the results. "Now you go right downstairs. I'll bet Papa is already waiting for you."

She followed a moment later in a gray wool dress to which a red corsage added just enough color. She went to the kitchen, cut some bread, and set out milk for the coffee. Then she set the table.

Reinier absently listened to the babble of his little daughter while he observed Marion's movements. The desire crept into him to draw this girl out of her shell, to find out whether her peace was true peace, or whether fire and temper were hidden behind those modestly lowered eyelashes.

When he returned from his nightly visit to the hospital, Marion was sitting, darning a worn-out sock under the lamp.

"I put Inge to bed," she said, raising her head toward him. "She was falling over from sleepiness."

Reinier laid his hat on the table and went and sat opposite her.

"Don't you ever stop working?" he asked as he grabbed at the sock she was working on.

Marion laughed. "I don't understand what kind of person Mrs. Everdings must have been," she said. "I don't believe that there was one piece of clean clothing left in this house."

"Oh, that's quite possible," responded Reinier without surprise. "She was sloppy, lazy, and brazen. It is a delight not to see her roaming through these halls anymore."

He took one of Inge's little socks in his hand and began to roll it up into a little ball. Marion took back the sock that he had let fall and bent herself over one of the holes. She wanted to finish that pair this evening.

Again Reinier observed her movements. He had never paid much attention to these little domestic housekeeping things before. He tried to imagine his mother, his meticulously clothed and coiffured mother, with a worn-out sock and a sewing basket. Or Magda!

To all appearances, he was now buried in his paper, but he was actually reveling in every minute of this peaceful rest. With an emerging desire to safeguard this generous atmosphere as much as possible, he broke the silence. "We must talk, Miss Verkerk. You came here as a companion for Inge, but today your demonstration of the art of housekeeping was commendable. You told me this afternoon that you always worked alone at home. We hope that Mrs. Everdings has disappeared for good from our horizon and I'm terrified at the prospect of having to look for a new housekeeper. Before we place an ad for a cleaning girl, could you possibly be convinced to take the reins in hand? Think it over."

His voice sounded convincing. Marion, who had spent the whole day sympathizing with him because of the loneliness of living in a house grown cold from the lack of a loving touch, could do nothing more than mutely nod her head. This change, after all, would be an improvement for her.

"Excellent," exhaled Reinier, and then she, too, recovered her voice.

"I frankly don't know what I would do the whole day if it were otherwise," she said seriously, but in her eyes twinkled a bit of humor. "It just isn't good for a child to have attention all day long. The raising of a child must take place unobserved."

They laughed together at this logic. "And she advertises herself as a nanny," he said, shaking his head.

He took care of the financial arrangements, and Marion went to look after the coffee.

After this conversation, they seemed to feel somewhat freer with each other. Reinier told her all the lovely little things about Inge that a father tells. Marion could sense how much he loved his little daughter. He didn't say anything about Magda.

Marion lay awake for a long time that night. As she thought of home, a silly little tear rolled over her pillow. Angrily, she whisked it away. Then she closed her eyes, and without words, prayed for wisdom to fulfill the task that God had placed in her open hands.

❧ Chapter 3 ❧

The days were piling up. Marion had not succeeded in becoming accustomed to the quickly changing moods of her employer. One moment he was romping through the house like a mischievous boy with Inge; a while later he could sit with a dark expression on his face, shut up within himself, and give short, snapped-off responses to her comments. In the beginning, she had retreated, wounded by his sharp tone, as a snail withdraws into its shell. But now that she had observed him somewhat longer in his daily ins and outs, understanding was beginning to dawn in her: This man was fighting his way through life. His existence was a continual struggle. He had no fixed point in his life on which to fall back.

His sarcastic outbursts did not concern her as much as his whole existence, of which she just happened to be a part. In a sudden moment of insight this was made clear to Marion, and since that time she had handled his moods. She had armed herself against them, and now he could not hurt her. His character had been awakened at its very roots. A great longing for coziness lived within him, but there was an internal conflict whose content and scope were unknown to Marion and which always hunted him out of his rest. How could she know how much Reinier had lost his balance, now that the atmosphere in his house so closely approximated his earlier ideal?

How ill at ease he felt under the searching looks of Magda, which were directed toward him with awakened curiosity—mysterious looks that he could not penetrate.

Marion had quickly adjusted to her new role. After a few days, Toos made her entrance. Toos was the part-time maid who spoke with a delicious Brabant accent and was the epitomy of congeniality.

After a few days, a letter came from Mrs. Everdings, which Reinier had let Marion read with a wink of understanding. It was an epistle written in marginal Dutch, in which the sender proclaimed her right to two weeks' retroactive pay.

Reinier wrote a money order with a smile. "I wouldn't fight with her for a thousand guilders," he decided. With a powerful stroke of the pen, he closed the Everdings chapter.

Marion stored these words with the scarce compliments that now came to her after that spontaneous reaction of the first day.

Then came the day her possessions arrived. When everything was in its place, she remained standing, holding in her hand the small Bible she had received on the occasion of her profession of faith.

She thought about her father, who as long as she could remember had read a portion from this book after every meal. "It has been given to us so that we may be strengthened," he had once said to her. That had been years ago, but it was one of the sayings of her father that had fixed itself in Marion's memory.

She looked up the text in the Gospel of Matthew where it is affirmed, "You are the light of the world. A city set on a hill cannot be hid . . ."

Mr. Van Herewaarden did not read the Bible. Marion wondered if the words in his letter, "I am Protestant," only meant that he was not Roman Catholic, the meaning given to the word by so many here in Brabant. But what about the beautiful old Bible that stood in the other room? Was that only an heirloom to him?

Wasn't there a task lying before her here? For the first time, she understood the full implications of the expression, "You are the light of the world." She slowly made her way down the stairs and into the salon with the little Bible in her hand. She leaned against the bookcase and continued to ponder. It would be difficult to talk with Mr. Van Herewaarden about these things. Was she shying away from it? Had twenty-one years under the breath of God's Word not strengthened her?

She sunk her teeth into her lower lip. "You are the light of the world." Was Jesus looking at her now? Marion closed her eyes.

Then she heard the car turn through the gate. With an almost embarrassed movement, she laid the little Bible down. She looked down at it intently. Then, carefully, she reached down and picked it up again. She stayed standing there until she heard Reinier coming through the back room, then she looked up, right into his amused glance.

"So," said Reinier—and Marion knew this was coming—"in quiet solitude?"

"If you want to call it that," she replied. "My father always read to us from the Bible after we ate. I miss that here."

Then she laid the small leather book down in the bookcase and walked past him into the kitchen.

"Miss Marion!" Reinier called her back, curtly, commandingly. She halted and looked back. He continued, "I don't want you to lack anything here. The Bible should be read in this house. May I request that you see to that task from now on?"

As she stared at him, startled, he added, "I mean it. Your Bible is a closed book for me. As far as I am concerned, it contains incomprehensible, bellicose stories and heavy treatises on sin and punishment. It doesn't speak to me. But I am convinced that you know how to find your way to the good things that it also undoubtedly contains."

Marion hesitated for a moment, but when he remained silent, she went back to her work.

Alone in the kitchen, she stood thinking over his words, the breadboard in one hand and the other on the doorknob.

What did he mean? Was this just more of his sarcasm, or was he just trying to tease her? Or was there some sincerity in his words? Had she begun to fear too quickly?

He was, however, completely earnest. When Marion folded Inge's napkin after supper, he said with unmistakable impatience in his voice, "Well now, Miss Marion?"

She caught his hint. A warm blush crept up her neck, and he cursed himself for his manner, yet he sat patiently until she had taken her place again and slowly paged through the small book.

He wanted to know in which words her joyfulness was rooted and where her tranquility found its source.

Then Marion read. She read the same chapter as before: " 'And Jesus, seeing the crowds, went up on a mountain, and when he had sat down, his disciples came to him.' "

Then followed the beatitudes, which were so comforting for Marion but sounded so strange to Reinier. After the first couple of verses, Marion had conquered her nervousness. It was so grippingly beautiful.

" 'Blessed are those who mourn, for they shall be comforted; blessed are the merciful, for they shall receive mercy; blessed are the pure in heart, for they shall see God; blessed are the peacemakers, for they shall be called sons of God.' "

It was quiet in the room. Inge sat, leaning motionless against her father, under the spell of the unusual, her little head resting on his sleeve.

Suddenly the voice of Marion sounded again: " 'You are the light of the world; a city set on a hill cannot be hid. Neither does a man light a lamp and put it under a bushel, but on a lampstand so that it may shine for all those who are in the house. So let your light shine before men, so that they may see your good works and praise your Father who is in heaven.' "

Now Marion shut the Bible, and they prayed together, Inge innocently, with her stiffly folded hands, the two adults with their heads full of swirling thoughts.

The quiet hung in the air long after they had opened their eyes. Inge tried to make a figure from the forks and knives and was completely absorbed in the game she had invented.

The comments that Marion had expected never came. Every night she repeated this little ceremony, and every afternoon, as Marion read from the children's Bible, Inge hung on her every word. Perhaps Reinier was listening with equal intensity. Was there someone in his tender youth who had laid out for him the secrets of salvation? Marion did not know, but it had given her a shock of joy when he had come home with a brand-new children's Bible and handed it to her with the words, "We must be fair, Miss Marion. What we receive is also for Inge."

Yet he was not apparently open to the Gospel, which he heard each day. Sometimes in the evening he tried to provoke her into an argument by making sensational comments about church and belief, but he continued to have the unpleasant feeling that she was in control and that, with her short, naive answers, she was boxing him left and right about the ears. And so the autumn passed.

One evening, as Marion sat down at the table with a bad headache and a pale, drawn face, Reinier commanded that she remain absolutely still. To the vociferous delight of Inge, he washed the dishes himself. When Marion, with a weak protest, attempted to get up out of her chair, he laughingly commanded, "Sit down."

In her heart, Marion had to admit that when he was in high spirits he was very attractive. Like now, playing with Inge with the washcloth, with which he carelessly mopped up the water that had splashed out of the sink. Then he swung Inge over his shoulder and said, "Give Miss Marion a kiss, little gnome. Then Papa will deposit you in your little bed."

He went whistling up the stairs. After Inge had put on her flowered pajamas, she was allowed to turn somersaults on Papa's big bed. Panting and tired, she finally lay down under the covers. But when Reinier attempted to tuck her in, she bounced back up again. "I stiw have to pway, Papa," she admonished, and Reinier stood and listened to the words of the little prayer that Marion had taught her. Just when he thought she was done—after her monotone: "Father awso in this night, over Inge howd your wight"—there came hastily tumbling after, "an' over Mama in de hospitow, an' over Papa, an' over Miss Mayion, an' Toos. Amen."

Magda first.

Such things make you soft, thought Reinier, as he slowly descended the stairs. Magda—from whom the child had never found enough love or leftover care. The grim look settled around his tightly pursed lips. The problems he battled day and night stood before him again, as big as life.

*　　*　　*

He had once quietly informed Magda that she couldn't do anything without self-interest. But what about him? Had the turbulent love of their courtship not shrunken to a handful of obligations?

Wasn't there enough love and warmth in him to continue loving her in spite of her sickness, in spite of the fact that she had not granted him the fulfillment of his beautiful dreams?

He balled his hands into fists. Oh, that lovely, blond child in the other room. She had taught him so much in these months!

There must be a power in life, an affection which grows within against all oppression, a love which gives without questions, that blesses when cursed, that when reproached, does not reproach in return. But he—Reinier Van Herewaarden— how grossly he had fallen short in his love for his wife!

He had cared for her, but he had not prayed for her. He wanted to change her, but he had never tried to understand her. He had loved her, but never forgetting himself.

As Reinier walked into the room, Marion asked innocently, "And is the gnome in bed?"

He looked at her as she sat there smiling in spite of her headache. Which devil had gotten ahold of him? Was it the devil of rebellion against the hand which he felt slowly closing its grip around his life? The hand of One whom he had to recognize as his Master?

"You have taught her a very touching prayer," he said with a forced laugh.

Marion sensed that the good mood of a few moments ago had inexplicably departed. A feeling of sadness overcame her. She did not answer.

Reinier continued. "Our beloved Lord must be more fond

of me than I thought," he said lightheartedly. "Otherwise He would not have sent me such a little minister."

He hated himself for these words, but he spoke them, nevertheless.

Marion lightly rubbed her forehead with a tired gesture. She ignored his last comment, which, as she well understood, was a reference to herself.

"It doesn't really matter what we think of Him," she said. For the first time, he heard a sharp undertone in her voice. "What He thinks of us is more important." With that she stood up, not waiting for his answer. As she left the room, he cursed under his breath.

A few minutes later, Marion heard the car drive off.

Before he had reached the hospital, Reinier's mood had changed. A chilly feeling of sorrow for his words slowly crept up within him.

Magda received him with a sad nod. "Sit down, Rein," she said wearily.

He remained standing and looked at her.

"Why are you staring at me?" she asked, slightly irritated.

"Have you had a lot of pain today?" he asked in return.

She shrugged her shoulders. "I always have pain."

"Inge prays for you before she goes to bed at night," he said softly.

The corners of Magda's mouth quivered slightly for a moment, then she asked sarcastically, "Prays? Did she learn that from you? Are we fulfilling our religious duties so scrupulously now?"

Reinier turned away, wounded. *I deserved that,* he thought. *I speak the same way to Marion, but she doesn't back down.*

He sat down on the edge of Magda's bed.

"No," he said with difficulty, "I have very little to offer her in that area. It was Miss Verkerk, the one I told you about."

"Oh, yes, your new housekeeper," she said with feigned

indifference. "I could have guessed. She is perfect, after all. Isn't she?"

Reinier shrugged his shoulders, "Who's perfect? She takes excellent care of Inge, and I'm very happy about that."

Magda let the subject drop. When saying good-bye, however, she said, making it sound somewhat like a command, "You must ask Miss Verkerk whether she is going to visit me tomorrow. I would like to meet her."

Reinier promised to do it. There was no other choice. He would gladly have spared Marion the cynical cross-examination to which he suspected Magda would subject her.

When he arrived home, he found the house dark. Marion had gone to bed.

As asked, Marion went to visit Mrs. Van Herewaarden the next day. It was a cold day, late in November. The air was ice blue, slightly frozen. She had decided to walk the half hour to the hospital. It was wonderful to walk alone. She had left Inge in the care of Toos, who considered it a real treat to be able to spend the afternoon playing with Inge in the Warbler, since she herself was still very young.

Marion was in a cheerful mood. Her headache was gone and the sarcastic storm with which her employer had departed the day before also appeared to have been an overreaction. Now she would see Mrs. Van Herewaarden for the first time. In the pictures she found about the house, Marion had seen that she was a very beautiful woman. It was a different beauty from Edith's, a refined, aristocratic beauty.

Mr. Van Herewaarden had never told her much about his wife. Marion knew that she was twenty-eight years old and had already lain sick for three years in that tall white building.

Magda had a lovely private room in the hospital.

But Marion was surprised at how impersonal the room was. There was not even a picture of Inge next to her bed. Could it be possible that this woman, who came from the wonderful atmosphere of the Warbler, did not need to surround herself with that atmosphere here as well?

She extended a hand to Magda and introduced herself as if she were a little girl. "Marion Verkerk, ma'am."

The two women stared at each other, probing, examining, appraising.

Magda's first reaction was *Heavens, what a child!*

She motioned for Marion to have a seat, and then she spoke. Marion listened with amazement at the musical quality of her soft voice, which was beautiful and yet not engaging. It seemed to hold everything that lived beyond the island of her bed at a distance.

"And," said Magda, "are you able to put up with my demanding husband? You should know that not a single housekeeper has been able to last with him!"

As she spoke, she gestured with her delicate white hands.

"I don't understand," said Marion simply. "We have had no conflict yet. I don't find him at all demanding."

Magda laughed a short, thin laugh, "I take it you don't know Reinier," she said.

She wondered if Mrs. Van Herewaarden was right. Perhaps she didn't know him. It seemed like such an absurd proposition that she smiled slightly. Not know him? She, who folds his pajamas, who darns his socks, who irons his shirts, who makes his bed? She, who for nearly three months now sat opposite him day after day at the table, listening to his stories about personnel problems and competition? She, who knows which vegetable he likes and which music he loves; who has observed him, and left him alone in his dark moods; who has rolled in laughter with him during his playful outbursts; who every time enjoys his little romps with Inge, her

35

little gnome? Oh no, in this Mrs. Van Herewaarden was surely mistaken. She knew every facet of his difficult, complicated nature. He had become a part of her life.

And here lay his wife, talking about him with such a cold and scornful tone in her voice that the corners of Marion's mouth trembled in silent defense.

Magda also was thinking of Rein. Rein during their courtship, in love up to his ears. Rein on his yacht, Rein on his black mare, Rein behind the piano, Rein against the background of the old castle.

She was a fool to think that it would always stay that way. What a grand future she had imagined for herself, with glamorous parties, with much gleam and glitter. And she, the baroness of Herewaarden, the hostess, floating about the rooms of the castle, through the lovely portrait gallery, a noblewoman among noblewomen!

Then began the disenchantment: Reinier's stubborn insistence on carrying out his own plans for the future, much different from those she had imagined.

Her lips curled back slightly in a disparaging little laugh. He wanted to turn her into a common little housewife, just like the rest of them; in a common house, and preferably with half a dozen little ones clinging to her skirt to make her old and tired and ugly before her time. She never felt happy in the Warbler. He had simply not understood that he had taken away from her the setting without which she did not want to live, and that was why she was now pining away.

He drove her crazy with his stories about the factory, which did not interest her at all, and with his wanting to sit at home and let all those visits and receptions, where she wanted to be, simply fly by. She asserted herself, she fought to get her way, but he hadn't given in.

Then she became sick less than a year after the birth of the child she had waited for without love. Deep in her heart, she knew, "This is my punishment."

Because during the long, difficult months when she was carrying the baby, it had slowly dawned on her: "I wanted the House of Herewaarden, with its whole entourage, more than I wanted Reinier."

And he knew it. She felt that he understood it. The silent grief in his eyes had not escaped her.

If only he had scolded her, if only he had reproached her! But he remained kind and obliging, a gentleman in every respect. She felt as though it were a double defeat. "He is a better person than I am," and resentment grew in her against his visits, his acts of kindness, his whole personality.

He also had to work through the disappointment of his life. She had watched his handsome, boyish face grow somber. She noticed his first gray hairs; she recognized his loneliness, his dislike of the silent house where there was no one who wanted to listen to him.

It gave her a small satisfaction, a sweet revenge, which she fed for many months.

She opened her eyes and looked at Marion, and Marion returned her look.

"You sure knew how to rope in my husband," said Magda in a rather hostile manner, with a sudden intense desire to wound this innocent child, to see her cheerful eyes grow dark.

Marion's mouth set. "I don't know what you mean, ma'am," came her firm reply.

"He has changed since you came," Magda continued, every word a drop of gall. "He isn't lonely anymore."

"I don't know what he was like before," said Marion, regretting that the conversation had taken such an unpleasant turn before it had even begun, "but you need not worry that I will take away his peace of mind."

Suddenly she caught the drift of Magda's comment and anger flashed in her eyes. *Bah! What a silly bit of nonsense this was. This insinuation about a man who makes the greatest sacrifices for his wife and has never said an improper word about her.*

Magda felt weak. Reinier had not been unfaithful, and she knew it.

"No," she spoke softly and urgently, and Marion was frightened by the fanatical look in her eyes. Without noticing, Magda began to address her informally. "No, you didn't take away his peace of mind. But you have given him back his peace of mind—if he ever had it, that is. Something has changed about him, something I don't recognize, something I can't understand. Something pious, something . . . of God. Now I am the only one who is miserable and alone. And that is your fault."

Marion listened speechlessly as she continued with the same suppressed passionate tone. "And you taught Inge to pray. I won't have it. Do you understand? I won't have it!"

She fell back onto her pillows and a great compassion filled Marion. There was more to this, she understood; years of grief were hiding behind this. "But why, ma'am?" she cried out. "Why may the child not pray for you? What harm could the prayer of a child ever do?"

Magda pushed her hand away. "You don't understand," she said flatly. "No one does." She fell silent again, her thoughts confused. *What am I doing? Why am I talking to this stranger so much? Why am I exposing myself? Why?*

Then she spoke once more, but actually to herself, with a tired, monotone voice, revealing only an occasional spark of its former fire.

"I don't want pity. I don't want it. No one loves me. My father and mother are dead; I have no more friends. I have no right to the love of that child, because I hated her before she was born. I lost the love of my husband years ago. I could tolerate his concern because it was a duty for him, day after day. But now, but now . . ."

Suddenly she turned to Marion with a flashing, piercing look.

"Now he is trying to give me more than he has. He is trying to love as he did before, but he can't. I noticed. I notice everything. They think I'm half dead, that I'm no longer interested."

She laughed quickly, a short, humorless laugh. "I notice everything. But I don't want it. I don't want any pity. I don't want any compassion. I want to be hard, hard as a rock. How else would I be able to tolerate the pain and loneliness?"

It had been a long time since Magda had said so much at one time. Marion still did not understand her very well. Had Mrs. Van Herewaarden lost the love of her husband? But how? Did he really no longer love her? Was that perhaps his eternal struggle, that he wanted to feel love and affection when there was no more spring from which love freely flowed?

How should Marion respond to this confession of Mrs. Van Herewaarden? Should she hopelessly seek for a gap in the wall of hatred and unwillingness that Magda had built up around herself?

She thought of the Man of Sorrows, the Savior, who lays His strong, kind hand on the head of the lonely and bitter, like this woman, and this image gave her the courage to say carefully, oh so carefully, "You say that you have no right to love. But can we speak of rights when it comes to love? True love is unselfish. All else is not love. And loving is something that we humans can only approximate. There is One who truly loved, but no one can lay claim to that love. It was for those who had lost everything and didn't know how to find their way back. Do you know who that Man was?"

Magda nodded, almost imperceptibly. She was so tired, so tired. Her head lay still on the pillow, and Marion realized that this conversation had been too great a strain for Magda. She laid her cool hand on Magda's forehead and straightened the sheets. Her voice was soft, barely audible, as she whispered, as though to a child, "Go to sleep now. Go to sleep now. Don't think about hate anymore. Love always wins in the end. Love always wins. Go to sleep now."

She said many other soft things, comforting things that later she could not remember.

It calmed Magda; in a miraculous way it calmed her. The nervous pull of her mouth relaxed, and her breathing became more even. When Marion saw that she had fallen asleep, she tiptoed out of the room.

A few hours later, as Reinier took the stairs three at a time, one of the nurses hailed him.

"Your wife is sleeping, sir," she said. "The visit this afternoon probably tired her out."

"I won't wake her," promised Reinier as he continued toward her room. He carefully opened the door and saw that she was indeed asleep. He sat down and looked at her face, which bore a much sweeter expression, now that she was resting.

He sat there for several minutes, silent, surrendered to his thoughts. Fifteen minutes, a half hour; Magda still had not stirred.

A powerful tenderness grew in Reinier. There was something indescribably beautiful in this being silently together. He thought about what Marion had said when he had asked her, "What do you think of my wife?"

"That she is hungry for love" had been her reply, and it struck him like a lash. He did not dare inquire further about the nature of the conversation that they must have had that afternoon.

He slowly stood up, and carefully, very carefully, pressed a kiss to Magda's forehead. She stirred slightly, and he held his breath.

"I know who you mean," she mumbled. "But are you sure that love always wins?"

She had been speaking in her sleep, for when she turned over on her other side, she was asleep again. Reinier left the room. He mechanically walked down the empty halls, his nails pressed into his palms.

Marion, he thought. *Marion.*

❧ Chapter 4 ❧

The long corridor leading into the toy store was full of children.

Inge was entranced by the display window, and Marion allowed her to look awhile. As she stood slightly behind Inge, her glance fell on a young man who stood tucked away in the corner of the entrance, a sketchbook in his hand, skillfully sketching one line after another. His keen eye moved repeatedly from the paper to the teeming children, searching with barely suppressed impatience, for the little boy he was recreating on paper.

It fascinated Marion, and she continued to look at him. *What a nice head he has,* she thought admiringly. *You don't see such a face everyday.*

Jaap Dubois suddenly slapped his sketchbook shut. Had he felt Marion peering at him? He looked at her, and Marion blushed and looked down.

What a ridiculous figure I must make, she thought, somewhat flustered. *How could I so foolishly stare at that man?*

"Inge!" she called to the little girl, in an attempt to salvage the situation.

But the little one was far from finished looking. "Just a minute, Miss Mayon," she said absently, her attention already gone.

The young man took a step in Marion's direction. "This is priceless, ma'am," he said, gesturing with his head toward the children.

Marion raised her eyes. "Yes," she said spontaneously, "I see that you were inspired."

Jaap Dubois looked with interest at the refreshing face that was lifted toward him. He leaned confidentially toward Marion. "If you promise not to tell anyone, I'll let you in on something."

His eyes twinkled.

"I didn't come here to draw at all. I had to buy Saint Nicholas Day presents for the whole family. But there are so many choices here, and I understand so little about these knick-knacks, that I didn't dare venture into the lion's den. Then that little boy came along, and I was distracted." He made a powerless gesture with his thin brown hand. "I couldn't walk away."

Marion nodded with understanding. "Yet, in the meantime you are just as far from home as when you began," she remarked practically, and Jaap laughed.

"Exactly," said Jaap candidly, "and that is why I am now going to ask you a very bold question. Could you perhaps give me a little advice on my choices? Gert and Marlies are still so small, and still believe so much in the existence of the good bishop, you can't just palm a chocolate frog off on them."

"With pleasure," responded Marion, who was beginning to

be uncomfortable with the situation, "but first you must tell me who Gert and Marlies are. Your children?"

"Spare me!" yelped Jaap. "Gert is my youngest brother. He is five, and Marlies is the youngest of all; she is just three."

Marion saw that Inge had disentangled herself from the mass and was coming toward her.

She quickly whispered to Jaap, "One condition: Work tactfully when my little gnome is around. She also still believes in good Saint Nick."

Jaap winked. The conspiracy was born, and the presents were bought.

After half an hour, Jaap Dubois had heard about Marion's work at the Warbler, and she was roughly familiar with his family.

They bought presents not only for the two little ones, but also for little Bram and Koert, for Laurens and Ronnie, for Father and Mother, and last but not least, for Grandmother.

With loving inflection, Jaap had said, "Something very nice for Grandmother."

When they were outside again, they looked at each other a little awkwardly. Somewhere a clock tower chimed. It was high time to go home. *Too bad,* thought Marion in silence. *We may never see each other again.*

Jaap extended a hand to her. "May I say 'until next time' Miss—uh—"

"Marion," said Marion with a blush. "Marion Verkerk," and she laid her hand in his brown, supple hands.

His fingers closed almost nervously, but they held her hand firmly as he continued. "I already mentioned that I am called Jaap, haven't I? Jaap Dubois, but for you, just Jaap."

His eyes were laughing as he enjoyed her blush. *I think you are a treasure, Marion,* he thought. *Don't think that I would just let you go like that!* He stood for a moment and watched her walk down the street, hand in hand with Inge. A plan arose within him, and he smiled boyishly.

I'll have to talk this over with Koert, he thought. *A beard and a red suit might just flatter me.*

Then he strolled the long way home to Forest Cottage, where his mother was waiting for him.

Several weeks before, Mr. Van Herewaarden agreed with Marion that this year's Saint Nicholas Day party had to be a real party for Inge. One evening, Reinier came home with a giant doll, "shamelessly undressed," as he had apologetically remarked when he opened the box.

Marion was put in charge of supplying a full wardrobe. Reinier watched with fascination as one piece after another came from her hands. Now the present lay handsomely dressed and hidden away in a safe place.

Every evening Inge sang her little song by the fireplace and faithfully set out her little shoe for Saint Nicholas. It was all still very serious business for her, and the adults took it all in with happy fellowship.

It was now the third of December, only days before the anticipated arrival of Saint Nicholas. Marion had just cleared the supper dishes from the table and Reinier sat reading to Inge when the telephone rang. He put Inge down and picked up the receiver.

"Good evening, Saint Nicholas," Inge and Marion heard him say. The child impulsively grasped her father's hand. Reinier listened for a while and nodded now and again.

"The situation is still not entirely clear to me, but I will gladly take you up on your offer for my daughter's sake," he said. "We'll see you soon, then, Saint Nicholas." He hung up the phone.

Marion was not altogether free of female curiosity, and a couple of questions lay burning on her tongue, but Reinier kept her with Inge in uncertainty. He nonchalantly remarked that Saint Nicholas would be coming himself on December 5 to hand out the gifts.

Marion was restless those two days. There were many things occupying her thoughts. First, there was the visit to Mrs. Van Herewaarden, which loomed before her like a mountain. And now, that laughing, boyish face kept pushing itself forward, forcing her to think about him: Jaap Dubois.

Reinier had frowned a little when the mysterious caller had announced, "Saint Nicholas here," then continued. "My name is Dubois, Mr. Van Herewaarden. Jaap Dubois. I met Miss Verkerk with your daughter a few days ago, and we were talking about Saint Nicholas. I will be functioning as the good bishop for the pleasure of my little brother and sister, and if you would like to make use of my services, I am favorably disposed to coming by your home, as well. Perhaps the child will enjoy it."

Reinier had accepted. Dubois had to be a son of the grounds keeper Dubois who worked for his mother but lived somewhere in the forest in this area, miles away from the castle. As a boy, he had sometimes been there with his father, but then the children were still very small, he remembered.

And so the last few days passed.

"Shouldn't we also do something for Mrs. Van Herewaarden?" Marion had asked Reinier hesitantly.

Reinier looked up with surprise. "If you can think of something, that would be nice. But she has so few needs, and she isn't interested in anything. In any case, I give you a *carte blanche*."

Marion thought and thought. Finally she ordered a basket of pink hanging begonias and warmly colored cyclamen. A small collection of poems wrapped in white tissue paper had been laid in the flowers, and inside lay a picture of Inge, which Marion had had enlarged for herself, that showed Inge on the swing, with windblown hair and shining eyes—a piece of sparkling life itself.

The florist would take care of the delivery to the hospital. There was a card that went along with it: "A little surprise from Saint Nick," Reinier had written on it.

The enchanted night had come. When the bell rang loudly and insistently at quarter to seven, Reinier answered the door himself. The packages had been collected and were lying ready for the saint. Inge was completely unaware of the plot; she was full of anticipation.

In her heart, Marion was rather ambivalent about the idea of a stranger being present at the party she had so carefully prepared. Then Saint Nicholas walked into the room. Inge did exactly what was expected of her: She sang her little song and sat on the lap of old saint, her lip quivering.

Then old Saint Nick began to speak, slowly solemnly. His eyes were young and pressing, and it began to dawn on Reinier that this visit was intended just as much for Marion as it was for Inge.

Marion needed but a few moments to orient herself to this voice. Before Saint Nick's helper, Black Pete, began to hand out the gifts, Marion's warm blush had already betrayed to the saint that she had penetrated his disguise.

Inge was touchingly happy with her doll and actually had no attention left to give to the giver. As Reinier let the wayfaring guests out again, Marion sat with burning eyes, looking at the tasteful little book in her lap, in which was written, "For Services Rendered."

The rough sketch of a little boy's head was pasted on the inside—the little boy from the toy store. Marion recognized it at first glance and realized, *This is pure talent. He is no dilettante.*

After Inge had, with great pains, been worked toward her bed—"The dowwy has to come awong, Miss Mayon"—and

Marion sat down at the table with her embroidery, Reinier laid a small package in front of her with a brusque gesture. "That's for you," he said curtly, then he walked away.

Marion looked tenderly at the three books that emerged from the wrapping paper. It was the trilogy about which they had recently spoken. Once again, one of her heart's desires was fulfilled.

"For a thousand tender cares" was written in the first volume.

"I could get conceited," she said to herself, aloud. It was just like all the other years: Books, books, and more books for Marion.

She set her embroidery down and paged through her presents. Her thoughts wandered to the young man who had come for her—yes, for her—and had extended to her a small token of his attention with a look that spoke volumes.

On Magda's table stood the pink flowers, celebrating their brief existence; they lent something unusually bright and happy to the room

Yet happiness was far from Magda. She wept heartrending tears and gave Reinier only confused and incoherent answers. She had pushed the book of poems and the picture of Inge as far from her as possible.

Reinier went home crushed. He did not understand her; he had never understood her. He wanted so much to talk to Marion about Magda, but each time he postponed it again.

Until Sunday came. Marion had been to church as usual, and now she stood in her white apron, preparing the food. Inge was playing in a corner of the room with her doll. On a sudden impulse, Reinier stood up and made his way toward the kitchen. He closed the door behind him.

Marion stood stirring a pan, and to all appearances she went calmly on stirring, but she felt his presence keenly. While she had been working in the kitchen, and earlier, when she was in church, she had been occupied with angry thoughts. She had been to see Mrs. Van Herewaarden in the hospital for a second time that week. They spoke again with each other, but this time the conversation had been very different. Magda had asked her many mean and malicious questions. She had reproached her for the Saint Nicholas Day gift, knowing that it had been Marion's doing.

She had read the poems over and over, and she looked up one for Marion with agitated fingers: "Here. Don't you understand that you hurt me with such things?

> This is youth, an expectation,
> beaming and without end,
> bubbling like champagne
> which sings through the blood.
> This is youth, cheerful giving
> never asking in return
> with open hands and wide eyes
> like a child.

"I had nearly let go of life. What more did it have to offer me? But now it has been thrust before me again, warm and seductive. The wound has been opened again; the old pain is back. Why don't you leave me alone?"

Magda heaped reproaches on Marion, and yet she did not send her away. She clung to Marion and told her to call her Magda, like an old friend. There was a strange relationship between these two: They repelled each other, and at the same time were attracted to each other.

Marion thought a lot about Magda, and her indignation rose at the thought of her circle of friends, of the people who were allowing her to petrify in her coldness and emptiness

49

and who had quietly resigned themselves to her numbness. Reinier shared responsibility for this—especially Reinier.

Marion stood thinking about these things as Reinier silently observed her. And when he spoke, it was the drop that made the bucket overflow.

"The doctor has complained to me that my wife has been very upset the last few weeks," he said. "She is going downhill fast. He warned that she must not get too excited."

Marion turned, her eyes flashing. "Is that what the doctor thinks?" she burst forth. "Then I think he is a pathetically bad psychologist. Is it better that she lie there, freezing inside the walls of ice and loneliness she had built up around herself, and that she die frozen and numb, with no ties to life and no hope of life after death?

"Oh, sure, it's easier, for us, and maybe for her, too. If she is confronted again with life, with joy and play, with children and flowers, with want and need, she will experience more pain, and it will be harder for her to die. Be happy that she can cry again! Maybe now she can believe that a day will come when God will wipe away all the tears from her eyes.

"You have written her off as dead! What good does it do if she plays out her cold, forgotten life a few weeks more? She must fight to find her life again before she dies. She must unthaw, and unthawing always hurts. Don't you understand that?"

This was a different Marion, in her righteous indignation. Her eyes blazed, and a blush of excitement crossed her cheeks. This was Marion at her best, a flame, shooting high above the small, clear light that she usually was, constantly though quietly burning.

They were standing close to each other in the humid kitchen. The misted windows closed out the world.

Reinier clenched his hands deep in his pants pockets. His

eyes drank in her face. A great amazement burst over him. *Child,* he thought painfully, *how I love you.*

Later, he could no longer remember how the rest of the day had passed. It was a long agony. Marion did not receive much comment on her outburst. She could not imagine what she had awakened in Reinier: desire, pain, self-accusation.

That night brought him no rest. Reinier desperately fought his heart.

Marion, he thought. *Marion.*

It had finally come, his great happiness, but he had to kill it with his own hands. He was a married man, the husband of a woman for whose happiness the one he now loved had pleaded and battled.

How difficult it was to muzzle that little voice within which reminded him that Magda was so sick, that she would certainly die soon. *Then you will be free,* said the voice. *Then she will be yours.*

Reinier knew these thoughts were wrong. He pushed his face deep into his pillow, and his fists clenched under the covers. How sinful he was. How unworthy of the innocence of that guileless child. God would surely punish him for this guilty love, for this tainted desire.

He could already see the blow that would be given him. The house of the grounds keeper rose before him, and in it a blond lad, a lad that had become a man, Jaap Dubois. He had a right to Marion, the right of freedom and youth. She would be his bride; and for him, Reinier Van Herewaarden, there would only be loneliness.

The night seems so much longer when one cannot sleep.

He threw off the covers and stepped onto the cold rug. He threw open the curtains and looked deep into the frozen night. The stars twinkled high and silent above, and a sickle moon hung motionless in the air. How could the night be so full of peace when it was storming in his heart?

51

He stood there until the cold made him shiver.

His heart was mutinous, as were his prowling thoughts. *Why has God brought all this misery on me? Why has he given me a childhood without love, a wife without a heart?*

Love had burst upon him, a love a thousand times deeper and warmer than he had ever felt for Magda, and must he now stand by and watch another take this beloved child from his home without being able to do anything?

Under his watchful eyes, her love for the other would grow, and he would never be able to speak a word to her of his own love. He felt his jealousy of Jaap Dubois racing through his veins like a physical pain.

He forcefully calmed himself, and once he lay down, he suddenly realized how tired he was. Just before morning, he fell into a fitful sleep.

After that night he carried his unsolved problem with him like a lead weight. Yet he had mastered himself enough to be able to pass on to Marion the invitation from "Saint Nicholas," which he had stubbornly kept to himself for several days. An invitation for her and Inge to come and meet the children of the Forest Cottage. He told her about the old house in the woods, and she listened with great interest. After all, Jaap lived there!

Marion was, for the first time in her life, actually in love.

❧ Chapter 5 ❧

The grounds keeper's lodging was very old. On the mossy front wall, heavy iron letters and numbers were attached: "Anno Domini 1786." The shutters were painted black and yellow, as they were on all the buildings affiliated with the castle.

Surrounding the house were aged trees that dwarfed Forest Cottage. It seemed such a peaceful place, this grounds keeper's lodging, far off the beaten track, reachable only through a forest lane that was planted on the windward side with sturdy beech trees.

Still, quiet was often far from Forest Cottage. It should not be forgotten that eleven people lived here, eleven healthy, lively people, all of whom let themselves be heard from time to time. Grandmother fit in well with the quiet of the surroundings. She had fought her fight and enjoyed with a gentle smile the joy which the twilight of her life still had to offer.

Then there was the grounds keeper, with his heavy, penetrating voice, the voice of a clarion, and his wife, the stout, openhearted mother, Marie-Louise.

Next to Forest Cottage stood an old carriage house that had not been used for a long time. This was Jaap's domain, as the oldest son. He had his studio there and stoked his own potbellied stove. The carriage house faced a small meadow and a large window had been hewn out, through which the bright northern light tumbled in.

Jaap had a beautiful collection of art objects he had collected on the long trips he took. Grandmother's adventuresome spirit had taken up residence in him. He, too, was like a migratory bird, always beset with longing for the sunny skies, now only temporarily landing at his parent's home. If his yearning for the distant became too strong, he would simply depart for another country that could satisfy his passion for beauty.

This was possible because his work was in demand. He had no financial worries or many needs. All desire for comfort was alien to him. How different the children of one family can sometimes be!

Laurens Dubois was twenty-four. He was only a year younger than his brother, but his character was so much more balanced. Since schooldays, Ronnie had always been his girl, his friend, with whom he had built his future. The younger children thought that Ronnie was simply part of the family. They had been married a year and occupied a couple of rooms in Forest Cottage, that beehive of activity. It made little difference when the cries of little Jaap joined the singing and shouting of his youthful uncles and aunts.

Perhaps Grandmother was the only one for whom this noise ever became too much. But she had learned to get along over the years, and her heart was big enough to lend a place to all these rascals, large and small.

Koert was still a schoolboy, but he already felt like an adult.

His eighteen years rendered him very important in his own eyes. He was certainly the most boisterous of the bunch.

After him came little Bram, who was sensible and cautious. His position was unique in Forest Cottage. He belonged neither with the grown-ups nor with the children. This distinction held little honor for a young man of twelve years, who was already attending middle school, yet little Bram was able to move between the two groups with amazing facility, and was wise for his age.

Then there were little Gert and Marlies, the two stragglers and the favorites of all. If it is true that children born after the mother's fortieth year receive an extra dose of tenderness, then little Gert and Marlies were no exceptions to the rule.

Life for these two was still so rich and uncomplicated, so safe and full of happiness! They had their chickens and rabbits, the birds of the forest, the shy squirrels, which came bounding across the yard. There was the forest—father's forest—that was as big as the world. There was Grandmother, who always had pillow mints, and little Jaap, whom they could admire. The days passed so quickly for little Gert and Marlies.

And now it had snowed! That was a brand-new joy added to all the others. They could not get enough play in today.

On this day Marion, on her afternoon walk with Inge, entered the lane that led into the forest. When she rounded the bend in the forest lane, the sight that greeted her was like a postcard. The roof of Forest Cottage was covered with a thick layer of snow. The backdrop of snow-covered, wooden trees left her speechless. It was like a fairy tale!

Inge had already discovered the playing children. Little Gert was busy rolling a large snowball, which was to serve as head for the snowman under construction. He was panting under the load of his freight and looked distrustfully at the unfamiliar child who stood by the front gate. Yet his first impression did not seem to be a bad one. "Do you want to come and help?" he asked openly, and Inge eagerly responded.

Little Marlies also approached. She was just three, and Gert took on something of a protective air in her presence. "That is my little sister," he said to Marion. "Her name is Marlies, and my name is Gert. What's her name?" A round little hand pointed to Inge, and the acquaintance of the children was already made.

Marion was allowed to place the heavy snowball on top of the snowman, a job which was a little too heavy for the children. While they were reveling in their building and molding, Mrs. Dubois checked up on them. She stood for a while in front of the living room window, taking in the whole scene.

She recognized Marion. She had seen her once in the store with Inge, and another time she had biked by just as the two girls were entering the gate of the Warbler.

She knew the history of Reinier Van Herewaarden first-hand, and a great compassion for Inge filled her motherly heart. This poor child lacked a mother's love.

Mrs. Dubois had never found the proud Magda Merkel-back to be a very sympathetic figure, and she was sorry when the young baron chose her. But now that the young woman had suffered so greatly and had been so tossed about by life, Mrs. Dubois's compassion overcame her dislike.

When Jaap entered the room, she called him to the window. Surprise flowed over his face. "So, Mother, what do you think of my discovery?"

They watched together for a moment. Marion was getting warm. She had taken off her overcoat and stood there so open and carefree in her red jumper, her white wool shawl hanging loosely around her neck. Her blond curls lay tangled over her face. This carefree play in the snow made her blood tingle. The children were pleased to have such a large playmate.

Jaap did not remain long on that side of the window. His fingers were itching to join in. A moment later, Marion felt a snowball on the back of her neck, and when she turned around, she saw Jaap's laughing face behind her. She reached without a thought for the fluffy snow, and soon the snowball fight was underway. The little ones plunged in as well. Jaap shook himself off like a poodle. "Four against one isn't fair!" he yelled, and he came after Marion with a handful of snow, with the apparent intention of washing her face. He grabbed her arm, but she avoided him. A wild chase around the house began, until he was finally able to catch her by the shed.

Tired and panting from running, she rested defenselessly in his arms. They were both red and wet from the snow, but their eyes were laughing. A splashing, reckless happiness bubbled up in them. They were young, and the game was so old and so exciting!

Jaap forgot the snow that slowly melted away in his hand. He pressed a soft, light kiss onto her warm mouth and said triumphantly, "So, Marion, did you think I would run so hard for nothing?"

She pushed the wet hair out of her eyes and brushed the snow from her skirt. He watched her closely, his hands in his pockets.

Oh, to draw her like this! he thought passionately, and the stare with which he drank her in was almost gluttonous.

"Come on!" he said as he grabbed her hand. In front of the house they found the children, who had continued the struggle, as well as Bram, who had just ridden in on his bike.

Mrs. Dubois rapped on the window and held up a cup. Shortly thereafter, they were all sitting around the glowing stove, their tingling hands clasped around hot cups of tea.

After Marion had departed with Inge, Mrs. Dubois said to Jaap, "Is Marion aware of the history of Reinier Van Herewaarden? Does she know that he comes from the castle?"

Jaap shrugged his shoulders. He wasn't very interested. "If he hasn't told her, why should we?" he asked laconically. "And if she does know, she'll bring it up sometime." With that the issue was closed, as far as he was concerned, and his mother had to concede that he was right.

Ingeborg was full of delightful stories, and so her father got an idea of the snow party that had taken place that afternoon. He could hear the happiness in Marion's voice; he could see it in the light of her eyes.

Jaap, Jaap! rang in her head. Oh, sure, Marion had enough sense to know that one kiss did not constitute a declaration of love, but what did that matter? The future was a sunbathed garden in which everything was possible, a veritable wonderland. Saturday she would see him again; they were going to take a walk together.

By Saturday the snow had almost melted away, but it was freezing again, and an enchanting frost covered the earth. Every branch, every leaf had been provided with a lacy border, and an old, broken-down pile of chicken wire had been transformed from an ugly, gray pauper into a prim prince with lacy collar and richly pleated, white ruffles.

Marion's imagination worked incessantly. She saw the world in a new and brilliant light. Jaap was a charming escort, an amusing man of many words. And Marion knew how to listen. He knew the way through the woods very well. As a boy, he had wandered around here for hours at a time, a fact which he also related to Marion. Their syncopated steps clicked rhythmically on the frozen forest path.

He continually felt the need to take sidelong glances at her. Her hair was so soft and light against her supple red headscarf. His hair was also blond, but his had a deeper hue and ran the spectrum from light to dark blond.

And yet she's not beautiful, he thought. *Far from it.*

He had known women who left her in the dust as far as beauty was concerned—slender French women, elegant and graceful; Italian women, with their dark, wild beauty; women from lands where the veil was still used, cloaked in a mysterious aura of sweet, intoxicating allure.

Marion was so simple; she was as open as a spring morning, a walk through the snow. What unique power of attraction held him in her sway? Was it his own insatiable yearning for beauty that he found in her eyes? Was it her innocence that made her so desirable to him?

"Where are we going?" asked Marion, and he told her that their destination was Borg, a little village—actually just a hamlet—that contained an old seventeenth-century church he wanted to see again.

"When you stand in that old church, Marion," he said, "you feel transported to another place and time. It's as though the spirits of our ancestors still hover there, exerting their influence.

"Nowhere have I felt that as strongly as I have there. Not in Notre Dame in Paris, not in St. Peter's in Rome, no matter how much you might be impressed by the majesty of those buildings.

"Nowhere is that spirit so strong as in that little church close to home. And now I want to know if you also feel it."

They had walked for over an hour when the forest gave way to pastures. They stood motionless for a moment. The narrow church steeple projected above the houses, and a little farther, beyond the trees, the towers of the House of Herewaarden were sketched against the sky.

"Look, there's the castle," pointed Jaap. He bent over her, and as she followed the direction of his extended hand, his cheek nearly touched hers. He could smell the lovely scent of her hair.

This was the first that Marion had heard of the existence of the castle. "The castle?" she said, surprised and curious. "Is it far?"

"Yes, too far for today, if we want to visit the church, at least. But we can still go there some other time!"

They walked down the village street. While Jaap asked the custodian for the key, Marion stood looking at the front of the church.

Their steps echoed loud and hollow in the entryway. Marion said with wonder, "I thought it was a Catholic church, Jaap! You don't find many of these old Protestant churches here in this part of the country!"

Jaap explained that the church was connected with the castle, and that the barons had been devoted to Protestanism since the Reformation.

The stood silently in the nave of the church. There was indeed a very unusual atmosphere there. They silently allowed it to sink in. Jaap could feel that aura that inspired him so, that awakened and fueled in him the urge to create.

A soft sound in the back of the building made him turn around. The old wife of the custodian was moving about, dressed in the traditional dress of the region. She fit wonderfully into these mystical surroundings.

Jaap took a couple of steps in her direction; they spoke briefly. He then took out his sketchbook and the passion that stirred in his blood spilled out onto the paper. The dim light flowed gently over their heads.

Marion walked slowly down the aisle. On the walls hung many weapons and plaques with names, dates, and texts.

In a wing extending from the side of the chancel stood a large family grave. Marion perceived that this entire church bore the mark of the inhabitants of the castle. She spelled out the names that had been chiseled into the marble:

"Here lies Reinier, Baron of Herewaarden, died July 24,

1738, and his noble wife, Machteld Geertruida, died October 29, 1750.

"Soli Deo Gloria."

Marion, stunned by the name, read it over and over again, attached each time to different dates. Many, many generations lay buried here, but each time, that same name came back again; Reinier, Baron of Herewaarden. Suddenly many things became clear to her that she had previously simply accepted without understanding. Her difficult, reserved employer, to whom she had become so attached, in spite of his continual outbursts, must be a son of this noble family.

She forgot for a moment that she had come here with Jaap Dubois. Her discovery had taken complete possession of her.

Soli Deo Gloria were the words that dominated the graves, subordinating to themselves even the pompous embellishments.

Soli Deo Gloria—to God alone the glory.

Marion thought of Mr. Van Herewaarden's resistance to everything that had to do with God and religion—a resistance that in essence was weak. She had sensed that a long time ago. The way he listened so intently to the Bible readings betrayed him. All his mocking words could not erase or undo that fact.

Marion was warmed by the thought that she had been the one who had been allowed to show him the way back to this living confession of his ancestors: *Soli Deo Gloria.*

He was turning back, of that she was certain.

Perhaps he was already even farther than she thought.

Marion's thoughts also turned to Magda and Inge as she stood under the beams of the old church, where the past cried out from every stone, and here she accepted for a second time the task God had placed in her hands but now more seriously, more consciously than ever.

❦ Chapter 6 ❧

Wisely and wonderfully, God, the Chessman, moves His pieces. Gentle and tender is the hand with which the Good Shepherd leads His sheep.

After several fruitless visits, the church council of Dintelborg had placed the baptismal membership of Mr. Van Herewaarden and his worldly wife on the list of doubtful and, humanly speaking, hopeless cases.

Yet God had chosen an inexperienced child, a girl with a warm and loving heart, to point out to these two wandering sheep the way to the eternal Light.

The lessons through which a child of God must walk before being capable of bearing the assigned task are often difficult and incomprehensible.

For forty lonely years, Moses had to shepherd the flock of his father-in-law, Jethro, in order to be cured of his uncontrollable temper and learn patience for the difficult task of leading a disobedient and rebellious people out of slavery into freedom.

And so God teaches everyone.

For Marion Verkerk, these years of learning were the most somber years of her life. She had to nurture infinite patience in dealing with her burdensome mother; she had gradually learned not to respond to her baseless accusations. She had learned endurance and forgiveness, but never in all those years did she suspect where that path of self-denial might lead.

For each of His children, the Heavenly Father has determined a path. There are those whom He keeps on a path close to His heart and with tender care teaches the soft words of selflessness: "In the same way, let your light shine before men, so that they may see your good deeds and praise your Father in heaven." This is the *Soli Deo Gloria* that resonates in seemingly insignificant lives.

But God also has children to whom He seems to be indifferent, whom He allows to wander away, along their own alien paths. Yet, He does not let them go: Slowly but surely, He bends those paths with His loving hand, so slowly, sometimes, that the child does not notice. And one day those two paths cross: The one belonging to him who attempted in wild and rebellious defiance to keep his life for himself, and the other belonging to one who, through a long and wearisome struggle, has learned to walk on other paths.

Yet above that intersection, the Almighty sits enthroned, and wise and wonderful is the movement by which He draws those two lives together.

❦ Chapter 7 ❧

Suddenly Marion felt two hands on her shoulders and heard Jaap's voice whisper softly into her ear, "Are you coming, Marion?"

She returned to reality. "Yes, I'm coming," she replied in a subdued tone, but before she turned around, she cast one last glance at the grave.

Jaap pointed out a name to her, the last of a long series. "That is your employer's father," he said. "He was kicked by his horse while show jumping. That was almost twenty years ago, when I just a young lad like our Gert is now, but I can still remember the burial very well. The whole village mourned. He was very loved."

It's true, then! Marion thought, but she did not want to ask Jaap any questions. It wasn't that she did not want to hear more about the occupants of the castle. On the contrary, but in some way it seemed she would be betraying Mr. Van Herewaarden if she were to discuss this with Jaap.

When they were outside again, they realized that twilight was rapidly overtaking daylight. A veil of mist had settled over the village, and the world had become very small.

Borg had only one café; actually it was half of an old barn. In the pub was a large open hearth, and ancient plants stood on the windowsills. The room was dimly lit by a kerosene lamp, which disguised well the blemished old furniture. This was a good place to rest. They spooned their hot pea soup out of crude wooden bowls and laughed with each other across the table. They teased and joked with each other, carefully choosing their words so as not to injure this fragile air of growing happiness. Another hour and a half of walking still separated them from their homes, but the time did not seem long to Marion.

Her heart was so frightfully full. She thought briefly to herself, *I should be alone now in order to work through all this. We should be silent now.*

Yet Jaap's talking did not bother her. There was still so much in his life that was unknown to her, and she wanted to know everything about him. He was so sweet to her! They walked, pressed against each other. He stood still and pressed her into his arms, while her head fell back.

In the falling darkness he could see her eyes, frightened, yet with something of that feminine mystery in them, a slight laugh that robbed him of his last reserve. He kissed her, reckless and without inhibition, her childlike mouth, her wise eyes, her temples, and her honey-blond hair.

His hand tossed aside her shawl, and she felt his hot breath on her neck. "Darling," he whispered, but she remained silent, tremblingly, with a joy larger than herself, a joy that deprived her of all words.

When she returned, Reinier was ready to go visit Magda; Inge was already in bed. They exchanged a few simple words;

she blinking against the bright light, he with his coat already on.

Then, the silence fell around her once again, for which she was grateful. She took a long look at herself in the mirror, amazed, and then she sighed.

This was all so incomprehensible, so unexpected.

She sat in Reinier's favorite chair, leaning her head on the cushions, her ever-busy hands inactive in her lap.

Slowly the heavy beating of her heart calmed.

When Reinier came home at eight o'clock, he was in no mood for talking. He grumbled about the mist that made it so dangerous to be on the road. He stood in front of the fire and took off his gloves, stamping his cold feet on the floor so that the cups rattled.

"What weather!" he said, shivering. "How could anyone be taking a pleasure walk outside for so many hours?"

Marion gave a slight laugh that spoke volumes.

He fell listlessly into a chair, chilled to the very marrow.

Marion silently picked up his coat and hat and brought them into the hall.

"Where did you go?" he asked, just to say something.

"To Borg," Marion answered from the tea table, without looking up. "We visited the church."

"The church at Borg?" he asked with surprise, and suddenly a multitude of images came to life before him. He saw himself as a young boy again, walking with his father to the high, elaborately carved pew that overlooked the entire congregation. He had not been there for years. Had he developed an aversion to that church since his father was laid to rest in that old grave on that cold day in May? He had only been a child. But the baroness had been no faithful churchgoer after her husband's death, and so the two boys had also drifted from the church.

So Marion had seen the church at Borg! In his thoughts he

was standing next to her as she viewed the old grave. He knew its every line; when he closed his eyes, he could see it before him. He knew the history of most of his ancestors. How often his father had told him of an earlier ancestor who had borne his name. His father had been so attached to the House of Herewaarden and the history of the family.

Suddenly, while he reclined in his chair so quietly that Marion thought he was sleeping, Reinier realized that that love lived in him, as well.

Marion sat looking at him, her chin supported by her hand. How she had come to trust this face! The dark, thick hair, with its few traces of gray; the rugged, firm jaw with the dark shadow of his heavy beard; the sharp lines of his nose, which accentuated his serious gray eyes . . .

She felt caught when he finally looked up.

"Listen, Miss Marion," he said, and she hardly recognized his voice, it sounded so dark and burdened. "I will tell you a story.

"A long, long time ago, there lived a knight. He was called Reinier the Warrior, for he was a brave man. He fought until this land was free of the lords who enslaved it. He fought for the people, and the people loved him. When tranquility finally ruled in his domain, he departed on a long journey, for he was a warrior in his heart and soul, and tranquility made him sick. He came back to die, for he had become a leper in a faraway land.

"He died a terrible death, but his family survived him. He had a son who acquired the name Reinier the Pious. He founded a chapel in the woods to which he retired every morning to pray. In his time, a wave of spiritual fervor swept the land. The pope had called upon all believers to deliver Jerusalem and the grave of Christ from the Turks.

" 'It is God's will, it is God's will!' was the cry that blew over the lands. Reinier the Pious was also touched by it, and he traveled along on the dangerous journey to the Holy Land, leaving behind the lady of the castle with her small children. Like Count Floris the Second, he succumbed to the plague in the mountainous desert of Asia Minor, which the army of crusaders ravaged.

"His son grew and lived with his children and grandchildren in the castle that the people from the surrounding areas had built for Reinier the Warrior out of thanks for the tranquility he had brought to their lands.

"There were knights who spent large sums of money on the beautification of the castle. There were some who collected great treasures, and there were others who squandered them.

"During the Eighty-Year War, on the third of May, 1590, the day on which Breda was taken through treachery by the Spaniards, the people of the House of Herewaarden celebrated because an heir was born. He, too, received the name of *Reinier,* the name his forefathers had borne and which his descendants would bear.

"He fought many years later for the freedom of the seventeen provinces of the United Netherlands under the banner of the Subduer of Cities.

"He was also the one who built the church at Borg, which was completed the same year in which the Peace of Westphalia was signed. On the cornerstone he had the words engraved *Soli Deo Gloria.*

"Did you see that?"

He looked at Marion, and she nodded. She found it difficult to realize that these things had actually happened.

While he was relating these things, she had seen herself, the little Marion Verkerk of years ago, with folded arms and stiff blond braids, listening to her history lesson at school.

Crusades, the Eighty-Year War, the Peace of Westphalia— it all sounded so familiar, and yet she had trouble connecting them with the man who sat relating these stories so realistically, as though he had personally observed the earlier Reiniers in their activities and inactivities. She understood that it was the history of his ancestors that he was telling, and that fascinated her a great deal. He used but a few words, and sometimes he would be silent for several minutes, but in Marion's lively imagination, the persons he described came alive.

Reinier slowly picked up a pipe, and as he tamped the tobacco into the bowl with his thumb, he said, "I'm not boring you with these old stories, am I?"

When she insisted that he was not, he continued. "Centuries passed. The modernization of the world did not leave the castle undisturbed. Especially over the last fifty years, a great deal changed. Around the turn of the century, candles were still burned as lighting, but that time is past. The carriages were replaced by cars. Electrical lamps now light the entrance lane, and the old harpsichord has been replaced by a radio.

"In the time of transition, another heir was born. The early years of his life were very happy. There were always people standing by to fulfill his every desire. His father was a good and noble man, from whom he learned a great deal. He often took the young boy with him on his horse when he visited the tenants, and he taught him to be friendly and helpful, and to look down on no one.

"When the boy was older and went to school, they often took long walks together, and on Sundays he took the child with him to the church at Borg. Now and again his mother also went along, but mostly she stayed at home with his sickly brother, Diederick, who had asthmatic bronchitis in addition to being born lame.

"So little Reinier became a daddy's boy. His father was an outdoorsman, his mother a salon figure. He had few attachments to her.

"When he was ten, he suffered his first heavy blow; his

father received a fatal kick to the head from his own favorite horse, the ash stallion, Gray. He was only thirty-six.

"He was brought home with heavy wounds and lived only a day.

"Diederick did not yet understand what was happening in the sick room; he was still too young. But Reinier wandered through the empty corridors of the castle with an unbearable fear in his heart.

"When he was called to say good-bye to his father, he whispered, and the boy would never forget these words, 'Be a knight, Reinier. Take care of your mother, take care of your little brother. Take care of everyone and try to be a good son of your father. And the Bible is for you.'

"Then they brought the boy away because his father was drained and death was no longer to be thwarted. The boy had an overwhelming need to cry out in his pain. He did not feel like a knight. He could not take care of anyone. He wanted only to be protected and comforted. He sought that comfort in his mother, but she was too preoccupied with her own grief to give him any attention. Then he turned away from her, and slowly he shut her completely out of his life."

Reinier fell into a long silence.

Involuntarily, Marion looked at the old family Bible, which was dusted every morning either by herself or by Toos. It sat there so uselessly.

Reinier followed her glance. His voice was louder and sharper when he continued. "The boy has not carried out the wishes of his father very well."

Then he began to speak again, and gradually his voice resumed its old subdued tone.

"He was something of a loner. When he left school, he usually turned aside into the woods. When he was older, and had his own horse, he wandered even farther. He sought out the tenants, whom he used to visit with his father, and spoke more openly with these simple people about his father—more openly than he dared with his mother.

"There was little joy in the castle those days. The empty place remained. The estate manager looked after things and consulted with the baroness, and she silently bore her sorrow for her husband. She had difficulty expressing herself and expected no openness from others. With great love and devotion, she cared for weak Diederick and raised him with impeccable manners.

"Reinier, who was four years older, escaped as much as possible from the straitjacket of formalities and obligations, but he was not always successful.

"One day they were expecting an especially important visitor. The baroness carefully instructed her oldest son. He held before himself, as he often did, the last wishes of his father, and resolved to conduct himself as a knight, a worthy member of the court, and to be a good escort for his mother.

"But he was sixteen, a period of upheaval in his life. The visitor was so tedious and spoke in such a monotone, and it was spring. His heart longed for the outdoors.

"In the middle of the conversation, he ran out into the woods. He ran until his feet hurt. Then he threw himself down on the moss and listened to the sounds of the spring evening.

"There lived in him such a strong yearning for happiness that he could have cried. But he was sixteen and wanted to be a man, so he did not cry. He simply lay there and thought of his father and his mother, whom he had once again abandoned in a crunch, and an intense hatred for himself grew within him.

"But he so despised the life he was required to lead. He missed the hand of his father on his shoulder, and he reproached his mother for being so closed, even though he marveled at her resolve and her understanding of her obligations.

"With his head in his arms, he dreamed of a future sparkling with sunshine and joy, glittering with happiness.

"And as he lay happily in his dream, a bird began to sing close by in the bushes. Ever stronger and more beautifully it sang, and its song became the accompaniment to the young boy's desires. It was the warbler that sang. Years later he could still hear the trills within, and the little songbird became the incarnation of his great desire.

"That was the reason he later named his house the Warbler, but perhaps that was his greatest mistake."

Reinier's last sentence broke off, and he bit his lip. Marion could not perceive the depth of his feeling. For her it was simply the confirmation of her suspicion that the marriage of Mr. and Mrs. Van Herewaarden had not been happy.

She had followed his story with careful attention, and she was little surprised by the odd way in which he related it to her. How could she know that Reinier had anxiously maintained the third person in order to deprive the tale of its warm personal character?

He did not understand how he had come to the point of dredging up all these memories; but sometimes a person feels a need to get things out, to take someone into his confidence, and to find a listening ear! He had been working things through for too long on his own.

He told many other things about his life—of his youth, full of friendships his mother considered unacceptable; of the disastrous year at the aristocratic boarding school; of his socialist tendencies during his high school years; of his entire resolute struggle to be free. But he said nothing of Magda.

When Marion lay in bed that night, she reflected on the story told by Mr. Van Herewaarden. "Still," she said pensively to herself, "it would be nice to be able to tell the history of one's ancestors."

She knew nothing about her grandfather, except that he was called Job and owned a grocery. With him, her knowledge of her ancestry ended.

Will Inge inherit the castle? she mused to herself. *No, Mr. Van Herewaarden will surely remarry if Magda dies.* He was still young, and who knew how many sons he might have? She could not imagine a woman who would suit him, but she soon cast aside such idle thoughts. Then her thoughts returned to Jaap and circled around him. With a smile on her lips, she fell asleep.

Reinier paced the room for a long time, the empty pipe clenched between his teeth. Now that he was an adult, he realized what a difficult child he had been for his mother—an *enfant terrible*, always rubbing against the grain, always stubbornly pursuing his own will. What drove him on? A yearning for something out of his grasp? Was he really asking that much from life? To work hard; to achieve something with his own hands. A wife who wanted to be his friend, and children to play with. A place in the world where he could be himself. Yet everything had broken off in his hands. A plan rose hesitantly in his mind, and as he made his way upstairs, he began to work it out. It calmed him. *Tomorrow,* he thought to himself, but Sunday had already begun. Somewhere in the night, a clock tower struck two.

❧ Chapter 8 ❧

As Marion descended the steps the next morning in her luxurious dressing gown—a birthday gift from Father and Mother—she heard a door open along the corridor above and, as she looked up, she saw the sleep-tossed hair of Mr. Van Herewaarden bent over the railing.

"Miss Marion, may Inge go with you to church this morning?"

"Yes, of course," she said with surprise. "Are you going out?"

"Yes, I am going out," he answered curtly, and she bit her lip. Yes, it was rather forward of her to blurt out such a question!

Later, while she was sitting at the table, Inge noticed that Reinier already had the car waiting outside. "Are you going to the factory, Papa?" she asked.

"No, my child," he assured her. "Papa will be back before dinner. This afternoon we will go for a nice walk together."

After a few moments, they saw him ride away. Marion knit her brow. Where in heaven's name could he be going at such an early hour? Marion threw her cape over her shoulders and, taking Inge by the hand, walked through the quiet morning streets to the church. Here and there they came across another churchgoer, but the quiet was generally intense. The mist had not yet risen.

Reinier rode down the Rijkstraatweg in the direction of Borg. As he approached the village, he overtook several farmers, who strolled without haste in their Sunday best toward the church.

He parked his car behind the building and entered through a side door.

He did not sit in the elevated, carved pew, but in the back of the church, where a few pews were held open for newcomers. There he slid himself in and observed the people who came in. Most of them he knew.

The old custodian's wife caught a glimpse of him and was taken aback. "Well, well," she mumbled to herself. "Well, well." Shaking her head, she shuffled slowly out the back toward the residence of the custodian. This she had to tell to her husband.

Reinier winked amiably at her when she later pushed a songbook in his direction. "How are you, Mrs. Brandsma?" he whispered.

"Fine, baron," she responded shyly, a bit awed.

Reinier felt wonderfully at home among the weathered tenants and small shopkeepers of Borg, all of whom he knew by name and nickname. This was a feeling he never had in Dintelborg, a feeling of being at home among one's own people.

Old Reverend Gerritsen climbed into the pulpit, and the

service began. Not everything that was said sunk in to Reinier, for there were too many things going on inside of him this morning. He avoided looking at the elevated pew, where he knew his brother Diederick was sitting. He had thrown a glance in that direction when Diederick came in, leaning on the arm of the estate manager.

It was the Sunday before Christmas. Reverend Gerritsen spoke of the longing of Advent, and slowly Reinier fell under the spell of his words. " 'As a deer pants for streams of water, so my soul pants for you, O God.' "

But it was not until after the "amen," when the organ began to play, that he was overcome by a radiant joy. These sounds he understood. They had been extracted from his own most intimate feelings. " 'O my God, my soul is downcast within me . . . Deep calls to deep. All your waves and breakers have passed over me . . .' "

Deeper and deeper the tones sank. The organ had its own voice now, its own heart. It was crying out with him, it knew his pain and his desire.

" 'O my soul, why are you cast down?' "

But then, in the midst of the mourning bass, a singing treble voice broke loose. Climbing, rising, ascending to unknown heights, a jubilant song of celebration. The prelude yielded to the singing of the congregation. " 'Then I ascended to God's altar, to God, my God, the source of joy . . .' "

The psalmbook lay open before him. His eyes followed the words, but his entire soul lived in the music which washed over him. He was transported by it and plunged again into its depths. " 'Then I will join with joyful voice, and sing the praises of His care, which after fleeting times of anguish, forever comfort my despair . . .' "

The song ended with a trill, like a gasp of exhilaration.

A deep sigh escaped his lips, and after Reverend Gerritsen

had spoken the blessing, Reinier slipped quietly out of the building.

His car rushed past the churchgoers and onto the street. In fifteen minutes he was home again, happy to find it still empty. He stood by the window, looking over the withered garden, and within him the song still lamented and rejoiced. *I must hold on to this!* he thought fiercely. *If I only hold on to this, then I will manage. Then I can win the struggle.*

He walked into the salon and, for the first time in a long, long time, opened the piano. He sat down and looked awkwardly at his hands. How long had it been since they had played? They would certainly be stiff and hard to control. "I won't play," he said aloud, and he did not. He feared he might diminish the majestic echo of the organ that still resonated in his ears.

He sat before the instrument, sunk deep in his thoughts. And so Marion and Inge found him when they arrived home. He was friendly, but quiet. Marion also had her thoughts, so their coffee time passed in near silence.

After they had eaten and Marion stood to get the little Bible, Reinier held her back with a curt wave of the hand. He pushed the plates and bowls to one side of the table. Then he stood up, carefully withdrew the old family Bible from the bookcase, and laid it down before him. He opened the heavy hinges with difficulty. A strange smell rose from the old book.

Inge slid out of her chair and went and leaned against her father's knee in order to get a better look.

Marion grasped something of the solemnity of the moment and waited with great anticipation for what had to be about to happen. Reinier looked for a moment and then he read—hoarsely and slowly through the difficult Old Dutch letters—the forty-second Psalm. " 'As the hart panteth after the water brooks, so panteth my soul for thee, O God.' "

Several times Marion saw his eyes brighten as he read.

And how beautiful it was after the lament, "O my God, my soul is cast down within me," to hear the breakthrough of the triumphant, "By night Thy song shall be with me, a prayer to the God of my life."

When he had finished, a slight bashfulness hung between them.

Reinier had done this on impulse, still under the influence of what he had heard that morning; but already doubt began to rise in him. *Should I really be doing this? Should I really be applying these words to myself? Isn't this simply the temporary swell of a sensitive man?*

Inge fiddled with the copper metalwork which bound the Bible, and Reinier carefully removed her fingers.

"Would you like to see the family tree?" he asked Marion. She walked around and stood behind him, looking over his shoulder.

During French domination, because of a lack of space, a couple of thin sheets of parchment were added to the book and were immediately betrayed by their unique color. With decorative letters at the top of the page had been written the words: *Si Deus pro nobis, qui contra nos?*

Strong words from a firmly believing family.

"Have you studied Latin?" Reinier asked. Marion shook her head, but with her knowledge of French, she had already made out the words.

"If God is for us, who will be against us?"

"The hymn from Romans," she said, and in her thoughts she finished it. *"He who did not spare His own Son, but gave Him up for us all—how will He not also, along with Him, give us all things?"*

Why was it that suddenly her interest in the family tree dissipated and a few furrows appeared on her forehead directly above her nose?

She mumbled, "Very interesting," and then turned away

and began to collect the dirty dishes. As she washed the dishes, she again reviewed the events of that morning. Inge had been a sweetheart. She had turned around a few times, but for the rest, she had behaved herself admirably.

Marion had seen the Dubois family come into church: Mrs. Dubois with Koert and Bram; Laurens and Ronnie together; Mr. Dubois in the elders' pew. Only Jaap was missing. The youngest were at home with Grandmother, she presumed. But Jaap—where was he?

During the service she had mulled this over and over in her mind, and the sermon was not able to lift her spirits.

While leaving the church, she felt a hard tug on her sleeve—little Bram. "Hello, Marion!" he said, beaming. "Know what? The snowman is still there!"

They spoke with each other for a few moments, and Marion was not able to resist casually asking, "Isn't Jaap here?"

"Jaap?" asked Bram, surprised. "He never goes to church! He only went along when Laurens got married."

She did not pursue it, but it had left her with a sensation of coldness, disappointment, and a heavy feeling of uneasiness. A shadow had suddenly fallen on her sunny path. Marion tried to chase it away. Perhaps Jaap went to another church. Perhaps his carefree spirit had trouble adjusting to the strict regimen of the Christian life. But that he might not believe in God, she could not even consider. Not when he had been so overwhelmed by devotion in the church at Borg and had spoken of it with respect, yes, almost reverence. How could she reconcile this? Was it only the beauty that he loved? Was beauty his god, art his master? So she brooded and piled assumption on assumption.

Her surprise when Mr. Van Herewaarden had reached for the Bible and the emotion in his voice when he read from the Psalm led her attention away from her mulling for a moment. Yet when her thoughts fixed on that shout of joy from

Romans: "How will He not also, along with Him, give us all things?" it ran through her like an electrical shock. *All things. That also means earthly happiness. But I would never be completely happy with a husband who did not, with me, believe in God.*

This bewildering certainty completely threw off her sense of peace. For Marion Verkerk knew, oh so vexingly well, exactly where her limits lay. While she angrily wrestled with the dishcloth, she heard her father's voice, warning, "Be not unequally yoked with an unbeliever, my child."

With an impatient shrug of her shoulders, Marion gave him an answer. She tried to think of Edith.

"Come on, Mar," Edith would say without a care. "You're always so gloomy. He doesn't go to church and you do. So what? Split the difference. Who cares?"

Edith took such things so lightly. But Marion intuitively felt that there was greater weight in her father's warning because his words were in such agreement with the words of the Lord: "Whoever loves father or mother, son or daughter, more than me is not worthy of me.

Marion knew it all too well. She wished she didn't know it so well.

You are unwise, Marion disputed with herself. *What are you worried about—one silly comment of a little boy?*

Marion was unable to convince herself, however. A warm tear fell into the dishwater, because one more voice had forced its way into the discussion, a soft tormenting voice rising from her subconscious that told her that little Bram was right, indisputably right.

She grabbed for her handkerchief. Gone! She angrily swept along her eyes with the dish towel.

"There you go again," she scoffed at herself.

But the voices would not be still.

The furrow between her eyes remained, even when that one voice appeared to be the strongest, the warmest voice of all, that husky yearning voice which whispered into her ear, "Darling."

And so Marion began the Christmas holidays.

This Sunday was not only unusual for Reinier and Marion. At the House of Herewaarden, a slight uneasiness had also crept in.

As the estate manager, Heckert, helped the squire into the shiny Buick, and when properly uniformed Albert had taken his place behind the wheel, Heckert said in a subdued tone, "Did you notice that your brother, Reinier, was in church?"

"Certainly," answered Diederick, stiffly.

In his mind, the estate manager cursed. *He did not get that from a stranger,* he thought grimly. *The baroness can also end a conversation at the outset with one timely word.*

Heckert had been working for the Van Herewaardens for years now. He had seen both boys grow up, and it had made him sad to see Reinier leave the castle. He got along better with him. That boy had more character and willpower. Weak Diederick did not lack for willpower, but he had inherited more of the formal, stiff air of his mother. Unfortunately.

And yet the estate manager would be surprised later when he heard the conversation which took place between the baroness and her son.

One of the girls had served coffee, and when she had shut the door behind her, Diederick began, "Mama?"

"Yes, Diederick?"

"You may have three tries to guess who was in church this morning."

She pensively laid a white finger against her fine nose and said, "Perhaps the wife of Doctor Meertens, who has been sick for so long?"

"Wrong!"

"It is rather difficult, you know, Son. Do I know him or her?"

A half-smile glided over his face. "Very well."

"Well, I believe I shall have to give up."

"Reinier," said Diederick flatly, waiting for her reaction.

"Our Reinier?" his mother cried out.

"Yes, our Reinier."

How easily he was pulled back into the family circle through that simple little word *our*.

His mother saw her child, her oldest, before her once again: the image of his father. As a boy, he could lie for hours dreaming in front of the hearth, leaning on his elbows. Later he always liked to be sitting high on his horse, and it gave her pain to see him thus, so young and carefree and reckless. She was afraid of horses, since her husband came to his end through one.

Reinier had always remained a stranger to her. How much sorrow he had caused her by his foolish, unmannered friends, his rejection of her way of life.

The white letters: VAN HEREWAARDEN LEATHER MANUFACTURERS, painted on the walls of his factory, had been a constant irritation for her.

Why did he have to bring down and make common the old aristocratic name in this way?

The baroness had many grievances against her son, but still he remained "our Reinier." He was, after all, still her child, her firstborn son.

When Reinier lay dying, he had told her, in broken, gasping phrases, "Think about the boy, Ingeborg. About Reinier. He needs a lot of love."

Often she had thought that he had been confused by the pain, that he actually meant Diederick, the weak one.

"He needs a lot of love."

She turned these words over and over in her mind, and

over and over again after all these years. No, Reinier could not have been confused. He knew her. He knew how her heart was drawn to her youngest child, that she did not understand the independent, headstrong character of his oldest, his namesake.

That was why he warned her, but had she followed his advice?

Lady Ingeborg looked at her youngest.

"Did you speak to him?" she asked.

Diederick shook his head. "He vanished immediately. I asked Albert, and he said that he drove away like one possessed. I don't think Reinier has had it very easy, Mother."

She thought about his last statement for a moment. "Do you know how Magda is?" she asked.

"In October I spoke with the director of the hospital, and he told me that she does not have much more than half a year. And that she does not appreciate visits. Otherwise I would have gone."

His mother looked at him reprovingly. "Why have you never told me about this?"

"You didn't ask. You never talk about them," Diederick answered. She took it as a reprimand and fell silent for quite some time. After a while, however, she began again with the same topic. "How long has it been since Reinier has been here?"

"Almost a year," said her son. "Mr. Herkert had to speak with him about the mortgages. On your birthday he only sent flowers and a letter."

She nodded. "It is not good this way, Diederick," she said, and in her proud voice there was a hint of complaint, a hint of injury.

"Well then," ventured Diederick, "invite him here for Christmas or New Year's Eve . . ."

"Must I . . . ?" the baroness began. Her proud heart struggled against her motherly heart. "Must I be the one to take the first step?" she had wanted to ask, and Diederick had read the question in her eyes, even though she had not finished it.

It was a few days before she arrived at the point where she could pick up the telephone and dial the number of Reinier's factory.

Reinier sat behind his desk, immersed in his complicated computations, when the telephone rang.

"Van Herewaarden," his deep voice replied absently, but the words, "This is your mother calling," shook him.

Mama, calling on her own initiative!

"What is it, Mama?" he asked with unusual warmth, and she related the invitation for New Year's Eve.

"You must bring Ingeborg, Reinier," she said. When he was silent, she added, "Hello, did you hear me?"

"Yes, Mama," he answered in a businesslike tone, but his thoughts were racing: Marion. Should he leave Marion home alone on New Year's Eve? She had stayed in Dintelborg for the holidays especially for him and Inge. No, he could not leave her.

"I gratefully accept your invitation, Mother," he said, "but on one condition. Miss Verkerk must also come along. She is fully part of the household: Inge would not want to leave her behind!"

Now the baroness was silent for a moment. Then she conceded, although not with her whole heart. "If you think it is necessary, then it must happen. How is Magda? Would you please relay to her our greetings?"

Reinier promised he would; then he put down the receiver with a hard clap.

The figures still lay before him, but he was far away. This had been so completely unexpected!

He was glad that he had included Marion in the invitation.

His thoughts returned to Christmas, which had just passed. Marion had been unusually silent, he had noticed, and he did not speak a great deal, either.

But he did play the piano—Christmas songs for Inge, parts of Tchaikovsky's piano concerto, and Schubert's lullaby, to which Marion had sung. That wonderful, tender melody, the soft singing words! They can heal a man, but can also break him down.

He had thought a great deal about God. Or was God thinking a lot about him?

❧ Chapter 9 ❧

It was December 31. Marion had dressed for her visit to Borg. She slowly descended the stairs, feeling a little nervous. After all, it was not every day that one went to a castle, the guest of a genuine baroness!

The car was already waiting in front, and Reinier honked the horn impatiently. Inge sat next to him, beaming with pleasure. Marion stepped in and Reinier drove out of the front gate with an elegant turn.

Marion asked, "Are you going to the hospital this evening?"

"I was planning to go from Borg after dinner," was his reply. "By car it is not very far."

Marion played with her gloves. *He is in a good mood,* she thought. *Do I dare?*

She opened her mouth a couple of times, but she could not summon the courage. Reinier had observed her in the mirror. "Did you want to say something?" he asked with amusement.

Good guess, she thought, and then she said aloud, "How would it be if you took Inge with you this evening? In all the months that I have been here, her mother has not once seen her, and that cannot be good. I thought that New Year's Eve would be a good night to rectify old mistakes."

"Hm," Reinier muttered. He did not tell her off, nor did he say it was out of the question.

Marion leaned back against the seat. She was glad she had gotten it out. She had been walking around with it for so long!

The conversation moved on to other subjects, but Reinier had heard her. As he helped her out of the car in front of the broad steps, he said without further introduction, as if nothing lay between their former conversation and now, "Would my wife appreciate it? She never asks if I am going to bring Inge along."

"You know the way I work" was her only response. Reinier reflected for a moment. "Good," he said. "We will try it."

Then the broad doors were opened, and an elderly house servant appeared before Marion's eyes.

The hours that followed were like a dream for her. She was deeply impressed by the surroundings and envied her employer the ease with which he could move about here. Of course, this was his parents' home, and he was born and raised here. Marion came from a middle-class family. Although hers was an environment of cultured and educated people, it was nothing like this superaristocratic world. When she looked at the baroness—the very image of grace and distinction—then she understood how it could be said of certain people that they belonged to a difference "caste."

The baroness was not old, even though her hair was white. She was fifty-six, and her eyes were still clear in her pale face. When she spoke, her hands spoke as well, in precise little gestures that were appropriate for her but would seem ridiculous for others.

Marion could hardly take her eyes off the baroness.

Magda also has some of this grace, she thought. *She also bears in her person something of this ancient glory. Could this indefinable quality be what they called "blue blood"?*

Whatever the case, she felt like a clumsy, crude commoner in these luxurious, elegant surroundings where every word—even of the staff—seemed duly weighed and considered.

Toos would die here ran through her mind, and a mischievous dimple appeared in her cheek.

Inge was a little shy. She stood leaning alternately on the knee of her father and that of Marion and was not terribly responsive to Grandmother and Uncle Diederick, whom she could only vaguely remember.

And yet the atmosphere was not forced. There was a sustained conversation. Marion looked for a moment at her boss. He sat there so sturdy and rugged and familiar, so completely different from his family.

He was indeed at home here, but not completely. His real home was the Warbler, where he could whistle popular tunes at will or play the piano for hours on end, where he could sit with his feet propped up on a footstool without embarrassment and joke to his heart's content, where he could laugh as loudly as he pleased.

In that environment, Marion could keep pace with him, but not here.

After an hour, Ingeborg had come around a bit. She performed her entire repertoire of songs as best she could, from "Here We Go 'Round the Mulberry Bush" to "The Lord Is My Shepherd," and stole all hearts with her innocence.

When the baroness left the room, silence fell.

Reinier gave his brother a friendly slap on the shoulder.

"Play something for us, Rick!" Diederick moved to the grand piano.

Inge looked with fascination at how he handled his cane. She went and stood by him and looked trustingly up at him. "Is your leg sore?" she asked with compassion. "The Lord Jesus can make you better again!" Her serious look reflected her sincere concern for him.

Reinier and Marion threw a furtive glance of understanding toward each other in response to Inge's loving concern.

Diederick's mouth took on a rather helpless twist. "Perhaps the Lord Jesus thinks it is better for me that my leg remain like this, my dear child," he said amiably. Then he played a children's song for her, which brought sunshine into the room and cleared the air a little.

As agreed, Reinier made motions to leave after eating.

"I am going to see Magda for a while, Mama," he said nonchalantly, "and I am taking Inge along. When we come back, she must sleep here for a little while. I don't want her to stay up the entire evening. It is not healthy, and she is not used to it."

And so Marion remained alone with Diederick, for the baroness retreated into her own rooms. Their initially stiff conversation became gradually livelier, and Marion got to know the best side of the slight, sickly looking young man. They spoke about history, and on that point Diederick seemed to be an expert. He had a broad outlook on and a sharp insight into world events, but he also related stories to her from earlier times, of people whom Marion still recognized from that memorable evening when Reinier described them.

But Diederick knew so many more details, and he related them so smoothly, with warmth and humor! He confided to her that he was busy writing down all these family traditions. There was documentation, but he had to glean it from old documents and yellowed diaries. Now it was about to become a comprehensive whole. He had been working on it for years already; it was his primary hobby.

Gradually Marion was losing the sense of pressure she had felt that afternoon. Before she knew it, Reinier and Inge were back again.

She heard his heavy voice in the hall and involuntarily stood up and walked to the door. He came in with his hat and coat still on. They stood in silence where they met.

Diederick sat forgotten in the extension of the salon.

The tension in Marion suddenly grew: How had Magda handled the unannounced visit by Inge? *If she made a scene, it is my fault,* she acknowledged. *I was the one who forced it.* These thoughts flitted through her mind in a fraction of a second.

In the hall she heard one of the servants talking to Inge; she must have been helping Inge take off her shawl.

With an agitated voice, Reinier reported what had passed. Marion felt privileged: He came to her, not to his family. To her, Magda's confidante. They bore the concern for her tortured body and tormented soul together.

"Then Inge gave her a kiss," Reinier continued, "and she began to cry. I had been afraid of that and stood by like a clumsy kid. But Inge said, 'Why are you crying, Mama? You are going to heaven, you know.' It sounded so trusting, so plausible. It even calmed Magda. 'Did Miss Marion tell you that?' she asked, and Inge nodded her head. Then she added emphatically, 'I want you to always listen well to Miss Marion.'

"After that she gave me her hand and said, 'Go now, Reinier. I want to be alone now. And Happy New Year.'

"She did not cry again, but I couldn't reply. How could I wish her a Happy New Year, Miss Marion, when we both know that she will die in this year? I just couldn't do it. I'm no cad. I stood in silence, and I think she read the desperation in my face.

" 'Go ahead and say it,' she said softly. 'Say Happy New Year. I am going to heaven, you know. The child is wiser than you, Reinier Van Herewaarden.'

"With that reproach I returned home. You're probably thinking that this is an interesting story for the last night of the year, but I had to get this off my chest, and you know us better than anyone."

It had gushed out like a stream; Marion had not been able to get a word in edgewise.

Diederick had not moved. Reinier had been unaware of his presence, but young Diederick had observed them with fascination: his brother, with his passionate gestures, and Marion, who looked up at him and listened with a hungry interest. There was so much warm companionship in this speaking and listening that he felt his own loneliness all the more sharply.

So this is what we have achieved with all our so-called "good breeding," he thought bitterly. *It has come to the point where Reinier must say to a stranger, a subordinate, "You know us best."* His fine mouth was drawn into a thin line, and his face became sharper, harder as a result.

The rest of the evening proceeded without any shocking events. They played more music and conversed. The baroness was an excellent hostess, and knew how to avoid controversy.

As midnight approached, she asked Diederick to read the ninetieth psalm, as was their custom. But Diederick extended the Bible to his brother. "That right belongs to you, Reinier."

To Marion's surprise, he did not resist. How meaningful the words sounded in these surroundings: " 'O Lord, You have been our refuge from generation to generation . . .' "

As they wished one another a happy New Year, Magda's shadow stood as large as life among them.

It was not long before they left for home. Reinier carried

sleeping Inge, wrapped in a blanket, to the car, and she slept on Marion's lap the rest of the way home.

In the light of the ancient lantern above the door, the baroness and her son watched the small procession depart, each thinking private thoughts. Diederick shivered.

"Reinier has become more settled," said his mother. "That young lady has been a good influence on him. A nice sort, didn't you think?"

Diederick did not deny it. But he did not have many more words. He was cold and tired and lonely.

In the car it was quiet. The fabric of mutual trust was strong and sound, and it needed no words.

⋖ Chapter 10 ⋗

Grandmother Dubois was seventy-six years old, and of those years, she had spent twenty-three in France.

As a girl, she had been named Jacobi Schollevaer. She lived in a strict Dutch city, and her parents were strict, upright people. Jacobi, with her adventuresome spirit and her longing for new horizons, sat at home day after day with her mother, behind tightly shut curtains. She felt like a caged bird. In those days it was not customary for a girl to seek out work, and the pointless existence that resulted bored Jacobi.

When she was twenty, actor Jacques Dubois entered her life. He was a member of a French theater group which appeared in the city where Jacobi lived. They met under romantic circumstances, and it was what they call love at first sight.

The talented Frenchman courted the Dutch girl tempestuously. Jacobi knew that her irascible father would never give his permission for her to marry an artist who was a Catholic and a foreigner.

But Jacques had already set his sights on the blond-haired girl, in whose eyes dwelt such a strong longing for freedom.

Adventuresome Jacobi fled her parents' home on a rainy night and within a few hours, the two were on their way to the south of France, where they lived for weeks in a flush of happiness. By letter, Jacques had asked Mr. Schollevaer's permission to marry his daughter, but he emphatically refused and charged Jacobi to return home immediately. If she didn't, he was going to come personally to get her.

This exchange of letters had lasted weeks, however, since the mail was not very fast in those days.

Jacobi had inherited much of her father's stubbornness, and she would not consider returning to that somber life within four walls. It was too late for that, anyway.

She laid her last trump card against her father, the tender secret she could hardly tell Jacques. She was expecting a child.

The permission came, accompanied at the same time by the report that Jacobi no longer had a home in Holland; she could stay where she was.

So Jacques and Jacobi married in a sunny village in the afternoon, and they lived for a few months in the exuberant exhilaration of love and happiness.

But as the months passed, the child grew within her, hindering her freedom of movement, thus making it more difficult for Jacobi to accompany Jacques on his tour. Jacques rented an apartment in which she could live from the money he sent her each week. He, however, had to leave again, for an actor is not the master of his own time, and the show must go on.

France is large, and the distances were such that Jacques could not visit his young wife for a long time.

The initial gleam of the adventure dulled. She was so alone and spoke the language haltingly, but she gritted her teeth, and in the absence of a husband, she brought her child into the world alone, a little Jacques Dubois.

The telegram she sent to his father was a proud cry of joy. He was, nevertheless, not very happy, as could be reasonably expected. His fickle heart had grown cold toward Jacobi, and he had turned his thoughts to another woman. He carefully phrased his revelation to Jacobi that his feelings toward her had changed, but that she need not be concerned, because he would faithfully support her.

It was a long time before the essence of the letter sank in, but when it did, the pride of the young mother was raised.

She swept the young child into her arms and had a long talk with him. "Darling," she began, "if your mother must bring you up alone, then forgive her for providing you with such an unfaithful father."

She wrote a letter in return, cool and detached, yet at the same time blazing with pride. "Keep your money for yourself, monsieur. If your son is going to be faithfully supported, it will be by his mother." She gave him the address where she had found work as a maid, and wrote to him that he could find her there if he should need her. "But let it be known that Jacobi Schollevaer will not take a single step in the direction of Jacques Dubois."

Her reaction had been strong and proud, but many nights she lay awake, small and crying, as she thought about her shattered dream.

It was in those nights that she also learned to pray again. She spoke often with the simple Catholic peasants and plunged deeply into the riches that can be possessed by the religious.

Jacobi worked for three years in the national tourist hotel, much to the satisfaction of the hotelier. The little boy had meanwhile grown into a robust lad who spoke fluent French and a bit of broken Dutch.

One late spring evening, when an emaciated, pale man arrived at the hotel asking for Madame Dubois, no one could enlighten him, for Jacobi worked under her maiden name. Nevertheless, he checked into the hotel, for he was sick and exhausted, ravaged by tuberculosis.

And thus the maid, Jacobi Schollevaer, found him, her ex-lover and husband.

The scene that followed was indescribable. Jacques Dubois, perhaps for the first time in his life, did no acting, but showed himself for what he really was: unreliable, torn by remorse, broken in body and spirit—a man in need.

Jacobi nursed her husband for the few weeks before he died. Her silent victory was that he had come back. At long last he had come back.

After he was buried in the small cemetery under the cypress trees, a void seemed to arise in her life. Her stay in France had no point any more. She felt driven by a new sense of duty. She saw her future life clearly defined: First, the boy had to have a Dutch education, and then they would return. With the few thousand guilders Jacques had left her, she was able to open a small boarding house in the Netherlands.

She continually kept this one purpose before her: to give to Jaap everything that lay within her power, to raise him to be an honorable and upright man. Only when she had disposed of this duty would she return to the sunny Provence, the land where she had lost her heart.

Although in France she had sought and found comfort in the Catholic Church, she gave Jaap a Protestant education, just as she had had as a child.

Jaap was easier to raise than she had expected. He grew to be a vibrant young man with a cheerful character, a believing and active member of the church. He had the nature of a

Schollevaer, interwoven with something of the sunny south, but nothing of the restless and hot-blooded man who was his father.

When he was twenty-one and had his own job, which made it possible for him to look after himself, Jacobi left Holland for a second time.

She was forty-two, a woman whose youth was irrevocably past, but matured by a life of giving and sacrifice, of living for a future which would not disappoint, because she bore the happiness within herself.

Twenty years she lived in the verdant Provence, in a poor village where the children called her Grandmother because of her white hair and friendly smile.

The old parish priest was her friend; the people were her family. She lived and worked among the people of Jacques Dubois and burned herself out in the service of those of whom he had said on his deathbed: "I have failed my people, Jacobi. I have served myself instead of the poor people who brought me into this world. I have failed miserably in my life. Make up to my people and my child what I have held back from them. God will repay you."

Through a regular exchange of letters, Jacobi kept up on the progress of her son. He had married a Dutch girl with the sweet French name of Marie-Louise. She had borne him children: Jaap, Laurens, Koert, and Bram, four sons.

When the fourth was born, Jacobi felt she had fulfilled her task in France. She was old, though only sixty-two. But she was homesick for her grandchildren, whom she had never seen, and she knew she had grown old as a result.

She said her good-byes to the village. The children of the village laid flowers by her door, and when she rode away on the rickety old bus to the neighboring station, they waved until she had disappeared from sight.

Grandmother never saw Provence again. But in the old

grounds keeper's cottage, she had found a new happiness: the tumultuous family of her son and his good-humored wife. Among them was the oldest boy, Jaap, who in his disposition, voice, and manners seemed to be the spitting image of the man with whom she had shared a few months of happiness.

The older Jaap grew, the more Grandmother recognized his grandfather in him, but also something of herself—the adventuresome, restless, irrepressible child that she had been in her youth. Whoever wanted to understand Jaap Dubois had to know the history of the audacious child Jacobi and the story of the fickle Jacques Dubois.

For he was their child—more than his father, who was a jovial double of his grandfather Schollevaer. There flowed through his veins the restless blood of the French artist; there burned in his eyes the inextinguishable desire for sun, wide open places, beauty, and passion. All of their pride and audacity, their unquenchable hunger for life, lay piled up in him.

One who inherits such a character must learn and suffer much before he reaches the heights from which Grandmother, after her difficult climb of many, many years, could review life with a smile and folded hands.

She had been washed to one side by the stream of life, small, bent Grandmother, with her thin, silver-white hair.

She still read and did handicrafts in her little corner by the stove, but she was hunched over and in pain from rheumatism.

Grandmother had a lot to think about. The children sometimes teasingly ask her, "Grandmother, what are you always thinking about?"

She would just laugh and go on spinning the fabric of her loving thoughts. They encompassed everything: the children and their parents, their friends far and near. They included the village in the French Provence, for everything that had crossed her life path, Grandmother lifted her thoughts.

She especially wove her thoughts around Jaap, however. Jaap, who knowingly alienated himself from the faith of his childhood. Grandmother knew the urges that dwelt within him, the good and the bad, perhaps better than he knew them himself. She was concerned about Jaap and knew that he, more than the others, needed someone who would remember him night and day in prayer.

At that moment, however, Grandmother was not deep inside her thoughts. The hubbub had begun to bubble up in Forest Cottage, for Jaap had just returned from a ten-day absence, and everyone had something to ask him or tell him. He had spent the holidays with a friend and fellow artist in Blaricum.

The day after his return home he met Marion in the village. *"Bonjour, Mademoiselle,"* his voice rang unexpectedly in her ear.

After a quick glance over her shoulder, she said with a slight fluster that she quickly suppressed, "So, are we back in the country? My sincere thanks for the New Year's Day card!"

Her voice had sounded slightly mocking. Jaap considered it a challenge. "Did you miss me?" His eyes laughed.

"Sure," she teased, "The good sir must think he is quite something! Did you think that I had the time to sit and think about absolute strangers?"

"Can you come to my studio tomorrow? Then I will let you see something beautiful!"

They talked together as they walked down the Rijksstraatweg.

Marion struggled to release herself from the spell he cast over her, but it did not work. Now that she was hearing his voice again, her worries of the previous week seemed unimportant and foolish to her.

With mixed feelings she visited the old coach house with the oak-beamed ceiling. Jaap welcomed her with a royal gesture.

Against one of the walls stood a couch with a beautifully

handwoven blanket thrown over it. On the window ledge stood a can with brushes and a brilliantly blossoming azalea, which reminded Marion of the little café in Borg. On the walls hung various drawings and oil paintings. The typical artist's attire—a corduroy jacket—hung carelessly on a nail. On the low table stood a bowl with spring flowers carefully arranged. There were books, a very beautiful floor lamp, and a single small sculpture. All these things were so typically Jaap that Marion immediately knew that she could fall in love with this room.

She nestled herself into one corner of the couch. "May I look around?" she asked. Jaap observed her with amusement as her eyes glided over his work. They fell on a small canvas that particularly struck her.

"Is that your work?"

"*Oui, Mademoiselle*," he acknowledged with a slight bow.

"Where is it?" she wanted to know.

"In Paris. It is a street in Montmartre, the old part of the city, right behind the Sacré Coeur."

Marion stood up and remained looking at the old street for a long time, her hands intertwined behind her back. After a while she sighed. "I would really like to see that. Have you been to Paris often?"

"Not often, but for a fairly long time. I lived there for a year."

"In the Montparnasse?" Marion asked with interest.

"How did you know?" he asked.

"Well, that is the artists' quarter, isn't it? I know because I have read a lot about Paris."

"I would love to show you all those beautiful things," he said. "It would be perfect for you to sit on the steps of the Sacré Coeur as evening falls. Many people do that. Most of the time they sit in silence, looking over the city below, where the lights slowly come on.

"Sometimes there will be someone playing a violin or a harmonica, a sentimental, sad melody, and then you can't do anything but love Paris. Paris is a magnet. As you sit there on the steps, and the melody dies away, you turn around and see the milk-white towers of the Sacré Coeur bathed in the light of hidden floodlights and outlined against the black sky.

"And the people you see walking along! Chic ladies and indescribably filthy beggars. People young and old, each one with private joy and sorrow. In Paris no one is alone, and yet nowhere is a person more lonely. Sometimes I am homesick for Paris, Marion.

"That is the misery of traveling a lot. You move from one homesickness to another, and nowhere do you ever feel completely at rest."

Yes, that was Jaap Dubois, from head to toe.

After that afternoon, there followed many afternoons and evenings in which Marion visited the coach house. Sometimes she brought Inge along, who thought it was wonderful to play with Gert and little Marlies. Marion also got to know some of the other sides of Jaap. She observed him as he worked, sometimes with his jaw set in a determined expression; sometimes with a look of satisfaction and a pleased glow in his eyes. She would sink deeply into her chair, and only occasionally would they exchange a word. Perhaps those were their most pleasant moments together.

Jaap also had days in which he did not so much as pick up a brush or set a pencil to paper. Then he would be restless and demanding, and would so turbulently overwhelm Marion that she sometimes had to fend him off, "No, Jaap, don't."

Although her affection for him daily grew stronger and more intense, she still could not bring herself to ask him about his relationship to God.

She was already feeling the repercussions in her own faith. Her prayers were more superficial; she no longer dared to descend into the depths or ascend the heights. She was drifting.

Just as "drifting" were Jaap's comments about his "religion": "something higher," "fate," "the eternal within."

These expressions deeply agitated Marion. They were so vague, so indefinable. She longed to hear something firm from him, something basic. The more she heard his perspective, the more she longed for the substantial words of the Bible, which hit their target and allowed no room for misunderstanding: "Jesus Christ was crucified for our sins and was raised for our justification."

But Jaap did not share this longing.

It was February before it came to a confrontation. But by that time the conflict in Marion's soul had become so great that her mood was constantly under siege.

Because there was more.

Actually she was not conscious of it until she received an engagement announcement from a friend from Amsterdam. With the card in hand, Marion realized that Jaap had never asked her if she would marry him. He had taken her availability as a matter of course, but they possessed nothing in common: no promises of fidelity, no plans for the future, no mutual life goals.

In the spontaneity of the first weeks this had not dawned on Marion, and even now the small voice of pride warned her not to draw too many conclusions from this matter.

In her weekly letters home she had spoken of her new acquaintances, but she had never written a word about her unique relationship with Jaap.

If he starts to talk about "later," then . . . , she thought stubbornly.

From that time on, a certain friction entered their relationship, at times hardly noticeable, but at other times growing almost into a fight.

It began on an evening in February, while Marion was looking through a portfolio of Jaap's drawings.

"Don Juan!" she suddenly exclaimed, half laughing, half serious.

He looked up. "What are you talking about?" he asked.

"Octavia," she said, "and Bianca, and Michelle, and Maria." Unmistakable sarcasm reverberated in her voice.

Jaap jumped up. He took the portfolio from her hands and looked at the drawing that lay before him. The Italian girl from Naples, warmly and seductively laughing, full-blooded, and wearing a minimum of clothing.

"*Mille grazie, Octavia,*" he had written below at the time.

Marion looked at him. "Were you in love with all those girls?" she asked earnestly.

But he wasn't sure if she was serious or simply kidding around. It made him unsure of himself. "Are you jealous?" he asked.

Marion did not answer immediately. "I wonder when my picture will be added to this collection" was her only reply.

"Don't be so banal," Jaap angrily snapped, returning to his work. Silly that he had not hidden those drawings, that Marion had to see them just now! Octavia . . . His thoughts turned to the nights that he had spent in her company. And Michelle, the petite Parisienne, that little thoroughbred. He looked at Marion through his eyebrows. *What a scoundrel I am,* he thought. *She is so unspoiled, so pure.* He suddenly felt the need to break something, something nice, something he was attached to.

At that moment Bram entered with two cups of coffee. "Are you coming, too?" he asked. "We are singing inside. Grandmother, too."

Jaap muttered something which could not be understood, and the boy retreated.

That bit about Octavia must have hit his Achilles' heel, thought Marion. *He looks as though he has been injured!*

She stroked his hair. "Shall we go?"

"You go ahead," he said curtly. "I'll pass on the musical frolic." His voice sounded contemptuous. "Ronnie Boonzaaier at the pump organ. Ronnie Boonzaaier, mind you, who is absolutely amusical. If *St. Matthew Passion* is being broadcast on the radio, she turns it off in order to sing Shepherd John songs. They can keep their commoner antics as far as I am concerned."

If Jaap Dubois thought that he had come to the right person with such a remark, he was miserably mistaken.

They sat opposite each other at the low table. With a resolute wave of the hand, she pushed the drawing material aside and out of his reach. Then she planted her elbows on the table and looked him in the eye. "You know what you are?" she asked, emphatically. "A twisted, myopic bully, with a mass mentality besides."

"So!" said Jaap, with a long look into her effervescent eyes. With shock, he forgot that he was offended. "So we don't know the young lady, after all. To what do we owe this pleasure?"

"I'll tell you." Marion picked up her gloves. "You are possessed by the conviction that Art, with a capital *A*, is the criterion of life, the point around which the whole world revolves. But you are quite mistaken, Jaap Dubois!"

He raised a declarative finger. "Not Art, Beauty. And if the world does not revolve around Beauty, what then?"

"Around God."

It fell out so unexpectedly, but the word erected a broad barricade between them. Now they spoke across the barricade, but it seemed that they understood each other less and less.

"God?" Jaap scoffed. "Great. Granted. But for me God is synonymous with Beauty. If He is perfect, He would certainly derive no pleasure from the music played by an organist of the caliber of Ronnie Boonzaaier on an out-of-tune pump organ!"

Marion shook her head. "You're looking at it all wrong.

You see God as some kind of art critic who evaluates everything that rings from the earth by your tastes and the tastes of your like-minded buddies."

"How do you see God, then?"

The questions flew like short growls back and forth.

"It is not a question of how I see God. It is a question of who He *is!*"

Jaap impatiently shrugged his shoulders. "Sure, sure, and who is He then?"

"He is a Father. A Father who gives talents to all of His children, and watches anxiously to see whether they will use them in His service. He has given Ronnie Boonzaaier a motherly heart and a cheerful personality, and she has most certainly developed those talents. But when she married Laurens Dubois she remained the same Ronnie Boonzaaier, and her lack of musical talent was not compensated for because her brother-in-law Jaap might take offense. But I assure you, Ronnie's listening to sweet little songs about Shepherd John has more value before God than your transported listening to *St. Matthew Passion.*"

She paused to catch her breath.

"So!" Jaap said again, and a barely discernible threat lay in his voice.

"Yes!" said Marion sharply, and in her mind she heard the lamenting choir from *St. Matthew Passion: "Wir setzen uns mit Tränen nieder."*

"Yes, because Ronnie at least believes what she hears and sings. But do you think your detached love of art will raise any echo? You think *St. Matthew Passion* is beautiful from a purely external perspective, but it does nothing to you within. Otherwise you would not so nonchalantly say that religion has had its day, as though the Christ of *St. Matthew Passion* had not risen and were not alive and would not come again!"

But Jaap did not give up.

"That is all very convenient for you," he said. "But with that theory, you undercut all art, because you cannot deny that beautiful is beautiful, and that a real difference exists between a truly beautiful work of art and well-intentioned bungling.

"According to you, all the Ronnie Boonzaaiers should just keep right on playing their pious little songs and composing their artless poetry, and so long as they believe the right things it will be beautiful. No, Marion, you can't mean that. Your tastes are too refined for that."

"I did not say that it was beautiful," she resumed, now feeling a little drained. "Before God it contains something beautiful. His concept of beauty lies on a completely different level. He measures with a different measure than we do. But if you begin with the basic conviction that all things are from and through and to God, then you get a different perspective on all those things.

"Then you can forgive the artless bungling, because in spite of their shortcomings, it is still their attempt to praise God through their music or song or whatever.

"That is not to say that those who have been given talent in that area should not make an effort to develop it! But you underestimate the danger of turning Beauty into an idol, because the beauty of earthly things is created, and what is created also passes away. And then you're left without a god—shattered, alone."

Jaap stood up, and Marion reflexively followed his example.

He laid his hands on her shoulders. "You say it so easily," he said hoarsely. "It all passes away. If that is true, then I could cry like a baby. Bach's fugues—gone. The choruses of Vondel—forgotten. The work of Michelangelo—shattered. The rose gardens of Capri—rotted.

All the beauty of the world gone. And you say it calmly,
Marion!"

It was a cry for help. He tweaked her cheek, but she was
hardly aware of it. A joy was welling up in her because she
could say it. "Yes, Jaap, it is passing away. That is painful. For
me, too, Jaap, for me, too! But we receive something in its
place—a new heaven and a new earth. You can read all about
it in the Book of Revelation. That is my comfort."

But she did not say it. She stood with her head slightly
turned and a smile was playing on her lips. What was she
looking at?

Slowly his grip on her shoulders loosened. He stood looking at her; at the slender line of her neck, at the profile of her
slightly parted lips.

"Nun!" he said roughly in order to control the lump in his
throat. "I thought that I had a woman with warm, red blood,
but it turns out that she is a half angel who can forget the
world she comes from without batting an eyelash. Come
here!"

He squeezed her in his arms. They were around her like a
vice. "I'll make sure you can't forget the world you come
from. Marion, be loyal to the earth." His voice trailed off into
a plea.

The sorrow and tenderness of his words tore at her heart.
She knew that she could not follow him. She had once given
herself to God, for better or for worse, and He would not let
her go. She no longer had a choice.

As Jaap's grip loosened, she backed out of his arms. Without a word, she grabbed her shawl and walked out into the
night.

She walked the long path home alone. He did not follow
her.

❦ Chapter 11 ❧

Magda was declining quickly. Her pale face had become ashen: her small hands a dull gray. Little remained of her classic beauty. Her glory had departed. She was now but a heap of misery—and now, just now, there began to beat in Reinier's feelings toward her a small, warm vein.

It was not anything to speak of yet. It was not love. It was only a hesitant tenderness, a protective friendship, as one feels for a small sick animal which was a nuisance in its short life, but whose defenselessness and helplessness tugs at one's heartstrings.

After New Year's Eve, Magda had become exceptionally tranquil. Her passionate outbursts did not reappear, nor did her bouts of crying. It seemed as though she was preparing herself for the last great struggle—the quiet before the storm. Deep under the quiet surface, something was at work, something frightening.

A great concern for Magda came over Reinier.

I should do something, he thought, *something to remove that final fear.* But no matter how confidently one strides through life, at the door of death, one still comes face-to-face with God, the only One who receives those last distress signals.

Magda had always remained estranged from God. She had even less room in her life for religion than he did, and he knew that. He was also aware that she knew well his own ambivalence and aloofness toward belief and the church. That was why he felt a great reluctance to speak to her about God, while at the same time he knew that that was the only way to provide Magda with the peace she needed in order to face death.

"I can't. I shouldn't," he fretted. "Marion should help her. She has something to offer her."

But Marion had become too preoccupied with her own affairs, while Magda was in trouble. She continued to visit, but her heart was with Jaap. She coddled her love and sifted her great problem. She had pushed the world around her into the background.

Her eyes were closed to the fact that Magda was hungering for words of comfort and security. One could only wonder what it would take before Marion noticed that she had abandoned her duty and was letting the precious few remaining weeks pass by, one after the other.

It was a good thing that she did not see the rare looks that Reinier was giving her of late, because they would have disturbed her very much. She did not know that Reinier's self-control was being tested to the extremes, that he was being driven into ever narrower straits, that his self-control was smothering him to the point of suffocation.

More and more he withdrew into himself.

On February 10, Marion would celebrate her birthday, and Reinier assured her well in advance that she was free to invite her acquaintances to the Warbler that evening.

Marion had no acquaintances in Dintelborg other than the Dubois family, yet she greatly appreciated the offer. She had already been shown so much hospitality at Forest Cottage that she thought it would be nice to play hostess for once.

Reinier had extended this courtesy to Marion because his mind told him he owed it to her. But he immediately sought a pretext to avoid the occasion, since he thought it would be unbearable to see Jaap and Marion together for the entire evening. So he confided to her that he would be conspicuous by his absence that evening because he happened to have a meeting on that same night.

Marion believed him. She had no reason to doubt his honesty. Furthermore, he had been out more frequently in the evening of late.

She felt a childish joy at the approaching party. Jaap was coming, of course, and Laurens and Ronnie would also be there, and Koert and Bram would come if they had finished their homework.

Two days before the party, however, her argument with Jaap took place, and as a result, Marion's mood changed. She continued to make the preparations, but she was nervous and felt under pressure; her friendliness was gone. Since her hasty exit from Jaap's presence, without so much as a good-bye, she had heard nothing from him.

When she woke up that morning, she heard the rain against her window. *That, too,* she thought sadly. She had no desire to get up.

No sooner had she come downstairs—it was still dark—when the doorbell rang loudly. The delivery boy from the florist stood on the front stoop and extended to her an armful of flowers. When Marion removed the thin paper, she let out a cry of surprise. She saw a wealth of spring flowers in contrasting colors; enough to mix something festive into her heavy mood.

With careful fingers she sought out the little white card, *INGE,* it read in large, awkward letters.

Oh, thought Marion, touched. *To think that such a reserved man has this in him, to make such a choice and then with endless patience to let a child sign her own name to it!*

Her sympathy for him again rose to consciousness.

There were more flowers: a single stem of white orchids without a card, even without birthday wishes.

Marion had not a moment's doubt that this was Jaap's idea. There was no question in Reinier's mind, either. Every time he followed Marion's glance toward the crystal vase, he thought, *I must go away tonight, as far as possible.*

The delicate white flowers seemed to look down with exotic arrogance on the jovial colors of Inge's trumpet narcissi, tulips, and grape hyacinths. But Reinier couldn't help but think that the latter were more appropriate for a thoroughly Dutch girl like Marion.

The day seemed to creep along for Marion. She had a quiet afternoon because Inge went to play with the little boy next door, who was also celebrating his birthday.

She picked up a book, the first volume of the trilogy she had received from Mr. Van Herewaarden for Saint Nicholas Day, and she buried herself in it.

At four-thirty she jumped when the doorbell rang. When she opened the door, a cry escaped her, "Father!"

What a surprise! Once in the hall, she kissed him on both cheeks. His goatee tickled her face. He wished her happy birthday, but before he had finished, his voice fell away. Marion, the independent housekeeper of twenty-one years, stood crying against his gray overcoat like a little child.

He patted her clumsily on the back. "What is the matter now, my child? Tears? On your birthday?"

Marion wiped her eyes. "Yes," she said, feeling ashamed.

"It is just so nice to have someone from home here. It has been so long since I have seen you."

She helped her father with his coat. He looked at her for a long time. What was wrong with Marion? Surely she was not homesick? She had been so strong all these months.

After they sat down, he told her, "I had to go to Breda for a business meeting, anyway, so your mother and I said to each other: Maybe I could go to Marion's birthday party. Then I could combine the trips. And we were, of course, curious to see how things were going here for you. That is why you see me here at such a strange hour."

Marion stroked his balding head. Daddy!

How much greater their trust in each other had become since she left home.

Absence makes the heart grow fonder, she thought, and she repeated her thoughts out loud.

"But why don't you come home more often, sweetheart? You know you are always welcome with us."

Marion shrugged. "I don't know. It is so hard to get away. You see, if I leave, there is no one to care for them. And Mr. Van Herewaarden leads such a lonely life. Mrs. Van Herewaarden is deteriorating rapidly. I would feel I was abandoning them if I took time off for my own pleasure. Can you understand?"

Yes, Mr. Verkerk understood. He did not pester her. Marion had to do what her heart and conscience dictated. Then she would be traveling by a good compass.

He had much to tell her. "You know that I am going to retire next month. We were planning to leave Amsterdam and have already looked into exchanging houses with someone in the Veluwe. We did not write anything about this because we wanted to be sure first. But now it is definitely going to work out. What do you think?"

Marion not only thought it was nice, she thought it was fantastic!

"It will also be nice for Mother," said Father's calm voice again. "She does not handle the business of the city well. We will be settled in the middle of the woods just in time for summer, so it could not be better. Then you can come and stay for a good long visit. That is our only condition!"

Marion was enjoying this conversation with her father. Now that he was near her, she realized just how much she missed his kind face. And Mother, too.

She showed Father the flowers she had received.

"From Inge, Father. She is such a precious thing. She should be home soon."

Mr. Verkerk also noticed the orchids. "From whom did you get those?" he asked.

Marion blushed.

"From Jaap Dubois. I have written to you about him."

Fortunately, Father did not pursue the subject.

Then Inge came home, and shortly thereafter Reinier also walked in.

Marion's father stayed for supper.

After supper, Reinier excused himself. "I hope you understand. I do not like to keep my wife waiting. She is accustomed to my coming directly after supper."

While Marion cleaned up and put Inge to bed, her father looked around and admired the many beautiful pieces of furniture and paintings that lent the interior a distinguished air.

When Marion returned, he said to her, "You must honor your employer, child. He is a man of character, a true gentleman. You don't meet many people like that anymore."

"Yes, Father," Marion obediently assented.

"I get the impression that this man comes from a good background," Father continued.

Marion laughed lightly, "That would be true. He is a baron and has a family tree that goes back deep into the Middle Ages."

She could say this to Father. It would not make a difference to him. He did not evaluate people by their external qualities. Nevertheless, Mr. Verkerk was surprised. "You never told us anything about that!"

"No, that was on purpose. He keeps it to himself as much as possible. I have not known it for very long myself. The ancestral castle is in Borg, about six miles from here. I was there on New Year's Eve, but it was no picnic! I can well imagine why Mr. Van Herewaarden fled the fortress, because you can never completely be yourself there if you are not comfortable with court etiquette.

"But let's talk about something else. How late can you stay?"

"I have to catch the train at twelve past nine."

"Wonderful! Then you have a while yet. How are things with Edith? She seldom writes."

"Oh, you know how Edith is. She has never been much of a writer. She still seems to like it in The Hague. Now she is busy planning a trip to the Riviera with a couple of friends from work."

"Pff," Marion exhaled with awe. "She's bold! She does not even know twenty words of French!"

Mr. Verkerk laughed. "That's Edith. She will try anything, and she usually makes it through."

"When is this little party going to take place?"

"Early in the spring, I think. March, April—they have not yet settled on a date."

"Actually, it probably isn't such a bad idea to make vacation plans during this somber weather. At least then you have the anticipation. Oh, wait. I think I hear our guests, Father. Just a moment!"

She hurried to the door and opened it with a sweeping

gesture. It was Laurens and Ronnie. "Come in, come in." She motioned warmly.

"Jaap is on the way," Laurens announced. "He is lugging a mystery package, but you will see it in a minute."

Marion introduced her friends to her father. Ronnie gave her a package of lovely handkerchiefs, and with a penitent expression Mr. Verkerk also groped about in his pockets.

"That's just like you." She laughed. "To forget like that. If Mother knew, you would not hear the end of it."

Then she thanked him for the silver napkin ring he managed to retrieve from the recesses of his pockets.

The doorbell beckoned again. Marion was grateful that Jaap did not come with the others. She opened the door, and he saw her standing in the light of the copper chandelier, her blond hair seeming to flow. They stood and looked at each other for a moment, then Jaap extended his hand to her. "*Sans racune,* Marion?"

"Of course," and she promptly renounced her brooding of the last two days. "What does that mean?"

"I could at least have brought you home," he added, and then the door closed behind them.

On the road a motor started and a car squealed off into the darkness.

Jaap and Marion did not hear. He congratulated her carefully. His warm, cautious kiss and his pleading glances spoke a thousand words. "Forgive me my rudeness, Marion. I am so sorry."

And Marion was gladly ready to forgive him! His gift made her quiet: the painting she most admired of the old street in Paris!

As long as you keep producing such things, people will always forgive you, she thought.

She had a wonderful evening. The schoolboys came in with a rumble and threw everything into a commotion.

All too soon her father had to leave. As she helped him into his jacket, she said with regret, "I am sorry I cannot bring you to the train station. Please give my greetings to Mother."

Then they said good-bye.

"You have fine friends," said Mr. Verkerk at last. "Except that Jaap. He seems a bit of a weird duck. He is not at all like his brothers. Are you sure he has both feet on the ground?"

"Yes," she replied sharply, "squarely! He is just a little more intense than most."

At ten, Laurens and Ronnie left for home, and Koert and Bram walked along with them. Jaap and Marion remained behind together. He encircled her with his arms, carefully, as though he feared he would break her.

She did not know him like this. There was something humble about him.

"I would have liked so much to have been able to celebrate this evening with you alone," he said as he stroked her hand. "We still have so many bridges to build between us."

She laid her head against his chest. "Maybe we will understand each other better some day," she said softly.

Then his mouth found hers again. When he released her, she ran her hand over her forehead with some agitation. She looked at the painting, and then at the orchids.

"You have spoiled me, Jaap."

"For you, nothing is beautiful enough, Mari!"

For some reason, this pat response made her feel uneasy.

She moved a little, impatiently, as though she wanted to shake something off.

"You should go now, Jaap," she said. "I am tired."

Yet after he was gone, she did not go directly to bed. She slipped deep into an easy chair and thought and thought.

*   *   *

When Reinier stood up from the table in order to go to Magda, his bitter mood had nearly disappeared. His conversation with Mr. Verkerk had distracted him.

As he stood in the hall putting on his overcoat, his eye fell on a book that Marion had laid down in her haste to let her father in.

He picked it up and, after a brief reflection, slipped it into his coat pocket. *I will just go to the office and read,* he thought. *If only I really did have a meeting, then I wouldn't have to give in to these tormenting thoughts.*

Magda was waiting for him with some anticipation. "Did you think about it?"

"About what, Meg?"

"You were going to buy something from both of us for Marion for her birthday, weren't you?"

"Oh, yes," he conceded as he searched his pockets. "I haven't given it to her yet because I thought that you would like to see it first."

She bent over the small package. It was a fine golden necklace with a small opal.

"You don't think it's too expensive?" he asked hesitantly.

"No," Magda responded resolutely. "She is worth it. She has done so much for us already, Rein. I wouldn't be able to do without her anymore. Besides, I owe it to her. The first time she came to visit I was so mean to her. I have done a lot of mean things in my life, haven't I, Rein?"

He swallowed hard. "Ah," he said with difficulty, "you shouldn't think about that. Love only remembers the good things, Meg."

Again he used the nickname she had when she was in the prime of her youth. His tender concern for her seemed to see her more and more as a child and less and less as a woman.

He told her that Marion's father had arrived that afternoon and about Inge's candid comments about his goatee. His story released a painful smile in Magda.

As he got into his car, he thought, *Maybe I should go home. It was rather cowardly of me to plan this escape.*

Slowly he approached the house along the Rijksstraatweg. When he was almost home, he noticed the hall light go on, and he stopped. Before his eyes the scene was played: Two young people looking at each other, rediscovering; two hands grasping each other in a spontaneous gesture. When the door fell shut behind them, he bit hard on his lip, and with uncontrollable emotion, he forced the car into motion. He hurtled down the road to Breda, where he finally collapsed in a random bar.

It is lasting too long, he thought. *Two months this agony has gone on. I can't stand it anymore.*

He ordered a drink, and then another.

When he put his hand in his pocket, it butted against something cool and hard: the book. He paged through it.

Foolishness!

How could he ever have thought that he would be in the mood to sit and read tonight? His attention was drawn to a passage Marion had underlined. She did this often; he had seen it in other books, as well.

Inattentively he took in the sentences. He read them again with more attention, then shut the book with a loud clap. He recognized it as the first volume of the trilogy he had picked out for Marion.

Life often plays funny tricks on a man, he thought cynically. Against his will, he sought out the underlined passage again.

"Desire can be like a beautiful flower, which casts her perfume to the wind. Desire can be like a bubble, trembling in the sun, like a snowflake on the windowpane. Desire can lie deep and unknown, hidden under the distractions of the day: but suddenly it rises before us."

His eyes hunted through the lines, and there it was again, that word that made him want to curse: "We see reality, but behind reality, our desire continues to beckon. It is everywhere, and in everything, near us, within us."

Marion! he thought. *She underlined this. Did she also have a desire beckoning behind reality? Why can't a person ever be completely happy, not even her?*

When he finally left for home, he had drunk more than he could handle.

Somewhere inside he still heard a voice warning him: *Fool. You cannot drive like this,* but the warning was drowned out by the monotonous refrain in his head, which pressed in on him in a hundred different keys: *Desire can be like a beautiful flower, a beautiful flower, a beautiful flower; like a bubble trembling in the sun . . . a bubble, a bubble, a bubble . . .*

It is everywhere . . . everywhere, everywhere, everywhere.

He arrived home without incident, a guardian angel riding at his side. He did not bother to put the car in the garage, but walked directly into the house.

The light he saw was still shining behind the curtains drew him with an irresistible power of attraction.

He opened the door to the living room and saw Marion bathed in the glow of the lamp.

"Did you have a good time, kid?" It seemed an innocent question, but Marion sensed something different.

He is acting strange, she thought. *He never addresses me so informally.*

"Yes," she said quickly. "Thank you."

He stepped closer and laughed. He handed her a package. "The goodies aren't over yet."

She unwrapped the small box. He leaned over her, and she could smell that he had been drinking.

She looked at the fine necklace lying in the case, but it did not please her. The situation was oppressive.

119

She set the case on the table and dutifully repeated. "Thank you. It's lovely."

He reached for the necklace and said forcefully, "Come on. I'll put it on for you." His voice was husky. Before she could avoid him, she felt his warm hands on her neck. She looked at him, and the lust burning in his eyes frightened her. She felt weak. She resisted the feeling and stepped backward.

Before he knew it, Reinier heard her quick footsteps running up the stairs. She had fled.

The sound of the door slamming above sobered him a little. He turned and climbed the steps with the heavy tread of one very tired. Marion stood quietly behind the door of her room, listening to the sound of his footsteps.

Her heart beat wildly. With a quick motion, she turned the key in the lock, then turned away and closed the curtains.

Reinier heard the lock click shut and doubled over as though he had been punched. Without bothering to change his clothes, he fell into bed. "She locked the door," he said, half aloud, and the words echoed.

Everything had gone wrong. She had fled and locked her door.

His desire had withered; even the bubble trembled no longer. He had fallen and was broken.

With fists clenched, Reinier fell into a dull sleep that brought him no rest.

The car stayed out the entire night in wind and rain. In the salon, a thin gold snake lay coiled in the carpet, and the opal, the small, silent white tear, caught the light of the lamp that remained burning the entire night.

Marion's birthday was over.

✍ Chapter 12 ✍

At seven-thirty, the alarm clock went off and Marion reflexively reached over and pushed in the button to silence its rattle. She was vaguely aware of something unpleasant. Slowly her memory of the previous night came into focus.

I reacted ridiculously, she thought. *What actually happened? Nothing.*

In the sober, gray light of dawn, everything had shrunk to a trifle.

Mr. Van Herewaarden had only set aside the usual formal distance for a moment, but he had said nothing improper. Did she really have reason to walk away? And so Marion reined in the whole affair until it was less than nothing. And yet she was not completely satisfied with this extenuation of events. It was not what he had done that frightened her, it was the way he had looked at her.

Marion was no child. Since she had gotten to know Jaap better, she knew what that expression in a man's eyes meant.

She folded her hands behind her head—her favorite position when she had to think seriously about something. She tried to put herself in his position. She thought about that December evening, about the hunger for happiness that could be heard in his story. She realized how lonely he was. His wife had been hospitalized for more than three years but he was not a widower. He was incomplete. That was it. Could she hold him accountable for the burning desire she saw in his eyes?

"He was not himself," she decided, feeling relieved that she could reduce the whole thing to something insignificant, something that would be over and forgotten by the end of the morning.

She thought again on the words of her father: "You must honor your employer. He is a man of character."

Reinier did not appear at the breakfast table. She left the dishes on the table for him and went to work. She said to Toos, "Mr. Van Herewaarden is still in bed, so don't do anything to the bedrooms just yet."

At nine-thirty she sent Inge upstairs with a cup of tea, but she came back down almost immediately. "Papa doesn't want any tea. He was sleeping very hard, but he already had his suit on. Then I woke him up a little. Is Papa sick?"

Marion lifted Inge high in the air. "You are a wonderful little girl," she said. "Yes, Papa is a little bit sick. You go with Toos to get some vegetables. You may carry the bag."

They were barely out the door when Reinier came down the stairs.

Marion was busy in the kitchen when she heard him. She did not go out into the living room. In the dining room she could hear him rattling his breakfast dishes; a few minutes later the front door closed behind him. She heard the car drive away.

An hour later, a woman called from the office to say that

Mr. Van Herewaarden would not be eating at home that day. Marion knew right away that he was avoiding her.

Dinner was very quiet; Marion felt that something was missing with just the two of them.

Inge whined a little, "Miss Marion, I'm so bowed."

Marion did not have the energy to remind her about her Rs.

It woke something up in Marion. *My poor child,* she thought. *You are the one who gets the short end of the stick. Your father is a brooder, and your mother is a brooder, and when it comes right down to it, Miss Marion is a brooder, too. We sit—all three of us— wallowing in our own problems, and you get stuck with the bill.*

Marion hastily arranged a festive afternoon for Inge. She invited little Pim, the boy from next door, and the two youngest Dubois children, and they celebrated for a few wonderful hours. Marion let them blow bubbles, and later they played school.

As dusk began to fall, Marion sat in a chair with the children gathered around her and cut out paper dolls with lovely clothing and ruffled edges. They all clamored for one.

Gert hung over the armrest. Little Pim sat on a cushion at her feet; Inge leaned against her knee; and little Marlies, the youngest, sat in her lap.

It was Pim's high voice that suddenly called out, "Look Inge, there is your father! By the window!"

How long had he been watching?

When he came in, Inge immediately captured him with an elaborate account of the day which was periodically corrected and supplemented by the other children. He listened patiently to her story about blowing bubbles and how Marlies' blowpipe was so quickly broken, and he admired the drawings she brought to him. Then he gently shook off the children and removed his coat.

"Are you done being sick, Papa?" Inge asked.

He glanced timidly at Marion.

"Yes, little one," Marion answered for him. "We have forgotten all about that!"

You are a good sport, Marion, he thought. *I don't deserve it.*

He stood somewhat indecisively with his jacket over his arm.

"You know what?" he said. "These kids will have to be taken home, of course. How about I put them in the car and take them?"

"That is a good idea," Marion responded. "And may Inge also go along?"

"Of course. And the other young man. What is your name? Pim? Good, you may also come, Pim. We will be back in about twenty minutes, Miss Marion."

Suddenly everything was so ridiculously normal.

When they returned home, they sat down to eat, and Inge just had to demonstrate for Papa.

The bubble pipe went back into action, and it really worked! With her cheeks rounded and her face taut with concentration, Inge blew her successful number. Reinier had to carefully hold the delicately wiggling bubble in his hand while she called Miss Marion. She had to see it too!

As the kitchen door opened, the bubble burst. Reinier had invested all his concentration in the affair, and his shock was a great as Inge's when the shimmering treasure popped.

Marion had to laugh at the bewildered look on their faces.

"Did it go the way of all bubbles?" Marion consoled. "Don't cry, Inge. You will be able to blow so many bubbles in your life."

Although Reinier was initially relieved at Marion's attitude, it later began to irritate him. He did not know what to think about her. Was she really so naive and innocent, or did she know him so well that she chose this as the most appropriate role to play for today? He sat working at his desk with his back to her. Suddenly he said, "Will the accused still be summoned before the judge?"

Goodness! she thought, *why don't you just let it rest? Would not that be much better?*

"Why?" she asked with her guard up.

"Because he was inconsiderate enough to come home drunk on your birthday," he said as sharply as a razor.

Go ahead, thought Marion, *give the knife a twist. Don't spare yourself.*

"The accused has already been acquitted," she said as nonchalantly as possible.

But he would not let it drop. "Why?"

"Extenuating circumstances."

"I would rather you chewed me out."

"Then I am sorry that I cannot oblige," she said curtly.

He went back to his work. A little later he laid down his pen again and reached for the jeweler's case that Marion had lain on his desk that morning.

"May I give this to you again?" he asked. "Would you still like to have it?"

"Yes!" she replied spontaneously, and she immediately put the necklace on.

She wore it faithfully. Reinier frequently looked at the white tear against her neck, and it was a constant warning for him.

His life took on the old dreary routine again.

After a few weeks the events of that late winter evening seemed only a dream. Magda became more difficult. A visit was a trial.

Marion looked in on her two to three times a week, and she admired her boss for faithfully making the trip to the hospital every evening. Magda did not make her visitors feel welcome. The cancer was beginning to erode her nervous system; she was overcome with obsessions. She had bouts of anxiety, and she spoke of demons who were secretly watching her, waiting to get her. She reproached Reinier for not staying with her. It did not help to try to reason with her.

Marion also heard her confused stories. She often read to Magda to help distract her thoughts, and upon mutual agreement, they managed to have a radio placed next to her bed. Magda had never been interested in a radio before, but now she grabbed it eagerly. The music stifled the frightening voices for a while.

But the devil did not leave her alone.

Marion noticed that Reinier was greatly burdened by his wife's frame of mind. This had to end. His own nerves were beginning to suffer from the strain; he had reached the end of his strength. His unbridled outbursts were becoming commonplace. More than once Marion could barely refrain from making a sharp retort. She also noticed that in the evening Reinier often delayed going to see Magda. It had become a chore; he was so tired of it all.

One day in March, after supper, she read a passage from Revelation. She was not paying any attention to Reinier, and it escaped her that he grimaced as she read that Satan would be loosed from his prison.

The connection that these words made upset him. He could not bear it! "Silence!" he bellowed at Marion, and he slammed his fist down onto the table. His eyes spewed fire.

Inge began to cry.

Marion turned pale. She locked eyes with him and bravely held her own. Their eyes challenged each other, and miraculously, she won.

"No," she said with a small but determined voice, and she continued. Her voice trembled a little as she read, for she had not yet reached the core.

As she read, " 'If anyone's name was not found written in the book of life, he was thrown into the lake of fire,' " Reinier's hands gripped the edge of the table until his knuckles turned white and his eyes turned black with wrath.

But Marion continued, knowing what followed this chapter. She never knew where she derived the courage for this; it was simply given to her.

> Then I saw a new heaven and a new earth, for the first heaven and the first earth had passed away, and there was no longer any sea. I saw the Holy City, the New Jerusalem, coming down out of heaven from God, prepared as a bride beautifully dressed for her husband. And I heard a loud voice from the throne saying, "Now the dwelling of God is with men, and he will live with them. They will be his people and God himself will be with them and be their God. He will wipe every tear from their eyes. There will be no more death or mourning or crying or pain, for the old order of things has passed away."
>
> And he who was seated on the throne said, "I am making everything new!" Then he said, "Write this down, for these words are trustworthy and true."
>
> He said to me: "It is done. I am the Alpha and the Omega, the Beginning and the End. To him who is thirsty I will give to drink without cost from the spring of the water of life."

When she finished, the silence was as heavy as lead. Only the clock could be heard, tormentingly ticking the seconds away.

Inge's big eyes looked with fear from one to the other.

In such situations it is often the plain and ordinary things of life that bring resolution. The telephone rang, loud and urgent, and Reinier was called away for five minutes to discuss business.

The meal was ended without returning thanks.

127

Marion put Inge to bed, and tried to reassure the frightened child.

When she came downstairs again, Reinier summoned her. They spoke long and seriously about Magda, and the conversation continued when he returned from the hospital.

It cost Reinier a great deal to say it straight out. "I know I have often been terribly inconsiderate with you, Miss Marion. But I am being eaten up by nerves and guilt. This situation with Magda . . . I am responsible for it.

"Magda came from a totally nonbelieving family, and I was raised as a Christian. Centuries of Christianity lie behind me, but I thought I was wiser than my ancestors. I thought I could just dismiss God.

"And now that Magda is so terribly tormented by something hellish, something demonic, it cuts through me like a knife: 'You did not warn her when there was still time. You never spoke to her about God, about Jesus, who is stronger than death and the devil.'

"It accuses me day and night. It is destroying me, Miss Marion."

His dark eyes stared into the distance with an undirected, desperate look.

"But it is not too late, is it?" Marion carefully began. "She is still alive. God is powerful enough to give her in a few weeks what we have withheld from her for years. I have also failed. It will not help if we talk to her and try to calm her with all kinds of strange arguments. We must pray for her. But most of the time we are too occupied with our own desires, so busy that we never get around to praying for others. That is what has happened to me, at least."

In spite of the concern and tension, mutual honesty blew between them like a fresh breeze and swept away many of the old misunderstandings.

"When you read a little while ago," Reinier began again,

"the horror of it all grabbed me again. When you are healthy and everything is normal, then you think so little about the spiritual world. But now that Magda has this—this complex—I am beginning to take account of these things again. Satan. Hell. Damnation. They are such ghastly concepts, but they exist. For the Bible makes that clear. I once read or heard somewhere: 'Their blood shall be required of you,' and I continually have to apply those words to myself. It is a good thing that you read on, Miss Marion. You must read that last passage to Magda, as well. How does it go again, that part about the tears? You said it to me once last winter, too."

" 'God will wipe away every tear from their eyes,' " Marion said softly.

"Yes, that was it. I hope Magda can understand something of this before the door of eternity closes behind her. She has had so much to overcome in her life, Miss Marion. She inherited such a difficult personality, and because of her stubbornness, she has denied herself so many things." His voice cracked. "I know that she has often been rude to you," he continued. "No one knows her moods better than I do. You really have no obligation to us, but for Magda's peace of mind, I beg of you, please hold on for just a little while longer. Try to talk to her. Pray for her."

He paced up and down the room with long, anxious steps.

Marion was moved by his passionate plea for Magda because the emotion evident in his words was so completely selfless. In pleading his wife's cause, he had so forgotten himself that a warm rejoicing flowed through Marion. What a joy it was to possess the friendship and confidence of this man! For all his failures, he was so inimitably likable.

In the weeks that followed, he regularly spoke to Marion about Magda's problems, and she in turn related to him her visits with Magda. Now that he was able to open himself up in these conversations, he became much more balanced, and that was good for the atmosphere at home.

God did not take Reinier Van Herewaarden by surprise. For months his soul had been under pressure, and he had put up stubborn resistance until, with one last rebellious cry, albeit halfhearted, he conceded the battle. He was still groping and wobbling—his feet stood on long-unfamiliar ground—but he had turned the corner.

After nearly half a year of daily reading from the Bible at the table, Marion was relieved of her duties, and Reinier took them over himself. She did not express her happiness at this event, but accepted the change as a matter of course. He was grateful to her for this disposition.

Their friendship grew by the day; the relationship of employer and employee was hardly a factor anymore.

As a result of his tremendous concern for Magda, Reinier's struggle with his own personal desires was pushed somewhat into the background. The fire continued to smolder, but it no longer burst into flames. He had been granted a respite.

Since the visit to the castle on New Year's Eve, Reinier had maintained contact with his family. He went regularly to Borg, and the baroness had even visited the Warbler with Diederick a few times. He did not, however, confide in them, nor did he encourage them to visit Magda.

"Leave her in peace," he would say, and only Marion knew the sad contradiction that these words contained, for Magda knew no rest.

On a windy day in March, while a hatless Reinier was crossing the grounds of his factory, he suddenly stood face-to-face with a man whom he recognized with amazement as an old acquaintance. "Dubois, what are you doing here?"

Indeed, it was the old grounds keeper, as strong and sturdy as ever. The two gentlemen began to converse. Dubois related to him the reason for his presence, and spoke together about the man, an employee of Reinier, to whom Dubois had to relay a message.

"How can it be," said Reinier, "that we so seldom see each other? We have lived for years in the same place! Why don't you come in for a while? We can talk more quietly there!"

And so they sat a few moments later deep in the armchairs in Reinier's private office.

Strange, thought Reinier, *that I can see this man so completely detached from his family. For me he is not the father of Jaap, nor of the little tots who come to visit Inge. Dubois is part of my childhood.*

The grounds keeper had spent a lot of time with him when he was still a boy. He was a fatherly friend, his adviser, his confidante. He was the one who made him a bow and arrows, who showed him the best mushrooms, and taught him to distinguish bird calls. Dubois was always there if he needed him. The family that lived in Dintelborg, which he never saw, he was never able to identify with Dubois.

That was all years ago, and Reinier Van Herewaarden had changed. He was no longer young, but Dubois had remained the same in his eyes, and he regarded him with the same trust.

"No, we rarely see each other anymore. But you never go anywhere, Reinier. Sometimes I think you have become too much of a recluse. Earlier, you were everywhere. Sports clubs . . . I can understand that you don't care much for sports now that your wife is so sick, but still, you live in the world and you can't simply remove yourself from public life, my boy."

"Actually," Reinier replied, "it started years ago, after I was first married. My wife and I had different interests, and when you are always disagreeing about something, it loses something of its appeal.

"When she got sick, I had to stay home with the child. I could have gone out in the evening, but I did not want to leave Inge alone; I did not trust others. She was my only possession, and I guarded her almost jealously.

"Without noticing it, I became a hermit. I became bitter, did not trust others, and no longer associated with anyone.

"It got to the point that nothing mattered but my work. I no longer went to Borg, but I was not happy at home, either. I constantly had to find new housekeepers, and one made a bigger mess of things than the other.

"As you probably already know, I have had representatives from the church council visit me on various occasions, but I made it vividly clear to the gentlemen that I did not want anything to do with them. Now they leave me alone."

Dubois heard a note of disappointment in his voice. He laid his hand on the young man's arm. "And does God leave you alone, Reinier?"

A direct question—typically Dubois—no beating around the bush, straight to the heart of the matter.

"No," said Reinier, "on the contrary. He has kept Himself so busy with me that I now read out of the Bible every evening after supper, like a respectable family man."

Dubois was surprised. "Is that right? And we wrote you off. So we see once again that God does not need us. Why don't you ever come to church?"

Reinier shrugged his shoulders. "When you have not set foot in a church for about thirteen years, it is sometimes hard to find the way back," he said. "Besides, God and I have not completely buried the hatchet, Dubois. I am a lot worse than you think."

Those who recognize and admit their mistakes are not the worst, the grounds keeper thought, but he did not say it.

"How did you overcome the impasse?" he asked with interest.

"Marion," Reinier said simply. "She has turned my whole

world upside down. She . . . well, I don't have to tell you what Marion Verkerk is like."

Then he told him of Magda, of her fear and of his own feelings of guilt toward her. "What do you think, Dubois? Can she be released from her obsessions? She does not want to hear anything about forgiveness and reconciliation. She insists that Satan is going to demand her because she has wasted her life. I don't know what we can do for her anymore. And the time keeps getting shorter."

"Yes, that is a sad case. But there is still nothing to do but to walk the way of the Mediator. Tell her about Christ's love, which is precisely for those who have wasted their lives. Beyond that, you simply have to rely on God's mercy. And pray—you can always pray. I will pray for her, Reinier. For her and for you. That you can count on."

As they departed with a warm handshake, Dubois added, like a father, "I cannot tell you how happy I am that you have found God again, Reinier. But be careful that you do not pursue your own stubborn religion. Apply yourself to the existing norms, Son. The longer you stay away from the church, the harder it gets."

Reinier's mouth twitched nervously.

"Give me a little more time, Dubois," he said. "There are still so many things I have to come clean on. I . . . ah, I can't even begin to tell you, but there are still so many problems."

Dubois shook his head. "Don't tell me," he said. "I believe you. You are on the right track, but don't make God wait too long, Son."

That evening, the grounds keeper kneeled long beside his bed, but sleep would not come.

"Is there so much to pray for, Jaap?" his wife said softly from somewhere in the dark.

"Yes," he said heavily. "And we still pray too little, Marie-Louise."

With a few words, he told her of Magda and Reinier.

"I find it difficult," he concluded. " 'You never change,' the boy said to me, but he does not know how wrong he is. Life works on us daily, or rather, God works on us daily. We had no worries when our children were small. Do you remember?"

She smiled slightly. "Of course we did. But they were small worries."

They were both thinking of Jaap.

"Yes," Dubois whispered, "here I am, an elder in the church, and I admonish that poor chap, sitting in the midst of his misery, to get to church, while my own son . . ."

He did not need to go on. They understood each other now; they had spoken of their grief so many times before.

After a while, he began again, "When Marion came along, I thought, 'Maybe she will have some influence on him,' but I fear . . . He has grown accustomed to it, Marie-Louise. Maybe he needs a few hard knocks before he finds God, just like Reinier Van Herewaarden. But a man wants so to spare his children those knocks."

"We must leave it in God's hands, Jaap," she said. "He is a child of the covenant, just like the rest of them, and with God all things are possible. Just think of Grandmother."

"I know," he sighed, and he folded his hands over hers.

ᵛᶳ Chapter 13 ᵃᵛ

It was no wonder that Jaap felt slighted.

Marion went to the hospital every afternoon now, so they no longer saw each other during the day. In the evening she would still sometimes drop by, but not as often as before.

Whenever they were alone, Jaap expressed his dissatisfaction on this score, but his comments did not fall on good ground with Marion.

"Necessity knows no law," she said, "Can't you understand that? This summer I'll probably wear out my welcome."

"This summer . . . ," he said scornfully, "I want you now."

If there is one thing Jaap could not stand, it was waiting.

Marion sat in the family room of Forest Cottage. She had walked past the coach house, even though she had seen a light burning inside.

As she was playing with little Gert, the door opened and Jaap stood in the opening. "Are you here?" he asked with raised eyebrows.

"You can see that for yourself," Marion answered laconically.

"Close the door behind you, boy." Mrs. Dubois shivered.

Jaap stepped into the room. He grabbed Marion by a lock of her hair.

"Stay for a little while longer," Gert wheedled, but Jaap cut him off authoritatively, "Nothing doing. Marion is coming with me."

They walked the short distance to the coach house. Marion said nothing.

"You sure are quiet," commented Jaap.

"You act as though I were your own personal property," she said indignantly.

He held the door open for her and flicked on the light, "Aren't you?"

"No," she said. "Not on your life. I am tired of your constant carping, and it bothers me that you show so little understanding for the situation in the Warbler. Magda . . ."

He interrupted her. "I already know that story. But you know what you're forgetting? You are an employee, and you have a right to your own life. You get too involved in other people's problems. You don't have to take them all on yourself. When it comes right down to it, it is not your concern."

"You don't understand at all!" Marion felt drained. She sat down on the couch and leaned back. "I am tired," she said.

He stayed leaning against the doorpost and looked at her, critically.

"No wonder," he said harshly. "I already told you, you have too much hay on your fork. You have to get out more. I want to do your portrait, Marion. If you just give me a couple of afternoons a week."

"No," she said. "No, no, no. You are just trying to lead me

astray. I will not abandon Magda. It is only a matter of a couple of weeks."

"What about the evenings, then?" he said. "May I perhaps make an appointment?" There was a note of mockery in his words.

"Please, Jaap. Don't make it so difficult for me! Do you want me to just leave Mr. Van Herewaarden sitting alone every evening?"

"No, you can't do that. I already noticed that a long time ago."

"You cannot imagine how it feels to visit Magda. It is, in a word, nerve-wracking. Then to come home to an empty house and not be able to utter a single word to anyone all evening. That could drive a person mad!"

He did not pursue the subject, but came and sat next to her and put his arm around her shoulders. His gesture softened her again.

"Marion, you know how I want to paint you?" Jaap stuck stubbornly to his own topic. "Like 'May.' You know—the work of Gorter? Of course you know, a pink sheet draped around your shoulders, bare arms and feet, a flower in your hair, and kneeling in the spring grass."

He looked at her with his eyes half closed, as though he were already seeing the image that he was describing.

"Maybe it is not very modern, but something modern would be a disgrace with you."

He walked to the bookcase and picked out a red volume. He laid it her lap and pointed to a line, "Here!"

Marion read. " 'The loveliest, the blondest, yes, little May.' "

She pulled his head close to and rubbed her face against his shoulder like a kitten. "You are a devious flatterer," she said, "but I still love you."

So ended most of their fights. But the painting was not made; Marion held her ground.

Then André Wesseling appeared on the scene.

He was short and dark, and a little older than Jaap. He had piercing eyes and he was, from the first moment, hostile toward Marion. One would think that he had more French blood in his veins than Jaap, but that was not the case.

They did, however, meet each other in Paris, and now that the one lived in Blaricum and the other in Dintelborg, their favorite pastime was recalling old memories from the exciting time when they were living in the City of Lights.

André unexpectedly blew into Forest Cottage one afternoon, and Jaap invited him to stay for a couple of days.

That evening, when Marion entered the coach house, windblown and wet from the rain, she encountered this stranger.

Jaap introduced them with a mindless gesture, "André Wesseling, Marion Verkerk."

"You will have to watch out for this one, Marion," he added. "You can't trust him around women."

The dark man laughed loudly at this comment.

While Jaap helped her with her coat and she straightened her hair a bit, he followed her every move with his black eyes; it gave her an unpleasant feeling.

Jaap put his hands on her face. "You're cold," he discerned. "I'll stoke up the stove."

Marion sat on the couch and looked on as he rearranged the fire with the poker. He sat on his haunches, and the light from the stove fell over his face, his light hair, and his thin hands.

Oh, how I love you, she thought fervently.

"Are you also an artist, Mari?" André asked.

"Please call me Marion," she said, cutting off his intimacy.

Jaap frowned. This was not like Marion.

"Sorry, pal," he said to André. "I have acquired certain privileges with this young lady to which you have no claim."

"Right," he said with scorn. "I ask her ladyship to forgive

me for taking such liberties. Among artists we are not so particular. And my question?"

"No," said Marion. "I am only house, garden, and kitchen help, with no unique talents." She felt no need to be accommodating. This André was like a red cloth to a bull.

"She is being modest," Jaap called from another corner of the room. "She had more feeling for art in her pinky than most people have in their whole bodies. Try to discuss the arts with her sometime!"

"Do you write poetry?"

André could not seem to shake the idea that she had hidden creative powers.

"No," said Marion again. "Not even that. I don't paint, I don't write, I don't compose poetry, I don't play music. I am only interested in all those things, and with literature, it is more than an interest. But what difference does it make?"

Even with this, Marion was not able to hold him off. He forced a conversation, and Marion rendered her opinion on various matters. He expressed his own very unconventional views, and found himself in continual disagreement with hers. She was not intimidated, but the point of view of this artist, who causally thought he could throw out everything that he considered "common," angered her into defending things which even she had outgrown. But she could not bear that he, with the sweep of a hand and a cynical laugh, swept away values which, for many decent people with more character than he, were worthwhile and even precious.

She stumbled over the arrogant contempt he displayed for the environment from which he also seemed to come— hardworking, serious people, to whose strength and self-sacrifice he ultimately owed the fact that he had been able to see more of the world than they.

She said so, too, and included in her reproach Jaap, who until then had only shared in the discussion as an observer.

"You hold forth on their lack of a broader perspective," she raged, "but I would not give one red cent for your broader perspective. As long as it deprives the little, simple people of a place under the sun, I think your view is pathetically narrow. Jaap knows how I feel about this. We have discussed this before."

The atmosphere remained tense and agitated.

André did not seem to be the least bit bothered by her comments, nor was he upset when Marion ignored his suggestive comments. When she stood up and Jaap pulled on his jacket to walk her home, he held the door open for them with the same smooth, contemptuous expression with which he had greeted Marion at the beginning of the evening.

When they were outside, Jaap immediately opened the hostilities. "You could in the future treat my guests a bit differently!"

Marion shrugged. "How old is that guy, anyway?"

"André? I don't know, thirty-five or so, I think."

"Then it will be a long time before he matures," Marion said angrily. "I am glad that I don't have to live with such a person, because we would be constantly fighting."

"The feeling is mutual, I'm sure" was Jaap's retort, "because you were exceptionally accommodating tonight!"

The sarcasm dripped from his words. They walked on in silence. A little later he began again. "Why do you dislike André before you even know him? He hasn't done anything to you."

"I think he's a creep," Marion said, short and concise.

"A creep? That is such a female thing to say. Why?"

"I don't know," she searched. "He undresses me with his eyes."

Jaap laughed. "I bet he would like to!"

Marion pushed his arm away. "Get lost, Jaap," she said. "You are so vulgar!"

They stood before the gate of the Warbler. Jaap looked at her and saw that she was serious. "You and your scruples," he said, irritated. "Do you think that that prudish little air flatters you?"

"I couldn't care less," she stormed. "Do you think I am going to play a little flirting game with such a jerk for your pleasure? And you can keep your little witticisms for your Octavia! Good night!"

She turned her back to him, but he took hold of her arm and pulled her back. "You are not going to leave me like that," he ordered. "Are you still jealous of Octavia?" The conceit in his words escaped her, for her anger was already ebbing away. She was not yet able to resist his charm.

"Oh, don't whine," she said half unwillingly. "Will André still be there on Thursday? Then you can scratch me off your calendar."

"No, Marion, you wouldn't do that," Jaap said with a teasingly drawn-out expression. "That would be too humiliating. It would appear that you were afraid of him."

"Don't count on it," she added, then left him standing.

A wasted evening, she thought sadly as she walked around the house.

Inside it was very quiet. Reinier looked up over his paper as she came in. They chatted briefly about their day, and then a merciful stillness once again.

The stillness calmed Marion. She crawled into a chair by the fire and stared at nothing in particular. Reinier furtively observed her.

Where do things stand? he wondered. *Is she getting along with that painter or not?*

He could discern nothing. They rarely spoke of Jaap, and he did not want to ask, but he could not say that she seemed happy after she had been with him.

Reinier had heard rumors about Jaap that had raised his ire.

How did Dubois ever get such a son, for heaven's sake? he thought grimly.

TENSIONS INCREASE, the headlines of the newspaper declared, and that was the truth. The world was full of them.

When Jaap returned to the coach house, André was still there. He held a book in his hands, but when he saw Jaap, he clapped it shut immediately.

"Did you get the job done?" he asked. "Man, was I amused with that little witch, but I can't say that I share your tastes. I would definitely think twice before I started something with that one. You will spend the rest of your life locked up with that little piece of respectability."

Jaap was not impressed. He chuckled.

"She was tremendously annoyed this evening, thanks to you, no doubt. I get the impression that you are not completely sympathetic to her."

André smoothed his greased black hair. "You said that right," he readily admitted, "although somewhat understated. I repeat: Such little arguments are amusing, but look before you leap! What was the name of the girlfriend you had in Paris? Michelle? Yes, now I remember. She was much more the womanly type! Esprit, Jacques, esprit! Such an old Dutch aunt will always be a ball and chain. Forgive me for putting it so bluntly."

Jaap pensively filled his pipe. "There is a lot to that theory," he thoughtfully conceded. "But you are forgetting one thing. Michelle was an angel, and she had esprit, that I grant you. But Marion has brains. You must have noticed. I must say that I have seldom met a woman outside the country with whom you can talk."

André slapped his open hand down on the table.

"My boy!" he bellowed, "it is high time you turned your

back on this cold kingdom of frogs. Brains! If you want to talk, you can always find someone, but if you want to enjoy life, you need something spicier than brains!

"If you needed her for her money, I could understand it, but you are still lucky enough not to have to worry about money. If you really want to be tied down, then find a woman with some music in her, one that loves adventure, one with personality!"

"If you think that Marion lacks personality, you are sadly mistaken," Jaap interrupted him. "You don't know her, that's the problem. At first sight she is just your average kid, maybe even a little boring, but she is worth the trouble when she is really angry or tender."

"I do believe you are lovesick," said André, shaking his head, "but I don't see any chance of evoking such emotions in her, now that I apparently am on her black list."

Jaap looked at him with a puzzled look. Then the corners of his mouth began to curl and he said, "Try to make her mad. Say something about her faith, then she'll spit fire!"

"Aha." André whistled between his teeth. "Is she that type? Actually, that doesn't surprise me. But to tell you the truth, I don't think that you will see her back here again this week."

Jaap thought of the conversation he had just had with Marion at the gate of the Warbler.

He laughed a short, arrogant laugh. "Of course she will come back," he said. "She always comes back. She fights like a terrier, but when it comes right down to it, I can make her or break her."

"I'll keep my fingers crossed," André concluded.

৶ Chapter 14 ৶

André's loud, mocking laugh was the first thing that Marion heard as she laid her hand on the doorknob of the coach house. She drew her hand back for a moment, but immediately annulled her action by resolutely stepping inside. After all, what did she care about this chap? Let him do his worst!

Jaap's eyes brightened triumphantly when he saw her. He was unusually friendly, and even André said nothing provocative for the time being. That disarmed Marion somewhat. She had come "in full armor," expecting the conversation to follow the same course as previously. But Jaap and André carried out an animated conversation over their work, and Marion had to admit, in spite of herself, that what André said was interesting and even educational. He let her see sketches that showed her he was not without talent.

"What do you think, Marion?" Jaap invited, but she declined.

"I would like to listen for a change." She stood up to retrieve her handkerchief from her coat pocket, and when she returned, she stood behind Jaap's chair, lovingly running her fingers through his hair.

André observed the tenderness of her gesture. "When you've had enough of his mop, you can do mine," he said suggestively.

Marion looked at the helmet of black, greased-back hair above his sharply handsome but rather sleazy face. She could not completely hide her revulsion when she said, with forced nonchalance, "I would not dare!"

He sensed her disgust, and it released something in him that her cool resistance was not able to reach. A dangerous glow arose in his eyes. The signal had been given to open an offensive; Jaap had placed in his hands the weapons with which to strike this little shrew, who thought she could pass judgment on him with one glance of her big blue eyes. "Are you Catholic, Marion?" he asked neutrally.

"No," she said. "Why?"

"Because earlier this week you disputed my views on birth control."

"Oh, you mean that. But you don't have to be Catholic for that, do you?"

"No, apparently not. But why aren't you Catholic?"

Marion looked at him, surprised. "Because my parents raised me as a Protestant, and later I embraced the Protestant faith as my own. That seems pretty obvious!"

"Obvious to you, perhaps, but it seems like the greatest foolishness to me. If your parents were Catholic, or even Muslims, then you probably would have been, too!"

"That is very possible," Marion admitted.

"But then isn't it all ridiculously relative?"

Marion sat up straight.

"Except for one thing," she countered. "You say, 'if you happen to be,' as though anyone just happens to be born!

There is Someone who controls whether you are born among Muslims or Christians. And He does so for a purpose!"

"You must mean God?"

"That's right."

Something guarded had arisen in her disposition, like a mother bear protecting her most precious possession from the sudden approach of an enemy about to strike.

André laughed an icy, arrogant laugh.

"But my little child . . ."

"I am *not* your little child!" Marion brusquely interrupted.

He stopped for a moment, then resumed unimpeded, "Do you really think that if God exists, He bothers Himself with all the little details? The thought alone is exhausting! But even if that were true, then He has, if you don't mind my saying so, made a fine mess of things. Just take Christianity, for example. What a chaotic disaster that is! No, I sometimes get the impression that that God of yours has really let things get out of hand, Marion."

He looked at her with sympathy. "Even His most beloved little lambs are howling with the wolves in the forest. Tell me, how can it be that a pious little girl has fallen in love with an atheist?"

The friendly words dripped from his lips like poison.

Marion sank her teeth into her lower lip. She had the urge to pummel that smooth, smiling mask of a face with her fists, but she did not. She did not even answer. She threw a quick glance in Jaap's direction. He had not entered the conversation. He uneasily received her look.

You are going too far, André, he thought, forcing himself to say, lightheartedly, "You shouldn't get this girl so riled up, old fellow!"

"Why not?" André replied. "We like a good conversation, don't we, Marion? I'm curious to know what your defense is."

Her eyes spewed indignation.

"Me? Defend God against you?" she asked, and with her emphasis on the words *God* and *you,* he felt put in his place, which awakened in him the desire to hurt this child even more deeply than he already had. It was no longer a game, no longer friendly amusement, no innocent attempt to see how far he could chase this cat up the tree.

Suddenly it had become deadly serious. Marion had discerned the naked hatred of God in his being, and it had become useless to try to mute that hatred in good-natured play.

"That's really easy, to resort to that!" he derided.

"I can only suggest that you read the Bible seriously for once," Marion said, with affected calm. "That is the best way to find out who is really responsible for the mess in this world, and more importantly, who can help us out of it."

André raised his eyebrows. "Who, might I ask?"

"Jesus Christ," Marion said, and it sounded almost solemn in these circumstances.

"Aha, that Jew, you mean?"

"God's Son. And in His human form, a Jew, yes. But what difference does that make?"

"I don't particularly care for Jews," André said.

That is no argument, Marion thought uneasily. *He doesn't even deem it necessary to advance an acceptable argument for his unbelief. He is not below using the first inane thought that pops into his head to offend me.*

"I don't like Jews at all," he repeated. "I would be very uncomfortable if I had to be saved by a Jew. It is all a bunch of trash, and someday you will have a rude awakening."

Marion stood up. The pencil that she had picked up from the table broke in her hands with a loud, dry crack. Her legs were trembling. "Please, be silent!" she cried out. "You do not know what you are talking about! I pray that this comment will not be held to your account. You do not believe that you are dealing with the King of heaven and earth, but someday you will realize it!"

She grabbed her coat and began to button it with trembling hands.

She looked at Jaap with a long, pained expression. *An atheist*, the sneering voice echoed in her ears, and through which a trusted voice could be heard, warning her: "Do not be unequally yoked with unbelievers, my child."

Jaap turned away, ashamed. He made a motion to stand up, but then his eyes met the mocking eyes of André. He suddenly understood something of Marion's dislike for André. But the black, jeering eyes had power over him; he submitted.

"Come on, Marion, sit down," he said. "You're breaking the conversation off so abruptly. Don't you want to try to change André's mind?"

"No," she replied darkly, and again she bit her lower lip, so that a small red drop of blood appeared. She tasted her sorrow on her tongue.

"After all, doesn't it say somewhere, 'Be ready, in season and out of season,' " Jaap said, digging deep into his memory.

"Yes," she said, "that is what it says. But it also says: 'Do not give dogs what is sacred; do not throw your pearls to pigs.' That is what the Jew said"—she aimed her flaming eyes at André—" and it applies well here!"

The door slammed closed behind her.

Once outside, tears streamed down her cheeks as she stood in the shadow of the barn. Was she crying because of André? No, it was Jaap who earned her tears. Jaap, who had sat there like a spectator while that brute, that crude lech, tore apart and assaulted what for her and millions of others was greatest and holiest in life! Jaap, who quietly listened to his blasphemous language, and who, by his silence, concurred so emphatically that Marion, weeping and shuddering, suddenly became aware of the sin of loving him. And how she loved him! She could not hate him. She could not even judge him!

When she heard footsteps approaching, she quietly withdrew further into the shadow of the barn, but she had already been noticed.

It was the grounds keeper, who had taken a short walk with Koert. "Is that you, Marion?" his deep voice asked, coming closer. "What is this, now? Tears? You didn't have a fight, did you?"

"Oh, its nothing," Marion faltered. "It was—it was because —it was because of André."

The kind face of the grounds keeper hardened. Koert stood awkwardly next to him; indignation robbed his square young face of childishness.

"It was because of André," Dubois repeated. "That is true, but not true, isn't it, Marion? It was because of Jaap, wasn't it?"

How well he had perceived the situation! Again Marion fought back the tears. "Yes, because of Jaap, too," she softly admitted, but loyalty prevented her from expressing her grievances.

She looked around her, as if seeking an opportunity to flee.

"I will take you home, Marion," Koert said hoarsely, but his father laid his large hand on his shoulder.

"No, Koert," he said, "I will. Tell your mother that I will be gone for a little while."

The lad opened his mouth to protest, but his father's eyes had authority. He turned around and headed toward the front door. Once there, he cast a black glance over his shoulder at the lighted windows of the coach house. "Heroes," he murmured scornfully. "The two of them against one girl! Big men!"

Dubois walked next to Marion down the beech-lined lane,

"Give me your arm, child, and try to tell me what happened," he said gently.

She gave him a confused account of the conversation she had had with André, while at the same time sparing Jaap as much as possible.

But Dubois knew his son. "And Jaap?" he asked.

Marion winced. She did not answer; instead she asked, "Is Jaap an atheist, Mr. Dubois? André said that he was an atheist."

"Must you ask a parent such things about his adult children?" he asked bitterly and sadly. "What did Jaap say?"

"He did not deny it." Marion's voice was nearly a whisper.

The grounds keeper was long in thought. Finally he said, slowly and deliberately, "What I am about to say to you is very difficult for me, Marion. After all, he is my son, and I would have very much liked to have had you for a daughter-in-law—very much. But if Jaap comes between you and God, you must end it, my child. The most important things must be given greater consideration."

"But I love him!" It was a cry for help, but at the same time a warm and tender confession that challenged all arguments.

He looked at her profile. This child had much grief, he saw, and grief must be respected, so he was silent. But as he walked back to Forest Cottage after seeing Marion home, he thought aloud, "You have grief because of him, Marion, but sooner or later you will heal. But for me it will continue to chafe, for me and Marie-Louise. Because he is our child, and no matter how far he strays, no one can stray beyond a parent's heart."

He thought of his own father, the Frenchman he barely knew who had also rebelled against God, bowed before beauty, and made many women unhappy. He had been dead for over half a century, but his heritage was being revealed in Jaap.

150

The grounds keeper thought of the words of the holy law: "For I, the Lord your God am a jealous God, punishing the children for the sin of the fathers to the third and fourth generation."

He raised his eyes to the heavens. How difficult it was to bear those words! He sighed. The powerful shoulders of the grounds keeper carried a heavy cross.

Koert did not quickly forget his indignation. Since André was visiting Forest Cottage he was staying in Jaap's room, and Jaap was sleeping on a cot in the boys' room, where Laurens had formerly slept. Little Bram had long been asleep, but Koert remained sitting at the edge of his bed until Jaap appeared.

Koert looked so young in his faded pajamas, with his large, thin hands extending from sleeves that were too short. His face was red as he angrily said, "You guys were real brave, upsetting Marion like that and letting her stand outside crying! Instead of defending her against that ugly . . ." He stuttered after a word that would do justice to his fury.

Jaap stared at him, astonished. In his eyes, Koert was still just one of his little brothers, and the little brat, seven years younger than himself, was suddenly standing before him and throwing at his feet the accusation, that had, ever since Marion's departure, continually run through his own head, even though he did not want to admit it.

An irrational rage grew in him. Rage at Koert or himself?

In any case, the lad would have to pay for his audacity.

"Mind your own business," he spit contemptuously. "Punk."

His cold eyes glided over the boy's pimpled face and then down his thin neck with the pointed Adam's apple.

"You don't deserve Marion!" Koert hissed.

Jaap began to get undressed, sizing up his brother as he did. "You're not harboring a few aspirations of your own, are you?" he parried. He hit the nail on the head, and poor Koert's delicate, fledgling affection was exposed then and there with a mocking laugh. Angrily, Koert bent down and picked up the first object he saw—a shoe—which he threw, in the fire of youth, at Jaap. "Good-for-nothing . . . ," he said sharply.

The shoe flew by Jaap and smacked the wall. Bram was awakened by the noise, and Mrs. Dubois stood at the door.

"What is going on here?" she asked strictly.

But Koert said nothing. He lay down in bed with his face to the wall and pressed his lips together.

"What is going on here, Jaap?" his mother repeated. Jaap turned toward her.

"Koert threw something at me," he said. "But it was my fault. I was teasing him. I'm sorry."

"You are the oldest. Try to be the wisest, too," Mrs. Dubois reproached. She disappeared from the scene, turning off the light as she went.

Little Bram fell asleep again.

Koert reflected on the last words of his brother. *At least he is still honest,* he thought, relieved. Yet his admiration for his famous and well-traveled brother had been chipped. As he drifted into sleep he thought, *When I find a girl, she will have to be like Marion. But I would never make her cry, that's for sure!*

In the other bed, Jaap lay awake for a long time.

❦ Chapter 15 ❧

André had departed again, and everyone was relieved. Jaap had offered Marion his apologies for the scene André had made. He felt that he had been at fault, and with heavy legs he made his way to her. Much to his relief, she accepted his rambling apology immediately, without further ado.

"We are going to take a day off together!" he said with enthusiasm, and Marion immediately concurred.

She would not be missed for one day, and she wanted so desperately to wash away all the misunderstandings and complications in the peace of a day off.

In her heart she fought tooth and nail against the advice of Mr. Dubois: "End it." She did not want to heed his words; she loved Jaap and she would not give up on him. Desperately she clung to the last straw. After all, a miracle could still happen and make everything turn around!

Jaap had a plan. He knew of a glade that provided the

most enchanting view and could be reached by bus. They got off the bus near a picturesque village, and after walking half an hour, they reached their destination. The glade lay amid a stand of pine bursting with new growth, here and there broken by a group of oak trees already thick with buds. The water rippled and the sun lavishly poured down sprinkles of light. It was a virtual paradise.

They lay down in the dry grass. The sun immersed them in luxurious, caressing warmth as it only can on an unexpected, wandering summer day lost somewhere in the early days of April.

Marion sighed softly with contentment, like a cat purring on a sunny windowsill. "Just look at the sky!" she exclaimed, as her bare arm swept in an arc. "Have you ever seen bluer blue? Colors, Jaap! I can never mention a color without also thinking of something that expresses it. From now on I will never be able to say *blue* without thinking of this sky. Blue is the happiest color I know."

Jaap let her words splash over him like a bubbling brook. He was enjoying Marion's animated chatter. He lay with closed eyes, his face thrown up toward the sun. He was already getting brown. "What do you see when you think green?" he asked. "What does green express?"

"Tranquility," she said. "A stand of beech filtering the sunlight. A group of reeds with cattails and croaking frogs. The land. Do you know the poem by Buning: 'There is nothing greener than the Maas' "?

"No," said Jaap. "How does it go?"

She began to recite for him:

> There's nothing greener than the Maas,
> Banks and reeds and poplars proud . . .

And later on:

The wild duck ascends from emerald recess.
Though one can moor on many banks,
Greener banks can no one possess.

"Beautiful," he reacted. "And red, Mari?"

"Red is lavish, passionate. A bouquet of poppies, a bowl of cherries, a torch."

He wanted to prolong this play. The images that she evoked were inspiring. With each color she conjured up a miniature painting. He could see it in front of him.

"And yellow?"

"Yellow? Something sunny. Flowers—wild flowers. Irises, marigolds, buttercups. Or a field of ripe rye."

"And gray?"

"Gray is a moody color. The sea at dusk. A canal in Amsterdam on a rainy day. Old houses."

He was motionless. He did not seem to be listening to her, but the contrary was true. Like placing an order, again and again he dropped a word into her dreamy thoughts: gray, yellow, black.

"Black? The stark silhouette of a city against the evening sky. A singing thrush on the peak of the roof. The armor of a beetle climbing a blade of grass."

With her eyes she followed the movement of the insect in the grass. How its shields shone in the sun! Nature was a treasure.

Jaap appeared to be asleep. He lay completely still. Only the sounds of nature periodically interrupted the silence: the splash of water at the movement of an animal, perhaps a frog, perhaps a fish. Or were there no fish in the glade?

The pinecones snapped in the warm sun—a friendly noise—repeatedly bursting open with a cozy, crackling sound.

Jaap was also listening to the quiet. Finally he spoke, as though a quarter of an hour had not passed. "And brown,

Mari? Brown is such a dull color. Can you also create something beautiful with brown?"

"Of course," she said. "Brown does not have to be a dull color, it is an intimate color. The color of old furniture, an oak chest, the leather binding on an old book—things with a history."

The broken thread was picked up again.

"And pink?"

"Pink? A cradle. A blossoming apple tree. The butterfly-like ribbons of a little girl on Sunday morning."

"And purple?"

"Purple speaks of grief, sorrow. Heather blooming along the road, a velvet ribbon, the dress of an old woman with white hair."

"And white, Marion?"

She turned toward him, found his hand, and brought it to her mouth. "A branch of orchids," she said, and the words were like light, floating butterflies, which can be seen, but not caught. Their silky wings were too delicate, too fragile. He pulled her into his arms.

"Marion, you are a marvel," he said. "You paint with words. You see happiness everywhere. You distill beauty from everything. I should have you with me always."

She was lying with her head against his chest. She could feel his heart beating.

What a day this was!

An island, an island!

They walked for a while around the glade. A willow tree stood bent over, its branches dangling in the water.

How could anyone have a care in the world? Was there really a woman lying in a white room in the hospital in Dintelborg, eyes narrowed with pain?

Was there really a man with graying hair, sitting in his

office at the leather factory, consumed by the dark secret worming within, for which he could find no outlet?

Was there really a problem between these two young people who lightly walked along the path, the sun reflecting in their blond hair?

Life was so inexpressibly good these few stolen hours!

In the afternoon, they again sought out a place in the sun. Marion was a little burned. Jaap lay on his side, admiring her. He did not touch her.

She willingly submitted to his observation. There was nothing unsettling in his look.

André can go jump in the lake with all his talk, Jaap thought. *I love her, and she will lose that stolid religiosity once we turn our backs on this moribund country. What she needs is a good dose of French frivolity.*

Marion had closed her eyes and dozed until she heard his voice again. "Mari?"

"Yes?"

"I am going to ask you to marry me."

He watched the changing expressions on her face, and knew immediately that he should not have said this.

"Don't," she warned.

Her defenses rose in a lightning flash. For months she had looked forward to hearing these words, but now that they were spoken, she wanted to push them back into the secure silence of the never spoken.

Oh, the goodness of this day!

Ruined!

Now she had to return to her reasonable considerations. Now she had to rake up the differences the peace bestowed on this day was supposed to sweep away. The miracle had not occurred. Everything was just as it had been before, even though the ostrich had stuck its head in the sand for a day.

Oh, sure, the day had been a miracle, but a miracle of a

different sort than the one for which Marion in her foolishness had hoped.

She would have to take her positions once again. She had no choice.

But how difficult it would now be to argue. Had Jaap perhaps sought out this, the weakest link in her armor? This day, island of sun and tranquility, which knew no bounds and lay defenseless without the walls of vigilance which Marion had erected around her normal life?

But the words had already fallen; they could not return.

"Why not?" Jaap sought her reaction.

"I have too many principle objections to marrying you," she said matter-of-factly.

It all seemed like a joke. Would the sword hanging by a silk thread above them both now fall and separate them irrevocably?

"Like what?" he pressed.

Marion hesitated for a moment, then she chose to joke. "You look too much at other women," she teased and, almost unnoticed, ran her fingers through his disordered hair.

He laughed, revealing his relief.

"You tease," he said, and he kissed her.

Then they were silent again for a long time. Perhaps he felt it would be better not to broach this subject again.

It was Marion who began again.

"Jaap?" she asked.

"Yes, my love?"

"If you were to actually ask, Jaap, and I were to say yes, how would you envision our future?"

"That is not difficult to answer. Marry as soon as possible and then leave the country. It has already been too long. I desire you. I have always desired you, and you know it! I have courted your favor long enough. But my lovely is a little nun, who has her sights set on getting married."

It was not because I was so good, thought Marion. *God knows, I am also human, and my blood is just as warm as yours is. It was my pride that refused to let you make me like all those other girls whom you sketched with such animal warmth.*

Octavia, Michelle.

The girls who gave themselves completely—even though you did not say it, I understood it—over to your irresistibility, and of whom you keep but a smiling memory.

Michelle Langlot—a thoroughbred!

And Marion Verkerk? A nun? Oh, to be sure a sweet nun, but still, a nun. Do you really mean that, Jaap Dubois? It makes me laugh. Feel how warmly the blood surges through my veins!

Thus ran her thoughts, furious and tormented.

For months she had waited for the question which would set her apart from the other girls. Waited in vain.

But now, had Jaap's eyes been opened to the uncompromising beauty of her life's rule: "all or nothing"?

Had he understood that he could not have her as he had had all the others?

"I am going to ask you to marry me," he had said.

She pulled herself away from her thoughts and asked, "What is as soon as possible?"

"In any case, no later than next month."

All of her boiling thoughts, pro and con, were now veiled behind the resistance that her mind put up. "You are not wise! Next month. You cannot possibly mean that!"

He tilted her face up. She looked into his resolute eyes.

"Of course I mean it," he challenged.

His attitude irritated her.

"But why so soon?" Marion demurred. "I think that is so impulsive. We have only known each other for five months, and my parents . . ."

He interrupted her. "Quiet!" he said. "I already know what is coming—all kinds of arguments concerning common decency. But I want you to release yourself from all those little things for once. You will come with me as soon as possible, and I will teach you how to live. I will show you how wide the world is.

"Listen, Marion!"

He pulled her close to himself, and his voice was warm and persuasive in her ear. He told her of France, of Italy. The sunny hills of the Provence, the mountain vineyards, the village of Grandmère, the limestones of the Italian countryside, Lago Maggiore, Lago Di Garda, blue and shiny, like clusters of grapes.

He spoke on, and his story was one long torment for Marion. She longed for the life Jaap was depicting for her.

This was happiness, the unburdened walking along paths that always lead to new horizons; drinking the local wines in low-ceilinged inns, sitting on a marble patio.

"Wanderer, where are you going to? Where the wind blows me."

Mountains with eternal snow, lakes salted with white sails, the cloudless sky.

But above all, Jaap. Jaap, who would be beside her day and night. Not just an hour, not just an evening. Always!

She would be beside him while he worked, while he relaxed, while he slept. They would walk through the world hand in hand, two children in search of beauty, which can be found everywhere, if one has the eyes to see it.

Oh, how strong her desire was. It pulled, it drew, it pressed.

Yet Marion did not surrender.

There was a strength in her which resisted the desire.

There was a Man, with sincere eyes and such a wonderful voice, who said only, "If anyone would come after me, he must deny himself and take up his cross daily and follow me."

And there was a woman in a hospital bed, lips pursed with

pain,who cried out in anguish, "Don't go, Marion, don't go! The devil! Oh, Marion, he says that love has never won!"

There was a child who coaxed, "You will always stay with us, won't you, Miss Mayon?" and the sombre father of that child, who responded with a sharp laugh, "Miss Marion should know better."

When Jaap finished, she released herself from his embrace. A deep furrow appeared between her eyes. She sat up and wrapped her arms around her knees.

"It is a good thing you have not yet asked," she said with unmistakable irony, "because then I would have to ask you something which would make you very angry."

"But I am asking you, Mari," he pressed. "And I mean it, too. So what is there for you to ask?"

"Time to think," she replied without looking at him.

"Don't you love me?"

"Don't you love me?" Marion mimicked him with infinite contempt. Then she laughed, a sad laugh. "Far too much."

"But why, then? Are you afraid of an unstructured life of adventure?"

Marion shook her head. "You don't understand," she said. "If I had my way, we could leave tomorrow. But I can't leave. I can't leave as long as Magda is still alive. Under no circumstances. And after that, oh, it is so difficult. Mr. Van Herewaarden and Inge." *And God,* she thought, but her thought was not spoken. She covered her face with her hands.

Jaap continued to look at her for a long time. He honestly tried to suppress the anger that was rising in him. He did not succeed.

He cursed, which frightened Marion, because he rarely, if ever, did so. "You and that damned baron!" he burst out. "It is always that weeping widower and his housekeeping that stand between us. I am being consumed, waiting for that guy to be set aside. I give you a week, and not a day more. If you still don't know who you love most, then I am going alone!"

He lay down again, and so did Marion. She folded her hands behind her head. Her eyes stung. The sky was still as blue as it had been that morning, only the sun had moved closer to the horizon. *In a book, a cloud would have covered the sun in such a situation,* she mused. *But such is life. Everything is just as radiant, just as lovely.*

Their return trip took place, for the most part, in silence. As they took their leave in front of the gate of the Warbler, Jaap said brusquely, "Changed your mind yet?"

When Marion silently shook her head, he curtly announced, "Until next week, then. *Bonjour.*"

Reinier was upstairs and observed the cool departure through the window. Anger began to rise in him at this skirt chaser who was causing Marion so much pain. He had many times detected that she was not happy.

He descended the stairs and met her in the hall.

He saw how she wrestled with her tears, and without thinking, he simply spit it out, while taking her shoulders in his firm grip, "What are that guy's intentions toward you? If he thinks he can play a little game with you, I will gladly knock his brains out!"

Marion stared at him, her eyes round with fright. She swallowed a couple of times. Then she straightened her back and said quickly, with a confidence that seemed completely out of place, "You don't have to worry, Mr. Van Herewaarden. 'That guy' has asked me to marry him next month and, and . . ."

He released her and said abruptly, "May I then extend to you my congratulations?"

She said nothing, but fled up the stairs. It was a poor attempt on her part to create a happiness which did not in fact exist.

The day had not narrowed the gap. Deep in her heart,

Marion knew that it had been the inglorious end of her idyll with Jaap. This gorgeous, gorgeous day!

The scales had been tipped. Marion did not even need the mere seven days to think it over. Jaap would have to go alone.

She fell facedown onto her bed and wept without comfort. To deny oneself was the most difficult thing in the world.

✦§ Chapter 16 ❧

A week is a long time, tormentingly long, when one turns over again and again a decision that has been made.

The longing for sunny horizons had grown in Marion into an ache that would not be healed. Her mouth was set in a painful line. Reinier noticed it and hated Jaap for it.

He understood little of the situation, for Marion had not left him another opening to discuss the whole affair. Yet he discerned, more than once, that she looked like anything but the beautiful bride. That week she stayed at home evening after evening, and that also seemed odd to him.

They passed each other in silence.

Jaap was not to be heard or seen until exactly one week later. The telephone rang at nine in the morning.

"Hello, this is the housekeeper of Mr. Van Herewaarden," Marion answered punctiliously.

"Marion, you mean," the voice on the other end of the line corrected.

"Oh, it's you. Yes, Marion."

"Can we meet? I would really like to know where I stand. When can I speak to you?"

As quickly as possible, Marion thought anxiously. *The sooner this is behind me, the better.*

"Immediately, if you want," she said. "Can you meet me in fifteen minutes at the birch grove?"

"Naturally." She could hear his surprise at her businesslike tone. "But why don't you come here?"

"Because . . . ," she said stubbornly, and returned the receiver to its place. Let him think she was harsh. She knew better.

Not in the coach house. There were too many memories swirling in that place. It would be difficult enough to say good-bye.

Again she bit her lip. During the week, a painful swelling had appeared there.

She peered into the mirror at her face with its many lines that would betray her, her mouth, and the nervous trembling of her nostrils. "Be strong," she encouraged herself in the mirror. The face looking out at her tightened into a mask. Only the eyes disobeyed her command; they looked out at her with the look of a hunted deer.

It was not far to the birch grove. Marion was there much too soon, even though she had walked slowly.

Jaap was already sitting alongside the dirt road, his bike carelessly tossed up next to a tree. She went and sat next to him on the high bank.

"Do you have an answer?" he asked, curtly.

"Yes," she said. "You will have to go alone, Jaap."

He looked at her. "Is it because of that mob?" With his head he motioned toward the Warbler.

Marion shook her head. "Only in part," she said. "It is

mostly because of God." She bent over and began to draw figures in the sand with a stick.

It was very quiet in the birch grove. It lay near the main road, and the cars riding by could clearly be heard, but their noise only accentuated the stillness. No one came by. Who would be out walking at this hour of the morning?

The streams of sunlight pranced on the ground through the birches, naked and uninhibited as children.

Marion registered all these things in her memory with painstaking detail.

Jaap was still looking at her, now half turned from him in profile. Had he already lost her? He searched for words to win her back.

"Because of God, Marion? Why didn't you say something about it last week?"

"Because I was afraid. Because I am in essence a coward, that's why."

"Marion," he repeated. "Isn't love the fulfillment of the law?"

She nodded.

"And doesn't the Bible say that of faith, hope, and love, the greatest is love?"

She nodded again.

"And you love me, don't you Marion?"

She lifted her head for a moment. "You shouldn't have to ask," she said, hurt.

"But if that is all true, why don't you listen to the voice of your love rather than the voice of belief?"

His voice was pleading.

In her mind she analyzed his words with merciless clarity. *His argument is not compelling,* she thought sadly, and she said, not angry or irritated, but oh so definitely, "You should not appeal to things in which you yourself do not believe, Jaap. Furthermore, you are taking those texts on faith and love completely out of context. Really, I know what I am doing. Did you think I had made this decision on the spur of the moment?"

The stick ceased drawing figures in the sand. It stood still against the hard gravel of the roadway, and Marion's hands were clamped so tightly around it that the blood had to seek new avenues of return and her fingers turned white with bright red tips.

"But I can set you free, Mari," Jaap pleaded again. "I am not like André. I harbor no enmity—really, I don't. It's just that I don't personally feel the need for religion. I would rather stay out of it. But you may gladly . . ."

Again the merciless clarity of thought. Again her heart, which received the thoughts and signaled back, was saturated with a warm drop of pain. Again her mouth formed the difficult but deliberate words. "That is what you think, Jaap. But no one can remain neutral toward Jesus. You just mentioned a text about which you understand nothing, but I am going to give you a text which leaves no room for misunderstanding, and I hope that you will remember it. 'He who is not with me is against me, and he who does not gather with me scatters.' "

He looked at her hands, how they clutched the naked stick, and even more clearly than her stiffly recited words, they told him how deeply she was suffering—infinitely more deeply than he. It came to him as a shock. The thought in him that was already reaching for a pencil and a piece of paper in order to capture forever those hands, the image of extreme exertion, left him, and he saw how her mouth could not keep from trembling.

You are so radical, Marion, he thought. *Radical in your belief, radical in your love, radical in your refusal. You will be destroyed by your intensity one day.*

Against his will, his respect grew for the magnitude of this belief that made the impossible come to pass.

Young, passionate hands, made for caressing and caring, had chosen a hard, dead stick instead of the warm body of a lover, and a voice which could paint with words had stiffly but emphatically said, not only to him, but also to her own yearning and desire, "No."

He could find no more words.

Suddenly he was standing in front of her and extending to her both of his hands. She let him pull her up, and they stood eye to eye. In his hands she immediately balled her own into fists again.

He saw in her eyes the cry of sadness and had to lower his. Her look of sorrow pierced his heart.

"Marion, don't look at me like that," he said heatedly and then he foolishly added, "If there is a heaven, you deserve to be there."

Somewhere in the back of her head a small defense mechanism still remained that sounded the alarm at this heresy, but her thought was never transcribed into words.

Her heart had already given up the struggle. It had become sheer pain, and her mouth could only manage one last, stiffled, *"Adieu."*

She pulled her hands from his, turned around, and walked away.

His eyes went with her until she disappeared around the bend. The last he saw of her was a lock of blond hair.

He looked down at his empty hands, as if they still preserved something of her petite, slender fists which he had so lately held. He looked at his hands like a child from whom a favorite toy has unexpectedly been snatched. Then he turned quickly around and went home.

*   *   *

Life continued, and Marion was granted neither the time nor the leisure to surrender to her grief.

Toos came down with the flu, and Marion suddenly had to take on all the duties herself. Inge's cough, which had for days made Reinier uneasy, was diagnosed by the doctor as whooping cough.

Marion was dead tired by evening and fell immediately into a merciful sleep.

One afternoon, as she was leaving Magda's room, Reinier was standing in the hall, speaking to the medical director. She intended to greet them and continue on her way, but Reinier held her back. "Would you mind waiting for a moment? Then you can ride back with me."

He opened the car door for her, and as they rode the miles to the Warbler, he told her what the doctor had said about Magda's condition.

"She must be suffering far more pain than we imagined," he said. "Doctor Martin summoned me for a consultation. Time is running out for Magda, Miss Marion."

"Yes," said Marion softly. "You can see it."

When they went inside, it was stuffy and warm in the room. Marion threw open the windows and leaned on the window ledge with her arms.

Queen Spring had already come, with all her loyal subjects. Marion looked at the Japanese cherry tree from which the blossoms seemed to virtually drip in reckless exuberance. When she first came, the leaves were large and green. She had seen them turn yellow and fall to the ground; she saw them blown away by the cold fall winds. She had the seen the tree in winter's bridal adornment, but now the power of life had burst forth in all its beauty. It was a though spring was trying to make up for something.

Reinier stood next to her and followed her glance.

"When are you leaving?" He blurted out the question that had been burning on his lips for days.

"I'm not leaving," Marion returned, with no apparent emotion. She did not look at him.

"Why not?" The question escaped him, angrily and suspiciously. "Didn't you say last week . . . ?"

"Yes, I did say that." Marion carefully weighed each word. "But I have declined."

A wild joy ran through Reinier, a joy that just as quickly ebbed away and left only shame and regret. For a moment he had hoped that she had refused Jaap Dubois because she did not love him, but the taut defensiveness in her words and the pained expression on her face told him otherwise. Dozens of questions flew to his lips, but one by one were found too indiscreet to express.

Finally Marion explained on her own initiative. "It was because of God. Jaap is an atheist." Relinquishing these words was pure torture for her. Then she closed the window and made motions to set the table.

He remained before the window and slowly collected himself. But a new emotion made itself felt: compassion for her pain, and the need to say something that could soften or even remove the pain.

"And what now?" he asked pointedly, quickly adding, "If it is not too indiscreet of me."

"No," said Marion tiredly, "you may know. He is going to France. Perhaps he has already left. I don't know."

He turned around.

She held the silverware in her hands but did not lay it down. She stared straight ahead, as though she was seeing something Reinier could not discern.

"But why did it have to be this way?" he asked awkwardly. "Was there no other way? If you loved each other. Someone who does not want to recognize God can still be won for Him. Take me, for example."

I must be crazy, he thought. *Am I standing here pleading for that miserable kid instead of rejoicing that he has disappeared from the scene? Only because of the pain in her eyes, which I cannot stand to see. Only for her happiness, for her happiness.*

Marion shook her head. "Please, don't talk about it anymore," she said. "You don't hear me talking about it, do you? Did you think that that argument had not occurred to me? If I had gone with him to France, I would not have done it for his sake, not to win him for God, but for myself, only for myself. That is why it is better this way."

These were the last words they exchanged for a long time about Jaap Dubois.

Happily, something unexpected occurred that pushed all personal affairs into the background for the time being.

Reinier returned home from Magda the Saturday before Easter with great excitement in his eyes. He strode into the hall and threw open door after door in search of Marion, who was in the garden, kneeling over a flower bed.

When he saw her, he quickly paced off the yard, swung his long legs over the flower bed, and came and stood next to her.

"Marion," he addressed her happily, "the fear is gone!"

She did not need to ask what he meant. They were too involved with Magda for that, both of them.

She stood up and brushed the dirt from her hands. "How is it possible?" she asked, amazed.

"Let's go inside, and I will tell you what I know," he replied, and together they walked through the garden.

Reinier related his story. He did not know much more than the simple fact that Magda's disposition had changed. She was now at peace; morning had dawned after the cold night of fear.

Magda had explained with a few words, yet it was still obscure to him.

She had heard a voice that called her name, "My real name Reinier—Magdalene." And the voice said wonderful things which she could no longer remember. But it had made her feel joy and peace.

"Did she perhaps have a dream?" Marion asked.

"Maybe," he said pensively, and yet this explanation did not satisfy him.

He had asked her, "Were you sleeping, Maggie?" but she was not certain. "I don't know. I don't know if I was sleeping. I am so tired lately that I mostly lay here drowzy, drifting somewhere between waking and dreaming. Then I heard that voice—so clear, so convincing—and when he was finished, I heard music. More than that I don't remember. I must have fallen asleep then."

When Reinier arrived at this point of his story, Marion said. "Wait a minute. Did you say music? Could the radio have been on? It is almost Easter. Was there perhaps a meditation on Mary Magdalene?"

He stood up and looked through the radio listings. She came and stood next to him, looking over his shoulder. Suddenly it was all so simple.

Small neat letters solved the mystery: Recitation—Easter poem by Gerard Wijdeveld, adapted from the thirteenth-century poem "Pone, Luctum, Magdalene."

"Did you see this?" asked Marion.

Reinier laid the program guide on the radio. "You know a lot of poetry, Marion," he said. "Do you know this one, too?"

"Gerard Wijdeveld," she thought for a moment. "I don't know. I don't think so. Or maybe . . ."

She walked over to the bookcase and pulled a thin volume out of the row. *Passion and Easter Poems,* the thin letters on the binding declared.

Together they bent over the pages. Again their solidarity
with Magda surrounded them like a shelter.

Finally, it stood before them. A long verse in five stanzas:

> Cease your weeping, Magdalene,
> Let light and laughter dry your tears,
> The sad travail is over now.

They read the verse straight through with the same avid
attention:

> You must laugh now Magdalene,
> And let your grief fall from your face.
> All your guilt has been removed.
> The day is bright with joy and grace.
> Christ has won our liberty;
> From hell and death He set us free,
> Alleluia!

> Sing and dance now, Magdalene.
> From the tomb He has returned.
> All your pain is washed away.
> Jesus lives! His freedom earned.
> Jesus whom you lately mourned,
> Praise Him now Who death has scorned.
> Alleluia!

And then the majestic ending:

> Live again now, Magdalene;
> Live in joy, live in light.
> Jesus has appeared to you.
> Forever gone is death's dark night.
> Distant all its pain and sorrow;
> Love dawns bright o'er your tomorrow.
> Alleluia!

"Yes." Reinier sighed. "This must have been it. Can you understand that, Marion? For weeks we have held out to her the same comfort offered here"—he laid his hand on the gray cover—"but it seemed to go right past her. And now she has been gripped by the coincidental voice of a stranger behind a microphone."

"Yes," she readily admitted, "it is incredible. But she is the one who matters right now, not us. I am so happy that she has finally been released from that obsession! But now it could end very quickly, sir, now that the tension has been broken. She won't be fighting as hard anymore."

They both stood for a time lost in their thoughts.

The same thoughts. It was Reinier who put them into words.

"It shows an incredible lack of faith and gratitude," he said, "but I am very much afraid that the fear will return. Am I wrong for thinking that, Marion?"

She looked at him in surprise. "I was thinking the same thing," she confessed.

He looked down at her; she was a head shorter than himself. A strange emotion played about his mouth.

"My comrade," he said warmly, "you cannot imagine how much support you give me. You understand everything so well. Would you believe that it is often difficult for me to address you as *Miss*? I am afraid that I have exceeded my bounds tonight."

Marion shook her head.

She was proud of what he had said, for she had a great deal of respect for him and was happy to share his friendship.

"I would like to be your comrade," she said simply, "and you may call me Marion if you prefer."

And thus their relationship grew closer. In the last days of Magda's life, their solidarity grew into something very precious.

~§ Chapter 17 ∂~

The Easter holidays passed turbulently. Reinier and Marion took turns visiting Magda. When they arrived home again, each immediately felt the quick searching look of the other, a look that pleaded to know if there had been any change.

A few days later, Marion was called by the head nurse during the morning. Magda had asked for her.

Thankfully, Toos was better again. Marion passed on a few instructions and hurried off to the hospital.

The duty nurse met her at the door.

"Things are going badly for Mrs. Van Herewaarden, I am afraid," she explained. "We had a terrible scene with her last night. Apparently she had had a dream, and she screamed so, we could hear her all the way down the hall. I don't understand where she gets the strength. When she was so tired she could no longer scream, she simply sobbed. We have tried everything to calm her down, but she would not tell us what the matter was. When we suggested that we call her husband, she absolutely refused. She slept a few hours and when she woke up, she asked for you."

"I'll go up immediately," Marion said, and walked quickly up the stairs to the second floor. Carefully, she opened the door to Magda's room. When she saw Magda's pathetic figure curled up on the large bed, her eyes filled with tears. It gave the impression, now that she was resting, that she had already died. Her eyes had sunk deep into her gaunt face, which was ashen and spotty.

Marion knelt next to her, and her voice trembled with emotion as she softly said, "What is it, Meg?"

"I have to ask you something, Marion," came Magda's anxious whisper. "Something about Inge. Does she look like me?"

Marion reflected for a moment.

"Yes," she replied, "she has many of your features, and she also has many similarities of character."

Magda lay silent for a long time, her eyes closed, as though she had to think over Marion's response.

Suddenly her eyes flew open, and Marion saw the horror in her look. Her eyes had a tormented expression about them. There was pain in those eyes—more than physical pain—and Marion remembered the continuing fear of Mr. Van Herewaarden: "I am very much afraid that the fear will return. Am I wrong for thinking that, Marion?"

O God! her thoughts cried. *Has Magda not already suffered enough? Why could she not keep the peace which she has enjoyed but a few days until the end?*

She did not understand where Magda was going with her questions about Ingeborg, nor did it become clearer to her when Magda continued. "I have done wrong, Marion. I never thought of anyone but myself, and when I realized that, it was too late. Last week, when I heard that voice, I thought that everything was over and reconciled, and I was almost happy. But last night, that dream, that dream . . ."

Again the horror echoed in her words. She began to scream—pathetically powerless, endlessly exhausted.

Marion waited until her tears stopped. In the meantime she prayed frenetically. Her prayer summoned to battle a dangerous foe who, she was acutely aware, was not to be underestimated—perhaps Satan's final assault on the heart of the dying. In her prayer, she focused on a line from the Psalms which surged above the sea of her confused and chaotic thoughts.

The line went out like an SOS to God, over and over again: "Do not abandon the work of Your hands."

Magda related her dream. She spoke with long pauses, and Marion's body became stiff and sore from kneeling in the same position, but she was not conscious of it.

"I dreamed," said Magda, "that someone was speaking to me. I saw him. It was horrible."

She gave a description of the fear-inspiring figure in her dream, one so realistically and brutally detailed that Marion shuddered in unease. She made a vain attempt to get Magda to leave out the details, but Magda paid no attention to her suggestion.

She continued. "He said, 'You have done wrong, Magdalene Merkelbach, and you have been foolish, very foolish. Because you think that everything will be over when Jesus comes to take you away; but you are wrong. You have a child, even though you have always denied it, and that child will continue to live after you. In that child stir your urges, your selfishness, your pride, and that child has no one in the world but a man who has never understood you and who will understand her just as little. You awaited the arrival of that child with resentment and black thoughts, and did you think they would not also grow in her? Do you now have an idea of the kind of life your child will meet? It's all your fault, Magdalene Merkelbach, all your fault. And do you now think, with so much guilt on your hands, that you can just peacefully and quietly slip into heaven while your child must struggle her whole life with loneliness and evil passions?'

"He laughed, Marion, cold and jeering. 'No, you will refuse that cowardly grace. You cannot die peacefully with this on your conscience. You are better off coming with me and doing penance for making a man and a child unhappy.'

"Then everything of the last few months came back, Marion. All the things from which I thought I had been released. The demons, the mocking voices, a cacophony. All the terrors of hell were thrown open wide again, and I believe that I screamed in my fear.

"Then came the thoughts, like a refined torture. Not of myself, but of Inge. I have never been so aware of my child as I was last night.

"I know that Reinier loves her, but he also loved me once. His love for me is dead, Marion. I know it is, even though he still treats me amazingly well.

"The doubt slipped into my heart: *If I die,* I thought, *he might meet another woman, one who makes him happy, who awaits the arrival of his children with love instead of resentment, who is better than I am.*

"And then my child, the child of the loveless one, will he not hate her as the one who does not belong? Will she not become lonely and be driven by those evil urges which her mother left her as her inheritance?"

"No." Something in Marion's heart reacted, outraged. "No one comes between Reinier and Inge. No stranger, no matter who it is." She could see his face, as it often was, bent over the child, interested and devoted, but Magda permitted her no time to put her thoughts into words.

"It has worked well, Marion," she went on, "the poison that the devil gave me, because now that the night is over, my fear is that what he said is true. I have tried to fight against it, but I am so afraid. He was right, Marion. I have done wrong."

Again she cried, and Marion confronted one of the most difficult tasks her life had ever presented her with. She was very much disturbed by Magda's account.

She anxiously formed sentences that would be able to convince Magda of Satan's powerlessness against the risen Lord, of the smallness of her guilt when weighed against the love of God.

But Magda spoke again, her voice strangled with tears. "Will you keep in contact with Inge, Marion? I know that you love her. She is going to need someone who loves her. That is why I called for you, Marion, so I could ask you . . ."

"Of course I will," Marion soothed, but then outrage raised its head in her heart again, because Reinier had been so completely written off by Magda because she seemed to doubt his love for Inge and because she seemed to pay more heed to the scoffing voice of her dream than to the years of devoted love with which he embraced the child. And then came the words of defense, of warm solidarity, with which she painted his feelings for Inge. With her advocacy, she tried to convince Magda that her fear for Inge was unfounded, because her father would never leave her.

The conversation was not yet over when Magda had a heavy attack of pain. Marion was forced to leave her to the doctor's care, and she returned home, heavy with discontent.

What have I said? she thought sadly. *I spoke to her of the love of a man, when I should have spoken of the love of Jesus. Only He can overcome death and devil.*

Tears of helplessness burned in her eyes.

What if she dies today? she agonized. *And I have used the time to tell the wrong thing. Our love cannot remove her fear, only God.*

She had been long at the hospital. Reinier had, in the meantime, returned home. He had heard from Toos that Marion had left for the hospital several hours ago, and he had waited impatiently, pacing back and forth for fifteen minutes.

Then he called the hospital, only to find that Marion had already left. Finally he saw her coming. He opened the front door and received her with an anxious, "And?"

A flaming blush rose in Marion's face.

How in heaven's name am I supposed to tell him this without hurting him? she thought nervously.

"She had a frightening dream," Marion related. "I was with her for almost two hours, and she talked and cried the whole time. It was horrible. It was about Inge."

"About Inge? What about Inge? Tell me quickly, please, what you mean."

His tone was rude.

"She is concerned about Inge, about her future, because . . . because . . ."

He noticed shame in her look; he felt that she was trying to keep something from him.

"You're . . . ," he began, but at that moment the door quietly opened and Inge entered the hall, her innocent child's eyes wide as she observed the two having a strange conversation in the dark corner by the steps.

Reinier picked up the little girl and took her into the other room. "We will be right there, my little gnome," he said affectionately, and Marion wished that Magda could have seen how he stroked Inge's curls. That gesture would have removed her doubts about his love sooner than a thousand words.

Reinier closed the door behind his little daughter and turned toward Marion. He saw how she avoided his eyes. He put his hands on her shoulders and forced her to look at him.

"And now the truth," he commanded, and she no longer resisted. She told the truth of Magda's dream and her reaction to it. Only her promise to Magda did she reserve, although even she did not know why.

Initially pity played on his face, but slowly it tightened.

Inge, his little gnome, his princess. Could he forget her even for a day?

Wrath flamed in his eyes, and Marion said softly, "You see? I should not have told you. Now you are angry with her, and you should not really hold what she said to her account. Her mind has been deformed and twisted by years of suffering and pain."

"Oh, child," he said, burdened, "you don't know how long this has been developing. This didn't come to her all of a sudden. She has never taken my love seriously. She has stacked so much ice around it that all my feeling was finally frozen into a single obligation. Only the unspeakable spiritual distress that she has undergone in the last few months has melted something within me. And now she had to do something like this to me. She does not trust me with Inge."

She felt his hands beginning to bite down into her shoulders; then he let her go.

"This is a bitter pill for me, Marion," he concluded.

They went inside. The room greeted them with a certain stark neatness. The table was not set, the meal was not prepared.

Inge had gone into the garden. They watched her as she slowly rocked back and forth on the swing. The flowers were motionless in the heavy air, which spoke of rain.

"What should I do?" Reinier asked aloud. "What can I do except go to her? If only I could approach her, but I never have been able to. Those crazy ideas of hers—sometimes I think she has gone mad. But I must go."

"Do not wait until this evening," Marion pleaded. "She will not live long now. I felt it this morning, and she is so afraid. Do not be angry with her."

He sensed the sincere concern for Magda in her tone. "I am going. I am going immediately." He said it abruptly, as though he were acting against his own will.

He was already at the door before Marion realized that he had not eaten anything yet. What a strange day this had been! She called him back.

"You haven't eaten anything," she reminded him. "You cannot just run out."

"All right," he said, "give me a slice of bread. But please hurry."

His tone did not bother her; she could take a lot from him.

They walked to the kitchen, he following her. He looked on as she prepared something for him with those small, careful movements he knew so well from days, weeks, and months of being together.

How I love her, he thought with deep amazement. *What a strange day this has been,* he thought, too. *I am going to my wife, who is deathly ill, who will perhaps die today, tonight, tomorrow. I am going to her, but my heart remains here, with the other, whom I love—with Marion. Is this a sin? Could this be sinful? Is it deceit? Have I deceived Magda? She knows nothing of this. She does not suspect a thing. No one knows it. No one suspects, least of all Marion. She secretly suffers from her longing for that painter, the son of Dubois—silently, just as I silently suffer from my longing for her.*

He rubbed his eyes with a drained gesture.

Life is so odd, he thought again. *Everyone is unhappy—almost everyone. Magda with her complexes, Marion with her grief, and I with my guilty love. Thousands are unhappy, and yet in some way or another it could be different, beautiful. The key to the door of happiness must lie somewhere.* Once again he rubbed his eyes. *I am tired and dizzy,* he thought. *I think I might be getting the flu. Just what I need after all this.*

A few moments later he drove away. When he arrived at the hospital, Magda was no longer conscious. The injection the doctor had given her had not yet worn off.

Dr. Martin was just leaving his office when Reinier came by. He gestured him inside. "It is good that you are here, Mr.

Van Herewaarden," he said deliberately. "I was planning to call you, to warn you. We are afraid that it may end today for your wife. If you wish, you may stay here until it is over. She is still unconscious; I had to give her an injection a short time ago."

"Miss Verkerk already told me," he answered mechanically. "I would like to stay. I want to be there when she comes around."

"That could be hours from now," the doctor warned.

"I will wait," Reinier said flatly, and Dr. Martin wondered for the umpteenth time what feelings this man might be concealing behind his impenetrable face.

Shortly thereafter, Reinier stood before the window of Magda's room and remained there for a long time. He watched as the sky darkened and tried to remember the weather report. Wind and rain. Deep depressions over West Europe.

His thoughts coursed wildly through him, driven like the clouds. Outside, the wind picked up, and within him everything was swirling—images, thoughts, words of long ago. In these dark hours, many things took on a different hue, were cast up against new and deeper backgrounds, were seen from broader, unconsidered perspectives.

He came to know himself. He lost himself and found himself back again, immovably planted and staring toward the turbulent, cloudy sky. His whole being prayed, and miles away, in the Warbler, Marion prayed silently with him.

Looking at Magda's still face, something of the universal reality of the Gospel of redemption slowly broke through to him, for slowly that face was changing. It was as if a soft hand were passing over it, almost imperceptibly wiping away the suffering and fear.

Under Reinier's eyes, but beyond him, the miracle had come to its fulfillment in Magda. With bewilderment that at the same time was an odd, glowing enthusiasm, deep in his heart he thought, *We have made a mistake, Marion, you and I both. How furiously we worked to convince her by our words and deeds, but it is God who convinces, in His time, in His way, even while we sleep, even deep in the subconscious.*

When it come right down to it, He does not need us, even though we are involved in one way or another, on the sidelines, like breathless spectators.

He sat down next to this new Magda and looked down at the few possessions which had been given place on the table next to her. The large picture of Inge, a few books. He took the Bible which lay there into his hands and began to read.

He read in the Book of Psalms, and was magically caught up by it, so much so that he did not look at Magda for a long time. When Magda slowly and with great effort opened her eyes, she thought she was dreaming. She beheld her husband sitting motionless next to her, like a perfectly sculpted image.

But when he raised his hand to turn a page, she realized that it was real, and she also noticed the book he was reading. She closed her eyes again, now more tired than when she had opened them. There was an unfathomable peace within, which hardly permitted a memory of the frightful phantoms which had so recently tormented her.

And Reinier suited that peace as he sat there, silent, reading.

When she heard a sound, she opened her eyes again. She saw that Reinier had stood up and was carefully making his way to the door. She wanted to say something. She wanted to call out, "Don't go!" but her tongue refused to obey. She had no strength.

Reinier wandered like a sleepwalker through the halls to the office of the medical director, where he knew there was a telephone. There was no one inside. He mechanically dialed his own telephone number. There was a strong burning desire in him to make Marion a partner in what had taken place that afternoon.

She had spent the whole seemingly endless afternoon restlessly waiting for this telephone call, and when she finally heard it ring, she was certain. "That is Mr. Van Herewaarden."

"Marion speaking," she said immediately, and then came his voice.

"I will not be home for supper, Marion. I am staying here with Magda. I wish that you could see her now. A miracle has happened with her. No, I have not spoken to her. God is putting us to shame, Marion. He is doing it without us. No, you could almost say He is doing it in spite of us. Do you know what I mean?"

How inadequate words are, flitted through his mind, and he continued, "Ah, no, you couldn't understand, because you don't know what this long dark afternoon has done to me, do you?"

He fell silent for a moment, and Marion asked, "Are you still there?"

"Yes," he said. "Would you mind waiting up for me tonight? It might be very late, but would you mind?"

"As you wish, sir," she answered obediently, and for a long time thereafter she reflected with puzzlement on the things he had said to her.

"He is doing it in spite of us."

The small ripple was again engraved above her eyes and she thought hard until the depth of his words were opened to her. To have believed and been heard is marvelous, but to have failed and doubted and yet to see the fulfillment is pure grace.

Reinier had gone back upstairs. As he entered the room, he looked directly into Magda's eyes. In a crashing wave of tenderness he fell at her side, grasped one of her small, fragile hands in his own, and caressed it as one caresses a small wounded bird.

"Rein," Magda whispered, barely audible.

"Meg," he responded, and in this exchange much remained hidden. In it they admitted their guilt and forgave each other. They spoke of their sorrow, heavy sorrow, but also finally of their joy.

These two whispered names made so many other words superfluous.

Finally Reinier said, through his tears, "Do you want to see Inge?"

Magda shook her head, nearly imperceptibly. Her glance fell on the picture of the happy, life-loving child.

She feared for her no longer. Her anguish was gone.

She raised her left hand to him and said softly. "Take the ring. For Inge."

Reinier looked at the golden ring with the beautifully cut diamond, an heirloom. The ring had become much too large for Magda; it hung loosely around her thin finger.

"Take it," Magda whispered again, and he wept as he slipped the ring from her finger. He felt as though by this single act he were breaking the final band that held them together as husband and wife, as living and dying, as mortal and immortal—cutting the umbilical cord of their common existence.

"Give it to Inge," she said, "and tell her of Jesus, Rein."

She closed her eyes again, and Reinier waited motionlessly for a further sign of life. He dared not call her.

Finally she spoke further, after she had collected her tired thoughts, "Marion."

"Must I call her?" he guessed. Again she declined. He lowered his ear near her mouth to catch her words, "Tell Marion . . . that love . . . has overcome."

His heart skipped a beat in the sudden blaze of happiness this message kindled.

The light in the room around them was fading. The window was but a light spot on the distant wall, and the sounds from the surrounding rooms were unreal and far away.

Reinier sat with the small hand in his own.

Suddenly a heavy shudder shook her frail body. Magda lifted her right hand and placed it together with the other one in the warm palms of the man who sat vainly fighting against the lump in his throat.

Once more she opened her eyes. They shined large and bright in the falling darkness, and her voice came more strongly than it had before, with undisguised joy and surprise. "All my guilt has been removed."

Her hands then went limp in his, and yet they were not cold.

Reinier waited for a while, and then he stood up, carefully removing her hands from his own.

He called a nurse, and soon Dr. Martin stood next to the bed.

"What is happening?" Reinier asked, and the doctor explained to him that the cancer had reached the brain of the patient. It would not be long now. Perhaps she would last a few hours but she had, in effect, already died. She would not regain consciousness again.

"Thank you, doctor," Reinier said. "It is good. I will stay to the end."

It was another four full hours before death reached Magda. As he waited, Reinier felt the dizziness of that afternoon return with twice the force. He glowed with heat and shivered with cold in turn.

When everything was finally arranged and he was walking

through the streaming rain toward his car, it suddenly occurred to him that if he drove, he might well cause an accident. Although his hands were balled into fists in his pockets, he could not stop their trembling. He leaned for a moment against a wall to let a dizzy spell pass. Then, feeling dull and numb, he began to walk home to the Warbler.

Within minutes he was soaked to the bone, but he walked on, along darkened streets, past dark houses, to the lighted window behind which Marion waited for him. He felt broken, as one who had done heavy physical labor.

The midnight hour had long since passed, and Marion still sat waiting, her hands tightly clenched together. It was taking so long, so long.

Now and again Inge's cough tore the silence. She went upstairs, but the child had already fallen back asleep as she stood by her side.

The wind moaned against the walls, the rain slapped against the windows. The elements seemed to be in rebellion.

Suddenly footsteps sounded next to the house. Marion froze. Her tired eyes were fixed to the door through which Reinier would come.

And then he stood there, dripping with rain, his face drawn and ashen. As he removed his hat, water streamed from the rim to the floor.

Marion was taken aback by his face. Was he sick? His eyes were feverishly narrow, and his entire body was wet. Had he walked all the way from the hospital in this weather?

And yet they said nothing. Reinier reached out for the edge of the table with an unsteady motion, as though he were going to fall.

Marion was immediately at his side. "Sir!" she cried, concerned and anxious.

"Magda has died," he said, flatly. Then they were silent again.

What words could be said at a time like this? The strain of this death had filled the room to its remotest corner. Any word would be a word too many.

Reinier mechanically removed his wet coat, and Marion hung it in the kitchen over a chair. When she came back into the room, he was still standing in the same place. The moaning wind formed the obscure background of their silence.

He seemed to be searching for words. Marion sat down at the table, but asked him nothing. This pause did not last long, in fact only a few minutes, but it seemed like an eternity to her.

Then he spoke, with the same flatness in his voice. "I could not drive, Marion. I did not trust myself. I had to walk; I had so much to think about, so much to work through. And I am so tired, so tired."

Now that the warmth of the room surrounded him, he realized how terrible he actually felt, and a strange indifference came over him.

Marion had been completely put at ease by the telephone conversation they had had that afternoon, but now that she saw him standing there, so defeated, so tired, the flame of concern leaped up in her heart again.

The question burned on her lips. "Was she all right when she died? Did she say it was all right?"

She stared at the man until he was finally shaken out of his indifference and took notice of the desperate question that lay in her eyes.

He related with few words the events of the last hours, and surrendered Magda's message word for word, "Tell Marion that love has overcome."

The taut cord of her self-control snapped. She laid her head down on her arms and wept, first softly, without motion, but then with heaving sobs. All the bottled-up strain of weeks and months broke loose and Reinier's presence could no longer hinder her.

An overwhelming tenderness came over him. He lightly laid a hand on her blond hair. How completely void of desire was this touch. It was the distillate of friendship, of common pain. Marion quietly composed herself. She wiped her eyes and lifted her head, feeling a bit ashamed. They stood next to each other in the night-quiet room. It mattered little that Marion's eyes were swollen from crying or that Reinier's face was ashen and feverish. They were simply two persons who had endured something which would forever leave its imprint on their lives—something essential, something eternal.

Magda had died, and she had seen her Redeemer.

"We must get some sleep," Reinier urged. "Tomorrow will be a difficult day."

As Marion undressed, she heard Inge have a coughing fit and heard her father speak to her softly and tenderly. Then everything in the house was still.

She lay on her back with her hands folded behind her head.

The wind had stopped, but a steady rain still fell against the windows.

" 'Cease your weeping, Magdalene,' " she said aloud, and there was something celebrative in these words, like ringing bells on Easter morning. But the joyous bells did not ring long. Mingled in was another sound, a sound that had been there for weeks, and was but briefly submerged in a wave of seething emotions.

It would not go away. It resumed its place and grew and threatened to drown out the celebrative altogether. It was the lonely resounding toll of a dark and helpless grief.

Chapter 18

The days that followed passed like a dream.

Reinier got up the next morning even though he was unsteady on his feet and shivering from fever.

How in heaven's name can I stay in bed? he thought, fighting the sickness, and he set himself to the task.

There were so many things to be arranged. He sent telegrams to Magda's family. He telephoned left and right to Borg, to the factory, to the hospital, to the undertaker, and in between, he found time to talk to Inge.

The child took the news of her mother's death very quietly, which was not unusual, considering the circumstances.

Marion overtook her employer in the afternoon, as he stood exhausted, leaning against the doorpost, his head hidden in his arm.

He looked up as though he had been caught, and she saw the dark circles under his eyes.

"You are sick," she announced decidedly.

"Spy," he scolded, half irritated.

She laughed slightly. "Scold me if you will. It will not help to deny it. I noticed last night. You must go to bed with a glass of warm milk and anise, at least for an hour or so. You have time now, don't you? Everything is arranged, isn't it?"

He let himself be steered, still fuming and mumbling, "That accursed Toos with her flu. She gave this to me."

And yet he was glad that he followed Marion's advice. He slept soundly for a few hours, and when he awakened, he felt markedly better.

When he came downstairs, Marion greeted him with the announcement, "The cards are here, sir."

He took one in his hand, but did not need to read it in order to know what it said. He had dictated it himself.

Marion's eyes also moved over the letters, "Today, after a long and very painful illness, Magdalene Charlotte Merkelbach van Rooyen, wife of R. Van Herewaarden, died at the youthful age of twenty-nine."

And under it, in small, discreet letters, " 'God will wipe away all her tears.' "

Marion could not help but think of these words on the day of the burial, as she stood in the funeral home next to the open casket. Reinier had escorted her to the casket with a slight motion of the hand. They stood together for the last time next to the body of Magda.

As Marion silently took in her small face, ringed with soft, dark hair, and her once-piercing eyes, now closed, Reinier paged through a volume of poems he had gotten from somewhere. He knew that Magda's last words were in the book and he pointed them out to Marion. "All your guilt has been removed."

Then Reinier, with a powerful sweep of the hand, ripped a page from the book and placed it between Magda's hands. It was the page on which the last stanza was printed:

Live again now, Magdalene,
Live in joy, live in light.
Jesus has appeared to you.
Forever gone is death's dark night.

They stood for another moment, silently observing, then Reinier closed the casket.

Leaning against the door, he looked at the damaged book and said with forced heaviness, "Sorry for my vandalism, Marion. I'll get you a new one. I'll get you a hundred new ones if you like, but I had to do this."

Marion took the volume in her hand. "This missing page says more to me than a hundred books," she said, and she bit her lip, for she felt a sharp pain in her abdomen which she had also felt earlier in the day.

"Could you step aside, please?" she begged. He attributed her grimace to emotion and silently stepped to one side in order to let her past.

Marion was not going to Borg, where Magda would be placed in the old family tomb. She stayed with Inge in the Warbler, and it was a good thing. The procession had hardly departed when Inge had another fit of whooping cough. The child was so miserable. She lurched and heaved, and when the fit finally passed, she looked pale and tired. Marion put her to bed as early as possible.

When peace returned with the evening at the Warbler, Reinier said, "We should both get to bed early tonight. I still don't feel a hundred percent, and frankly, you look a little wilted, too."

In spite of the many impressions and emotions of the last few days, Marion fell asleep almost immediately. But in the middle of the night she was prodded awake by a sharp pain. She thought that the throbbing would pass if she just lay still, but it only worsened, until finally the pain began to frighten her.

Appendicitis, she thought anxiously, and innumerable thoughts shot through her mind. *Operation, hospital. What would happen here? Inge has such a cough. Oh, how miserable, that I have to get this just now! I haven't been sick all winter.*

Then these thoughts were swept away by a new attack of pain. As it diminished, she tried to get out of bed, which she was able to do, with gritted teeth.

Reinier awakened with the vague feeling that he had heard something unusual. *Inge!* was his first thought. He jumped out of bed and hastily pulled on a bathrobe. He walked to Inge's room, but she was sleeping quietly.

I'm sure I heard something, he thought as he walked back down the hallway toward his room.

Then he saw the strip of light underneath Marion's door. Feeling uneasy, he knocked on the door. When she did not answer immediately, he pushed the door open. He saw her sitting on one of the chairs, doubled over like a sick bird, her face chalk white above her dressing gown, her teeth sunk deeply into her lower lip.

"Marion!" he shouted, frightened. "What's the matter? What is it?"

"I think—appendicitis," she said with difficulty, and again she grimaced from the pain. "I feel so awful," she said softly, and two tears rolled down her face. "Why now?"

His brain was working furiously. He reviewed the situation and acted quickly. The first thing he did was to pick Marion up and lay her back in bed, dressing gown and all.

"And remain lying down," he commanded strictly. "I am calling the doctor immediately."

He looked at his wristwatch. It was four-thirty.

The family doctor was not at home; he had been called away a few hours before for a delivery. But there were several doctors in Dintelborg, and Reinier called the closest one, with success.

He dressed quickly and was barely ready when the doorbell rang. Doctor Adriaansen was still young. Blond and thin, he looked very much like a schoolboy standing next to Reinier.

After a brief examination, he was able to discern that Marion's suspicion had been correct. It was appendicitis, and the patient would have to be brought to the hospital as quickly as possible.

The hospital was contacted and an ambulance appeared relatively quickly.

"I will, uh . . ." Doctor Adriaansen bustled toward the vehicle. "They can pull up to the door, can't they?"

Reinier and Marion stayed behind together. She lay with closed eyes, her mouth drawn taut, and periodically she groaned. She had but one thought: *Let this be over soon.*

Reinier had to exercise himself to the extreme in order to remain standing like that, silently, without saying any sweet comforting things to her.

Doctor Adriaansen returned. "They can't get up the stairs," he said with jerking gestures.

Reinier gave him a devastating look. The mannerisms of the other irritated him, even though he could not say exactly why.

"I will carry her downstairs myself," he said with measured tones.

Marion was hardly aware of who picked her up and carried her down the stairs. Later, much later, she would vaguely remember a pair of strong arms that enclosed her very carefully and a dark face directly above her own. For now, however, she simply allowed herself to be carried to the car, weak and helpless, and was not aware of the voice that whispered with an almost rugged tenderness, "Marion, my girl."

Under the cold night wind she opened her eyes once again, her strong white teeth still embedded in her lower lip.

They helped her into the car, then Reinier took her hand and said, with forced animation, "Hold on, Marion. It will soon be over."

"Yes, sir," she responded weakly. Then the car rode away and Reinier found himself standing on the front step of his home in the gray light of dawn.

Doctor Adriaansen stood next to him, but Reinier did not notice him. The man had made a very unfavorable impression on him, and Reinier looked amazed at him when he heard him say, "Amazing what wrong conclusions a person can draw. I thought initially that the patient was your wife."

Do you really think I would let her camp out in that little room then, idiot? he thought grimly, but he said coolly, "You have indeed drawn the wrong conclusion. My wife was buried yesterday."

Doctor Adriaansen was shocked, and apologized. Reinier waved off his words with a thoughtless gesture. "It's nothing. You don't know us. You could not have known." He forced himself to say with some spirit, "I will not detain you any longer, Doctor."

The young man got the hint. He left, and on the way he thought to himself that he had seldom felt so powerless and inexperienced as he had next to this imposing figure, in whose voice he detected the barely disguised anger of a man who had been extremely provoked.

Van Herewaarden, he thought. *I'll have to find out what kind of a person he is.*

Reinier proceeded to have a rotten day. He set about his work until it was time for Inge to get up.

He dressed her himself and told her something of the previous night's events. Toos came at eight, and Reinier made her swear above all to take care of Inge. Then he went to the factory for a few hours. It had been several days since he had been there, and there were many things that had to be taken care of.

The office personnel avoided him, frightened off by the line of his mouth, which they incorrectly interpreted. That was one of the things which bothered Reinier most about it.

They are respecting my grief for Magda's death, he thought. *But my problems are of a very different nature from what they assume.*

He felt like an imposter because the grief for Magda, which was expected of him, had such a small place in him and was completely overwhelmed by his concern and desire for Marion.

No matter how hard he tried to banish her from his thoughts, he could not. He saw her on the operating table. He saw her in the white hospital bed with her mouth drawn tight from pain. It did not matter that he had told himself dozens of times that an appendix operation was routine nowadays. It was Marion!

A great feeling of unease fell from him when he was informed by the hospital that the operation had been completed and everything was proceeding normally.

Toos tried, with a nervous flush, to put a decent meal on the table, but it did not turn out for her.

Reinier felt sorry for her and chewed courageously on a tough potato, but Ingeborg unceremoniously pushed her plate away and asked pointedly when Miss Marion was going to be back. After lunch she again fell into a coughing fit. She threw up on her clothing and began to cry with evident self-pity.

Reinier decided to stay with her that afternoon. The child was miserable. The cough, which had already lasted for weeks, had left her pale and thin, and her father wondered who would care for her in the coming weeks. Toos was a good girl, but she was not in the least independent. He was not looking forward to leaving Inge alone with her, and he could not be home continually.

Could he bring Inge to Borg? No, his sick little gnome would feel terribly lonely there. No, not to Borg.

Buried behind the newspaper, he lowered himself into the many other problems which had arisen now that Magda was dead.

He realized painfully that things could not simply go on as they had, when Marion recovered. Sitting across from her each day at the table, sleeping under the same roof, hearing her voice, seeing her eyes, and then remaining silent and swallowing what was boiling up in him, no, that would be asking too much.

Fire Marion and look for another housekeeper? He could not even think about it. Besides, what reason would he give Marion? He shook his head. He should not think about it now. Perhaps a solution would arise. So much happens in life that a person cannot predict.

The following day, Mrs. Dubois called. Reinier listened, at first amazed, but then strangely at ease, to her robust, energetic words. "Perhaps it is very indiscreet of me to involve myself in your affairs, Mr. Van Herewaarden, but I just happened to speak to Toos Brinkman yesterday, and she told me that Marion had to be taken to the hospital. I got the impression from her story that the situation was too much for her, especially since Inge has whooping cough. She is frightened by the coughing fits; they are like two kids together. And you surely have work to do. If you would like, you may bring Inge to us. She may stay until Marion is better. The children will receive her with open arms!"

Reinier's initial reaction was to decline, because he immediately associated Forest Cottage with Jaap Dubois. But then his understanding took over, telling him that Jaap was far away in France and that the offer was indeed a solution for him. Still he raised objections.

"It is incredibly kind of you, Mrs. Dubois," he said, "but the whooping cough! It is contagious, and you have two little ones of your own."

She laughed. "Gert and Marlies have both had it. She can't infect them, and the others have also had it. So it would not be a problem!"

He hesitated yet for a moment, "If it really is not too much trouble . . ."

Then the irrepressible Marie-Louise considered the matter closed. She asked about Marion's condition, and the conversation was over.

Taken by surprise, a few moments later Reinier was driving Inge and her clothing to Forest Cottage, where she was gleefully greeted by Gert and Marlies. The children had not seen each other in the last few weeks, for Marion and Inge had not been to Forest Cottage since the breakup with Jaap.

After a pleasant chat with Mrs. Dubois, Reinier returned to his car. He already had the door in hand when Mr. Dubois rode up on his bike.

"Well, Reinier! What are you doing here?" he said with surprise. "It is good to see you!"

Reinier explained the situation. "Your wife is one in a thousand, Dubois," he said appreciatively, and the crow's-feet at the corner of the grounds keeper's eyes deepened.

"That is so," he confirmed.

Reinier drove back to the Warbler and reviewed the conversation he had just had. Not a single word was spoken of Jaap.

❧ Chapter 19 ❧

It was not going as well with Marion as it first appeared. She remained feverish, and her temperature went up very high, especially in the evening. She was not interested in anything and showed no interest in her visits.

The hospital was full. Marion was placed in a room not really intended to be a patient's room, and she lay there together with a young Indonesian girl named Sylvia. When Marion received visitors, Sylvia pretended to be sleeping. She was very sensitive and courteous.

The visits that Reinier made to Marion, a couple of times alone and a couple of times with Inge, were a great disappointment to him. Marion had changed. There seemed to be nothing left of the devoted concern she had always shown for the things which belonged to her task. She asked only disinterestedly about Inge, and when Reinier asked her if she would like a visit from Toos, she simply shrugged her shoulders.

Marion did not have it easy. The backlash had now come from the long winter of strain and worry, and especially from her breakup with Jaap. She continually had the crippling feeling, almost something physical, that she had borne something beyond her strength. She had been able to fend off Jaap; she had braved his anger and his affection; but she knew that she would be able to no longer.

Her yearning for him was great and heavy. It took possession of her to the neglect of all else.

If he came back now, she thought during her feverish nights, writhing under her covers. *If he came back now, or wrote, I would go with him. I would stay with him, no matter what the cost.*

God has asked too much of me. It cannot be His wish that we live apart. I do still love him, and he loves me. Why doesn't he write?

But then she realized that she was the reason, and she fell backward into a deep pit of apathy, in which she wanted nothing but to be freed from these tormenting thoughts.

On the first of May, nurse Toni pulled a page from the calendar with a cheerful smile. "Well, ladies, the month of blossoms has returned!"

"And I have to begin my first May in the Netherlands in the hospital," sighed Sylvia, in her slow, deliberately pronounced Dutch.

Marion said nothing. *May,* she thought. *May.*

It was as if deep within her a voice continually wailed, and she felt too weak to stifle it. There was no resistance left in her.

Jaap, she thought with great pain. He wanted to paint her as "May," sitting in the blooming fields! How fervent was the voice that flattered her within: "The sweetest, the blondest, yes, little May."

It had only been six weeks! His face was so vivid to her yet.

A sudden anger arose in her. Why did she have to miss him? Why?

How cruel God had been to force them into this separation!

Did she deserve this? Had she not been open about her belief? Had she not spoken desperate words to Jaap? Had she not prayed for him, fervently prayed? Oh, why could he not believe? Why Magda, why Mr. Van Herewaarden, and why not Jaap? Jaap, her beloved—in spite of his faults, in spite of his odd libertine views—still her beloved.

As the hours and days lengthened, the rebellion ebbed from her heart, but there remained behind a rancorous feeling of denial. The old resiliency would not return.

She was reanimated briefly by a visit from her parents. Reinier had informed them immediately of her illness, and now Father and Mother came from their new home in Garderen to visit her.

Marion cried when she saw them.

"Be still, my child," comforted Mrs. Verkerk, and she recalled how often Marion had comforted and cheered her when she felt ill. "Be still. When you are released from the hospital, you can come and recover with us in Garderen. We have only been there for a couple of days, so it is still rather messy, but you'll see how cozy it will be! Then you can regain your strength among the pines."

Marion wiped away her tears.

"I wanted to come and help you move," she said sadly.

Father described for her the move, the small country house they encountered, and the neighbors, Farmer Knol and his wife, who had so warmly welcomed them on the day of their arrival.

"Everything is so rustic, Marion," said Mrs. Verkerk. "You will enjoy it. It is just your kind of place. You can pick flowers right along the road! Completely different from Amsterdam! I am so happy that everything has been arranged."

Yes, Marion could see it. Mother was so enthusiastic.

Then she got a report on Edith, whose foreign vacation was almost over. A few days later Edith herself came, very fashionable, emphatically but carefully made up, dressed to the hilt.

She had become the chief buyer for a fashion house in The Hague, and you could tell, Marion thought.

Edith undoubtedly had a beautiful appearance. She was taller than Marion, her figure was lovely, and her face proportional. She was somewhat flirtatious, self-conscious, and carefree. She had not yet totally lost her vacation mood.

She had brought along lovely gifts for Marion, souvenirs from the Riviera—a beautiful book and a bunch of bananas. She babbled a hundred miles per hour.

Sylvia sat staring at her with wide eyes. She could hardly turn away her glance.

The stories of France interested Marion. When Edith told her of the natural beauty, Marion thought, *Jaap will enjoy that.*

As she described the picturesque little city, Marion thought, *Perhaps he has already sketched it.* And as Edith described for her some of the interesting characters, she saw him observing them with the hungry eye of an artist.

Then Edith changed the subject. Marion listened while her sister related her big plans. She planned to give up her job and go on and become a beauty specialist. In France she had visited a beauty salon. "Mari, you would not believe what I saw. I am so enthusiastic! I can go where I want, even in The Hague, and I can start right away. The course lasts a year. I can keep the same room. I really want to do this. It is really different, isn't it?"

Beauty specialist, thought Marion. *That is right up Edith's alley; just as long as she leaves me alone and does not try to use me as her guinea pig!*

But Edith had no intention of leaving Marion alone. She had already mounted her hobby horse and was intently examining her sister's face. She named a few technical terms that she had no doubt picked up in France.

"If you would just order that cream, Mari," she enthusiastically advised. "You could really have nice skin if you wanted to. And I don't understand why you don't do anything with your eyebrows! They're too light. If you would just put a little something on them, it would give your face so much more character. Then you would have offers!"

"Right," demurred Marion. "I can just hear myself: Nurse, could you please hand me my eyebrow pencil? The doctor is coming soon."

She smiled ironically. "I am pretty enough already."

"And who would dare to doubt it?" asked a dark voice behind Edith, who promptly turned around.

It was Mr. Van Herewaarden, with Inge on his heels. Marion introduced them, and moments later, Reinier and Edith were locked in intense conversation.

Inge stood next to Marion and told her about the games she and Gert and Marlies had played in the woods.

She only half listened, for her attention was drawn to the two others.

Edith surely is pretty, she thought, with a strange flurry of jealousy, for her intuition told her that a comparison was being made between the two of them. It suddenly dawned on her that Edith was right. She did not look very attractive—especially not now.

What had Mr. Van Herewaarden said when he came in? She remembered his words and blushed slightly.

Yes, she rebutted, *but that was before he saw Edith.*

She impatiently sunk her head into the pillow.

I am such a fool, she thought angrily. *What do I care if he thinks Edith is prettier than I am? She is, isn't she? And our friendship is certainly above such things!*

She turned toward Inge and asked her several questions.

They laughed together over a joke, but the laugh did Inge no good. She had one of her coughing fits again, and Marion was there immediately to take her arms and help her. Reinier also rushed over, and they exchanged a few quick words of concern.

The coughing subsided and Marion sank back into her pillow. She felt tired after having sat up so quickly. Apparently she was not up to it yet. She turned pale.

Reinier, still bent over the child, continued looking at Marion. "You must stay calm, my friend," he warned. "You may be sicker than you think. Will you promise me that?"

Edith stood watching. Inge came and stood next to her and with her hands stroked the flowery material of her dress. Edith did not respond.

"Does she have whooping cough?" Edith asked, her eyebrows wrinkled.

He affirmed that she did.

"Isn't that contagious?" She threw an impersonal glance at Inge, a glance that hit Reinier wrong.

"Yes, it is," he said flatly. "Come, Ingeborg, we must be going."

He extended a hand to Edith. "It was a pleasure, Miss Verkerk. I hope I have not exposed you to contagion by bringing my daughter along."

His voice was not completely free of sarcasm, and Marion, who knew that voice so well, heard it and measured the irritation hidden behind it.

You have put your foot in your mouth, Edie, she thought, not completely without perverse delight. *You shouldn't take out after Inge, or you'll get on the wrong side of him.*

Reinier returned his daughter to Forest Cottage and then turned toward his own empty house. Since Inge was no longer at the Warbler, he had taken to eating out. Toos did not have a great deal to do. She made sure that there was bread in the house, made his bed, and kept the house dusted.

Reinier spent the long, lonely spring evenings out on the veranda, the floor lamp behind his chair, and arranged his plans for the near future. Many ideas were angrily rejected; some were carefully considered and weighed. It was very difficult to make plans right now.

The evening was quiet and sweet around him. Somewhere, far away were the sounds of the street—a voice, a horn.

A June bug flew against the lamp; the paper rustled in his hands. If he wanted to have coffee, he would have to make it himself. So he made it himself, while his thoughts reposed with that blond child who held his heart in captivity and did not know it. More strongly than ever, he was aware this evening of how much he loved her. This, the evening that he met her sister.

Edith Verkerk was pure femininity, just as Marion was pure femininity, but with a completely different accent. He saw the dark, expressive eyes before him, the striking mouth, the noble disposition. *A dangerous woman,* he thought. *A woman who can make her wishes be known.* And she would have many wishes: admiration, luxury, comfort, beautiful clothing, and who knows what else? But would she also give? A dangerous woman, too dangerous because she had something of Marion's innocence in her eyes. Innocence that the keen observer could see was belied by the selfish curl of her mouth.

She involuntarily awakened in a man the desire to tame her. Yet this was but a fleeting thought. Infinitely more potent was the liberating blossom of knowing for certain that Marion was different! She lay there so small and withdrawn and insignificant, but her helping Inge was a reflex, just as the anxious recoil from infection was a reflex of the other.

You cannot deny yourself, Marion, he thought. *Your indolence may last some days, but you will come out of it again. I know it for certain now. The other person is too strong in you; it will overcome you—the warm, the giving. You cannot continue thinking only about yourself. It won't work.*

Shortly before Marion was released from the hospital, she had a conversation with Jaap's father that was especially gripping.

Sylvia had left the day before; the room was empty and cold without her.

When Marion heard footsteps in the hallway, she thought for a moment, *Would that be for me?* But she dismissed the thought immediately. It was the middle of the afternoon. Who would come?

But it was for her. The rectangular figure of Mr. Dubois filled the doorway, and Marion suppressed a shout. She had not spoken to the grounds keeper since the evening he brought her home. Then she had rejected his well-meant advice with a hefty "No!"

Mrs. Dubois and Ronnie had visited her, but they had brought the children along, and furthermore Sylvia was there. They tactfully avoided mentioning Jaap's name.

But now that his father stood before her so suddenly, so unexpectedly, and peered at her with those clear, gray eyes that seemed to look right through her, she knew she would not be able to hide anything from him. A great feeling of defenselessness came over her.

Dubois began with a couple of normal, encouraging words. He did not force a talk, but now Marion wanted it. All the things she had bottled up, which she could not express, not even to her parents, were looking for an exit.

"Mr. Dubois," she said urgently while she nervously buried her head into the pillow, "how is Jaap?"

"Well," he said in his usual quiet way, "it has been three weeks since he left. We have received a couple of postcards from him, but nothing more. Jaap is not a writer. We are used to that."

He answered only her explicit question; to the implicit, he answered nothing. Marion had to say it herself. Confidence cannot be extorted.

Then Marion spoke, somewhat defiantly, "You must be wondering why I have not been to Forest Cottage in so long?"

"I know why," he said. "Jaap told me a few things."

"Do you remember the conversation we had about six weeks ago?" she asked. "You advised me then to break up with Jaap."

"Yes," he answered, "I did, even though it hurt me to have to give you that advice. But you were not about to follow my advice, Marion!"

"No," said Marion forcefully, "I wasn't. Up to the very last moment I did not want to."

"And yet you did it." His voice was very gentle.

"And yet I did it. I had to. I was forced to act as I did, but it was terrible, Mr. Dubois. It was as if I were being torn in two. My mind and my blood fought against each other, and my heart did not know how to choose between God and Jaap. That was the choice, after all. But God forced my will to conform to His, and that did not happen without pain."

She began to cry softly, and he laid his hand on her arm. "And yet I am happy that it has gone this way, Marion. In the end you will be thankful."

She looked up at him immediately; her tears came no more. "Thankful?" she asked sarcastically. "Oh, you don't know the whole story. If you did . . . Hundreds of times I have wished to do these last weeks over. I would act differently, Mr. Dubois, no matter what it might cost."

He looked into her excited face and realized, *She regrets it. So that is it.*

He remembered almost word for word the conversation he

had had with Jaap a few weeks before, and he thought, actually somewhat baffled: *I saw this coming then, but did I do the right thing? She is so unhappy. I have taken a great responsibility upon myself.*

Marion bit her lip. She fussed with the sheet and said loudly, while avoiding the eyes of the grounds keeper, "I had always believed that God was love, but He is cruel and incomprehensible, Mr. Dubois."

"I have often thought the same, my sweet child," he responded, "so I cannot blame you for these words. But please take my word for it, Marion. God sometimes has to be cruel in order to convince us of the fullness of His love."

She lightly shook her head. "I don't know," she said doubtfully. Suddenly she asked, "Does Jaap know that I am sick?"

"My wife has surely written it to him," Dubois reflected. "She writes him practically everything that happens in Dintelborg."

Again he saw that searching puzzled look in Marion's eyes, and he understood. "Perhaps, Marion, you cannot understand why Jaap has not written to you? You did not think he was the type to allow himself to be knocked out of the game by the first rejection."

Marion nodded. *His address,* she thought feverishly. *I want his address. I can explain everything to him. I could.*

The grounds keeper did not, however, give her Jaap's address, and her pride prevented her from asking for it.

When Dubois left, she cried herself to sleep.

Somewhere in France sat a young man on the embankment of a sloping road. His back was supported by a sign on which appeared the words ROUTE DU VIN. This sign was frequently seen in this exceptional wine-growing region. A dazzling panorama was laid out before Jaap Dubois.

But he had little attention for the beauties of nature at this particular moment. He was reading a letter for the second time, and a particular passage in it brought a frown to his forehead.

"Mrs. Van Herewaarden has died. Marion has been sick for weeks now. She worries much too much."

He recognized the subtle rebuke from his mother. She thought differently about the whole affair than Father did. She would like to see things work out between Marion and himself.

But Father . . . he whistled between his teeth.

"A mixed-up, crazy case," he murmured. "Marion worries too much." Was she sorry now? It would not surprise him. The decision she forced upon herself was too hard for her. And what now? He cursed under his breath.

The old man could see this coming, he thought. *He should have been a psychologist. He missed his calling.*

He recalled the conversation he had had with his father.

"Jaap," he had said firmly, "you must promise me one thing, and I expect you to hold yourself to the promise like a man. As long as you have no intention of altering your life-style, you must leave Marion alone. Do not try to get in touch with her. Do you promise me?"

He had lowered his eyes before the honest, searching gaze of his father. One felt like a naughty boy under that glance.

"It looks like you think you need to protect Marion from me," he had mumbled.

Then the peculiar pull of his father's mouth smoothed and he said mysteriously, "Not from you, Jaap. From her own heart. What do you say?"

He had extended his hand to him, and Jaap had half-heartedly promised. He would leave Marion alone. He did briefly perceive the pain in his father's eyes, because he would rather let Marion go than change his own self-made religion, but he would rather not think about the pain.

Father was a powerful figure. It was difficult to escape his grip. It was easier outside the country.

A fiat. He would forget Marion. Was he the kind of person who would get down in the dumps over some woman? And yet—her eyes would not release him.

"Little nun," he mumbled as he got up. "Still, you did teach me a few things."

Marion received no letter.

✝ Chapter 20 ❧

The day arrived on which Marion was to be released from the hospital. Reinier would be picking her up with the car and bringing her to her parents in Garderen.

She sat next to him, wrapped in a blanket, and watched the streets of Dintelborg disappear behind her. Reinier did not say much. Marion was not sure what she had done to him. She realized that he had not been the same since Magda's death. He was calmer, kinder, more attentive. Or was that because she was sick?

After a while he began to talk. "Have you thought yet about what will be on your program once you have completely recovered, Marion?"

"No," she admitted. "To tell you the truth, I have not looked into it."

"Well," he continued, "I was planning to take a trip. Since Magda's illness began I have not taken a vacation, and now I would like to get away for a while. Can you understand that?"

Marion nodded. "But what about Inge?" she asked, as he expected her to.

"Exactly," he said. "That is what I would like to talk to you about. If you could see your way clear to agree, I would like to send you two together to the ocean for about six weeks. Inge has really gone downhill since she has had whooping cough, and you . . . Actually I feel a little guilty. When you first came to us, you looked like a healthy girl. But now you have such a pale face! Your stay at the Warbler has not done you any good."

Marion laughed somewhat sadly. "You are acquitted," she said. "The appendicitis did have something to do with it."

Yes, he thought, *as did all the rest.* But he stifled the impulse. He elaborated on his vacation plans.

Then the stillness fell between them again. Marion was tired from sitting. Reinier noticed it and said carefully, "You are getting tired, aren't you, Marion? Lean against me a little, if it is easier."

She did not answer, but on a particularly bad portion of the road, he felt the pressure of her shoulder against his own and saw that she had her eyes closed.

She trusts me. She trusts me implicitly, he thought, almost surprised. He set his jaw, and the frown above his eyes deepened. He tried to drive more carefully.

The rain tapped on the roof of the car; sometimes, under a tree, a large, heavy drop would suddenly fall. The atmosphere in a car could be so intimate.

"Ride like this to the end of the world," mused Reinier.

He shook his head at himself. *Fantasies,* his mind explained.

Marion opened her eyes.

"Are we almost there?" she asked. "I have never been to Garderen."

"Nor have I," admitted Reinier. "But I looked at the map

this morning for the best route. It will be about fifteen minutes yet, I think."

Indeed, after a short interval, the car stopped in front of a small country house picturesquely tucked away amid the pines and brush.

Then suddenly there was a great burst of activity about them. There was Mother, who embraced her and helped her out of the car, and there was Father talking to Mr. Van Herewaarden and picking up her luggage.

Everything passed like a film before her.

While she was being installed on the sun porch, she managed to hear over Mother's hasty, somewhat muffled noise, a hearty, trusted voice from the living room. "That daughter of yours? She has taken on a difficult task! She has earned a medal, Mr. Verkerk!"

And then Father's tranquil tone. "Our Marion does not do things halfway, Mr. Van Herewaarden."

With a blush at this double compliment, Marion began her cure in this outstanding rehabilitation center.

Was it the conversations with Father that made her blossom? Was it the delicious delicacies that Mother set before her? Or was it the air, the pure air of Gelderland, which she enjoyed with full draughts?

Whatever the case, she improved visibly. The color returned to her cheeks and fascination to her expression.

She became familiar with the surrounding area and became acquainted with the Knols, the neighboring family. Early in the morning she could be seen leaning over the natural wood fence discussing with the farmer the plants in his vegetable garden, and after fourteen days, she had taken in hand with Father the cultivation of their own garden.

But when the late flowers and grass had been sown and everything was finally in place, she was possessed by a certain unease.

Even the little spats with Mother began to crop up again. Had Marion lost her tolerance?

She began to long for her responsibilities again.

"I feel better," she announced one evening. "I am going to report back to work. Then Mr. Van Herewaarden can at least take his vacation. He has been greatly handicapped by all this loafing."

"Don't you think that is a little . . . ," Mother said carefully, "how should I say it? A little awkward? You a young girl with such a young widower? I don't know."

Oh, she meant it well, she was only thinking of common conventions, but to Marion it sounded very ugly, an insinuation, a stain on her pure character.

She looked at her mother with large eyes that grew darker and darker. "I take it that you do not know Mr. Van Herewaarden," she retorted sharply. "Ha, what an idea!"

For a brief moment, her memory of the events that took place on the night of her birthday surfaced, but that only caused her to reproach Mother more harshly. "I don't understand how you could even imagine . . ."

Mr. Verkerk intervened. He admonished Marion not to talk to her mother with such a tone.

"You don't know men," Mrs. Verkerk whined.

Marion laughed scornfully. "I just happen to know this one," she said, "and he is one of the few decent ones, as far as I can judge."

She whirled and walked away. She half heard Father testify to Mother that Mr. Van Herewaarden was, in his opinion, a gentleman in every way. "Besides, darling, the child is still there, and the maid. You should not overreact. Nothing is in fact different from last winter."

And so Marion returned to the Warbler but only for a few days, to prepare for the upcoming vacation.

Reinier would be going to France, Switzerland, and Italy.

He had many meetings with his procurement team, and Marion saw very little of him those days.

Inge was overjoyed about the vacation by the ocean. Rooms had been reserved for both of them on a small beach on the North Sea. But before they left for the sea, they were to spend a week in Garderen.

Marion thought it would be impolite if she did not pay a good-bye visit to Forest Cottage before her departure. She took Inge along, but the girl immediately engaged in playing with the children with whom she had so lately formed a family.

Marion hesitated a moment. Should she ring the bell? Or should she just step in as she had done over the winter? She decided on the latter.

The large room appeared to be dead. But no, there was Grandmother, much smaller, more insignificant than the last time Marion had seen her. Again she hesitated. Then she said, "Hello, Grandmother. Is Mrs. Dubois here?"

Grandmother looked up through her small, gold-rimmed glasses at the one who had entered. She showed no surprise.

She told Marion that her daughter-in-law was out visiting a sick friend. The older children were in school; the little ones were playing outside; and Ronnie and Laurens had a house in Borg. They no longer lived here, didn't Marion know that?

Grandmother was all alone, but it did not matter, she loved the stillness. Nevertheless, she thought it fine that Marion had come. Now they could talk for once.

"Yes, Grandmother." Marion nodded. "I must confess, I was not looking forword to coming here."

"I understand, child," the old woman said. "I understand it all too well. I have anxiously followed events from my spectator's seat outside the mainstream."

Her wrinkled hand stroked the smooth, white hand of the girl who listened silently to her.

"You have been strong, Marion," her small voice went on. "Stronger than I was. You have chosen the more difficult part. I thought I was choosing the most beautiful part—adventure, excitement, enthusiasm—but it turned out to be the more difficult."

She paused for a moment, lost in her thoughts.

"May I tell you my life's story?" she asked suddenly.

"Please, do," Marion responded, fascinated by the sudden openness of the quiet, always-smiling Grandmother, the comparison which she so naturally made between then.

Then Grandmother spoke of Jacobi Schollevaer, of Jacques Dubois, of a sunny, beautiful love that all too quickly lapsed into bitterness and disillusionment.

Marion listened breathlessly.

"I have taken great blame upon myself," Grandmother concluded. "A guilt which I will never be able to satisfy. My son has grown up, thanks be to God, into a man whom people can love without much effort. But Jaap, Marion—my old heart suffers so because of Jaap. He has reaped his grandfather's heritage, and who will be next? Perhaps Bram, perhaps Marlies; who knows what a child will become? A person can never undo what has already been done, Marion. I can only pray for them now, and who knows for how long?"

Her voice became strangely deep.

Marion gripped her hands.

"Oh, Grandmother," she cried with emotion, "I would have acted exactly the same as you did. I wanted to. I wanted to follow Jaap through thick and thin, but I was restrained. I couldn't. I am not strong. God holds me back so tightly that I sometimes feel like a prisoner."

Grandmother looked at her, her eyes blinking as she pronounced the unexpected words, "Then why don't you give God up, Marion?"

Marion was shocked at her words, words that forced her to

express her most hidden feelings. She sighed and shook her head as she said, "I couldn't, Grandmother. I love Him. Even though He holds me prisoner, even though He cruelly strikes me, even though He has taken Jaap from me, I still love Him. But I understand so little of life, Grandmother!"

The old woman heard the lament in the heavy confession of the young woman. She said to her with deep tenderness, almost solemnly, "You are a lucky child, Marion. It is a privilege when God wants to keep you so close to Himself. Thank Him for it, even if you do not understand it yet."

Deep in her thoughts, Marion turned back to the Warbler. She asked Grandmother to deliver her greetings to the rest of the family. *Will I ever see Jaap again?* she wondered to herself along the way. She did not know. She was not in a position to overlook things and accept them as Grandmother was. The years had not matured her yet; too many thoughts and desires were still seething through her heart.

The following day they would depart, Reinier earlier than the girls. He was taking the train to France, and the company chauffeur would be taking him to the station in Breda.

The last meal in the rather disorganized house felt strange. The plants had been taken out of the windows. They would be in the care of Toos's mother during these weeks.

Soon the curtains would be shut in front of the humble windows.

They spoke a little. "I will keep you informed of my address," said Reinier. "Will you write me regularly about how Inge is doing, Marion?"

Marion promised.

After eating, he sat for a long time with Inge on his knee. Marion noticed that saying good-bye was difficult for him. There had hardly been a day in which he had not seen his little gnome, and now it would be six weeks, a very long time.

When they heard the car drive up, he pressed the child wildly, almost violently to his breast and kissed her.

Then he sent her outside. "You go tell Mr. Brouwer that Daddy will be right out!"

Inge bolted out.

Reinier and Marion stood alone in the half-dark room, the thick, plush curtains holding out the sunlight. He leaned against the fireplace.

"I must go," he said, as though talking to himself.

"Yes, sir," she answered mechanically. Her glance swept over the furniture, over all the familiar surroundings. At that table she had cried when Magda died. There they had had many arguments and confidential conversations.

How I have come to love this room, thought Marion.

Reinier stood observing her. She was still rather thin and fragile, and the circles remained under her eyes. How drained she looked. He took a couple of steps toward her and laid his hand on her shoulder.

"We have an emotional year behind us, Marion," he said.

"Yes, sir," she again replied. She seemed to be blinking her eyes, and he wondered what she was thinking about.

"We owe you a great deal," Reinier continued.

She dismissed his comment with a gesture, but he went on. "You have helped me through a very tempestuous time, and I cannot thank you enough for it. And now I am asking more from you than duty requires. I am entrusting to you the most precious thing I have, my daughter. Will you take good care of her, Marion?"

She tilted her head slightly so that she could look into his face. Then she said openly, in a sincere attempt to put him at ease, "I think that, after you, I am the one who most loves Inge, Mr. Van Herewaarden. That will have to be guarantee enough."

Ah, Marion, he sighed within himself, *why must you always say the things that most press my heart?*

Abruptly he released her.

"All right," he said, "I trust you. Have a wonderful vacation. And good-bye!"

Then he disappeared. An hour later Marion and Inge were also on their way. The Warbler was closed.

ᷤ Chapter 21 ᷤ

The vacation flew by. The sea, the endless sea, which upon first sight brought Inge to a complete stop, slowly but surely wore the sharp edges off Marion's grief.

Each week, sometimes twice a week, there was a letter from Reinier.

The first couple of times, seeing the envelope post-marked France gave Marion a start. Could this be word from Jaap? She had become accustomed to the idea that no letter was in the coming; she had pushed her memory of Jaap deep into the furthermost recesses of her heart.

Reinier cut his own knot when his vacation was almost over and made his decision: He and Inge would move in with his mother at the castle. Many hours of consternation were not able to bring him a better solution.

He was not looking forward to going to Borg, but a small, hopeful voice encouraged him. Perhaps it was just for the time being. *You have a long, long winter ahead of you to win Marion for yourself. Perhaps next year.*

Then his thoughts ground to a halt, for he would first have to make his way through the mine field of dismissing Marion. How would she react? Would the friendship which had grown up between them, and which had been reinforced by their exchange of letters, be able to survive? It would be very difficult, because he could not reveal to her his reasons. Not yet.

Two days earlier than he had planned, he returned to the Netherlands. He stopped in Dintelborg for a couple of hours, but he only left a portion of his luggage there and went to pick up the car.

He departed directly for the beach where Marion and Inge were lodging.

With some direction from the manager of the rooms where they were staying, Reinier was able to quickly find them on the beach. It was a spontaneous encounter. Inge clung immediately to her father and could not be pried loose again. Reinier was pleasantly surprised that they both looked so brown and healthy again, and he complimented Marion to that effect.

She let her eyes pan the infinite water on which the sun had paved a golden path. She shoveled up loose sand with her fingers and allowed it to run out again, thoughtlessly.

Why do we have to leave so soon? The day after tomorrow! she mused to herself, and her ear registered once again all the sounds that had become so familiar and trusted. The shouting and talking of hundreds of children, like on a schoolyard, the warning whistle of the lifeguard, and in the background, the ceaseless breaking of the waves.

A little later they were walking along the sea, Reinier carried the beach bag and Marion carried a handful of shoes with the laces tied together. Inge hopped along in between them, both of them rewarded with a small, sturdy hand in their own.

Oh, how I will miss this, Marion thought over and over again. It was almost as though it was the arrival of Mr. Van Herewaarden that made her focus on their upcoming sad departure.

The next morning they were together early. It was a day of carefree joy, in which they were both children again with Inge, with so much natural familiarity that it surprised them all. They romped through the dunes, played tag, rolled in the warm sand, and finally lay exhausted in the cup of a dune. It was not long before Inge fell asleep, her dark hair sprayed over her father's sweater. The two adults lay looking at her with tender expressions.

Then Reinier said, somewhat muted, "She is going to look like Magda, Marion."

Marion frowned slightly. She thought about the scene a few days before, while she had been in Amsterdam picking up some things and Inge, frightened by the storm which suddenly blew up, had broken into such hysteria. Hours later she had again become frightened while she was sleeping.

"She had more of Magda than we ever imagined," she answered Reinier, equally muted. "I heard and saw something of it this past week, and it frightened me."

Reinier's eyes questioned her.

She related in a whisper what had happened. "Inge is more delicate than one would guess on the surface of things," she decided.

Reinier's eyes were fixed with fascination on the hand that she had carefully laid on Inge's curls while she spoke. The child knew this gentle caress; she did not awaken.

In this gesture of her lightly browned hand, which almost imperceptibly stroked Inge's head, Reinier detected the almost motherly love which had grown in Marion for his child.

He thought about the message he had to deliver to her today. His jaw set in pain.

And I am supposed to separate you from Inge, he thought, his eyes closed. *God grant that it be only temporary.*

This thought was more than a wish. It was a prayer, moving and heartfelt, a prayer with wings.

But the heart of the man with closed eyes was heavy with concern.

"Shall we walk down the boulevard?" Reinier asked.

Marion stood up.

It was their last evening at the shore.

Now I must tell her, he thought, smothering a curse. *Days like this should never come to an end.*

Marion was animated. She had enjoyed the carefree day in the sun, and she experienced this evening walk and the light conversation they had together as something very good.

The noise of the beach people was all around them: Young people whooped and sang, and in the background was the sound of the surf.

Reinier told her of the Côte d'Azur, of the fashionable beach life there, that was so completely different than here.

She walked next to him and thought with satisfaction how pleasant it was to listen to his deep, trusted voice again. They walked into town and stood still on a small, high bridge which spanned the canal.

Leaning on the railing, they looked into the dark water, which sparkled here and there where it caught a moonbeam. They were silent for a long time before Marion became aware of the silence.

"You certainly are quiet all of a sudden!" she said openheartedly. He looked down at her, and a dour tug distorted his well-formed mouth.

"I have to take care of one of the dirtiest jobs I have ever done in my life," he said. "That takes away a person's spirit."

224

Marion looked up at him, puzzled, the moonlight illuminating her face and large questioning eyes.

"Yes," he said forcefully, answering the question in her eyes, "a dirty job. I must dismiss Miss Marion Verkerk."

Marion turned her head and looked into the water, her hands clutching the railing.

Dismissed. That means away from Inge. That means that the hand of a stranger will quarter her sandwiches, that a strange hand will tuck her in.

Dismissed. That means leaving Dintelborg with its thousands of sweet memories, leaving the Warbler, which lay dreaming in a collar of flowers.

Dismissed. That means being sent away by a man whom she had thought was her friend, who had called her his little comrade and with whom she had struggled through months of concern and suffering.

Her mouth began to tremble. Reinier saw it and cursed himself under his breath. "Why don't you say something?"

"What am I supposed to say?" she asked, her voice trembling. "I'm sorry."

He balled his fists. *One word,* he thought wildly. *One word and I have messed everything up. She was not ready for it. I must have been crazy.*

He forced himself to search for a different approach, a different tone.

The distance between them was so dangerously small. He felt that he had to create distance in order to avoid a serious accident, and, perhaps intuitively, he found the words which immediately found their mark.

"I am sorry, too, Marion," he said, businesslike. "But that it is the way it is. We are breaking up house. The Warbler has been sold, and Inge and I are going to Borg. Hunting season is coming up, and then the old castle is irresistible. I was overcome by the temptation."

He listened with surprise at how easily it went for him, this speaking of words which were alien to him, which he did not mean. But Marion did not see through them.

"To Borg? And I thought . . ."

Something flashed through her eyes. Was it disappointment, or even a hint of disdain? He was not sure, but it made something boil in him. For a moment he forget to play his role.

"What did you think?" he pressed sharply.

She gestured flatly. "It doesn't matter. I have no right to meddle in your affairs."

As he opened his mouth to administer his retort, another thought shot through his brain, *Whatever she might think, her conclusion is wrong.* He saw it in the way she had reacted just then, in the indignation in her expression.

Let her think what you yourself suggested to her, a reasonable voice came from his consciousness. *As long as she draws the wrong conclusion, your secret is safe. Go through with it!*

He swallowed the words which teemed on his tongue. He said a few things, business things, which were only half attended to by Marion.

A few days in Dintelborg, pack things up, everything put into storage. *Go ahead,* she thought, hurt and angry. *As far as I am concerned, you are putting me in storage, as well. Inge, my child! I will miss you so, and how will you sleep if Miss Marion tells you no story about the big brown bear?*

Another thought floated through her, overshadowing the first.

You have become too attached to them. Always the same mistake, Marion Verkerk. Jaap Dubois was right. When it came right down to it, you were nothing more than an employee who could be fired, simply fired. Who knows, maybe he will even throw in a nice letter of recommendation.

Something in her eyes mocked him as she spoke to him of immaterial things that had to be said in order not to be impolite.

To Borg, she thought over and over again.

Had he not told her how he had fought for so many years to be free of the hated straitjacket? And now he was returning of his own free will?

Why? Why is he doing this? She felt he was betraying himself by walking into the camp that he had once turned his back on in fiery idealism.

Was the blood not able to deny itself, now that he had sown his wild seeds of youth? Would Lady Inge now have to enjoy an upbringing which Marion Verkerk would not be able to provide?

Oh, the ladies from the circle that she had on several occasions heard him describe as "the clique" would greet him with open arms.

Very desirable company, the handsome, fascinating, and above all rich widower, Reinier Van Herewaarden!

But Inge? What would Inge mean to such a woman? A ball and chain; at most a little fashion doll with a pretty little face to parade around the salons.

Marion was building steam. She knew that she was exaggerating and being unreasonable, but it gave her much-needed relief to run on this way.

Once back in the Warbler there was little else for her to do but pack. Everything would have to be packed away: the dishes, the clothing, the bedding. It hurt her to think that other hands would unpack all this, that within a few days, she would be forever locked out of this little community of which she was such an integral part.

In the lonely hours of her monotonous toil there was a constant dispute going on within her. Her heart brought up questions, and her mind answered, mercilessly sharp and cold at times, but her heart did not give up the battle.

What is going to happen to Inge now? her heart asked. *I did, after all, promise Magda that I would keep in contact with her.*

Tell that to Mr. Van Herewaarden, her mind mocked. *You should know better, Marion Verkerk. It would look rather ugly if you were to force yourself on them like that.*

But what should I do? complained her heart. *I can't just walk away the same way that I walked in. I am bound here by a thousand bonds.* "Our Marion does not do things halfway," Father had once said, *but wouldn't it be better to reserve part of yourself, your deepest, innermost self? Aren't you too vulnerable when you give everything?*

Of course, replied her mind. *You have gone about it all wrong again, Marion. And you were warned often enough. How often did Jaap Dubois say to you,* "You get too attached to people. Their concerns are not your concerns"? *And now you see; their life is not your life. They belong at home in Borg, at the castle, and you belong at home in Garderen, living off your father's moderate pension. Never forget that there is a gulf between you and that each should remain and live out his life on his own side of the gulf. Little Inge will slip through your fingers. Your friendship with her father will fade into the shadow of the dark year that you lived through together. The farther it is behind, the fainter the memory will be.*

You must be calloused, decided her mind. *You must not let any of your pain show when you say good-bye.*

And the mind had pride on its side. But the heart remained standing alone; it did not give in.

And so Reinier had to deal with a silent Marion for several days, who was polite and proper, who laughed when it was appropriate, but whose eyes shouted pain. Three more days, two more days, one more day. He was concerned about her disposition.

The distance is increasing, he thought, alarmed. *She has not even left yet, and already the distance is so great. Did I go about it wrong? Can I still restore what I had to rupture by taking this step? Or will she disappear from my circle completely, seek another job, meet other men, maybe Jaap Dubois again, who knew? Did it have to be like this?*

He shook his head. *Now or never,* he thought with resolve, and rode sooner than usual toward home, where he hoped to find Marion.

He found her in Inge's bedroom, which was bald and cold, where only the made-up bed suggested anything of home.

Marion stood with her back to him and straightened some things in a chest. He stood silently in the doorway for a moment, then he stepped in and shut the door behind him.

"Marion, I have something to say to you," he began.

She hardly reacted, with just a hasty glance out of the corner of her eye. "I'm listening, sir." She went on with her activities.

"No, not like that," he continued. "Stand up."

He closed the cover of the trunk and sat down on it.

"Come sit down next to me and hear what I have on my heart. I've had enough of you playing the mute all week. Is that clear?"

Her heart was pounding. *Leave me alone,* pulsed that heart, *I had to!*

But Marion raised her eyes and said flatly, "Excuse me?"

"Look," he began again, trying another tone, "I understand you better than you perhaps think. You are sad for Inge, to whom you must soon say good-bye. You cannot understand my decision, and you are harboring the nagging feeling that I used you and now am throwing you away. Isn't that right, Marion?"

"I have no right to criticize your decision," she stubbornly replied.

She looked at his hands, resting on his knees. On his right

hand he still wore his wedding ring; on his left sparkled the signet ring with the family coat of arms. It was a very beautiful ring, but for Marion it simply reinforced what she had been thinking these last few days. *Stay on your side of the gulf, Marion. Inge is a lady, and you are an employee. You collect your salary and beyond that you have no rights.*

"No right?" Reinier repeated. "What drivel. Of course you have a right! We made demands on you the whole year, and you have given everything you had. Haven't you earned the right?"

Her heart skipped a beat, it leaped up high, like a jack-in-the-box. *So that's it,* her heart thought, but it had become more careful; it waited.

But her mind took quite a clout. It could not handle this reaction of Reinier's, and so it fell silent.

Marion sat silently on the trunk, with folded hands.

Reinier continued with his speech. "I would love to tell you all my reasons, Marion, just as we have talked over everything for so long, like good friends. But I cannot. There are sometimes things in a person's life that cannot and may not be said. I am asking you something very difficult. I am asking you to trust me, even though I have not trusted you. Will you trust me, Marion?"

He turned her shoulders toward himself a little.

I am pleading for my happiness, he thought anxiously. *If I want to earn her love, I will first have to be worthy to hold onto her friendship.*

Marion could hardly pretend. Her heart could be read through her eyes; her mind had already retreated. And her eyes said so clearly, "I trust you, in spite of everything," that her raspy "yes" was almost superfluous.

"Thank you," Reinier said simply. "Later I hope I can tell you everything, Marion, because we have no intention of losing sight of you, Inge and I. She will still need you often enough, our little gnome, because she will receive very little spontaneous love in Borg, that I know. We will probably pull up to your door sooner than you think to kidnap you for a day."

His sincere tone completely disarmed Marion in the end. She gave in with her former laugh. "You may come. For Inge I am always available."

And so her departure from the Warbler was not as sad as she had imagined it would be. A breach had been opened, a breach called "later."

Of course, Marion still fretted a good long time over the possible reasons for her dismissal and Mr. Van Herewaarden's return to Borg, especially since he had so clearly made it appear that his attitude toward her had not changed.

She remembered what her mother had said back in Garderen. "Awkward," she had called it, a young girl living in with a young widower. "People are so quick to talk, child." Yes, Marion knew it all too well.

Did people really talk about them? That would be absurd. Nevertheless, absurd or not, it was just like Mr. Van Herewaarden to want to protect her from all slander and yet to be silent about its existence.

The first weeks in Garderen went by faster than Marion had dared to hope. She fit in well in the village, which vaguely resembled Borg.

She spent a lot of time with the Knols, whom she learned to appreciate for their openness and candor, which radiated from the faces of Mrs. Knol and the children. The farmer himself was somewhat stiffer, but Marion gladly put up with him, and he in turn stole glances of approval of how that "city girl" helped gather the plums and harvest the beans, a red bandana about her hair, and sometimes, because of the mud, wearing a pair of borrowed wooden shoes.

Marion enjoyed this natural life. In her memory, this fall held the smell of sunny, ripe fruit. She ate, tired and satisfied, delicious farmers' omelettes in the roomy kitchen of Mrs. Knol. She teased seventeen-year-old Rolf, who harbored serious plans of emigrating, and she helped him in the evening with his English lessons.

She frolicked with the children in the fields, and they taught her the way through the forest and showed her where the best blackberry patches were.

Every now and again Marion realized as she lay in bed in the evening, reviewing her day, that she had not dedicated a single thought to Jaap. She would then try to recall his face, but it did not come as easily as it once did. This made her sad. She saw it as a loss. Even the sharp, vivid memories began to fade.

But during the day everything was different. There were so many new things which demanded her attention, and if her thoughts slipped away to Dintelborg, they only remained circling around the Warbler, and from there they went to the House of Herewaarden where Inge now was.

She thought about Reinier's words before she left, how he had said, "I am naming you supervising guardian of Inge, Marion," and the other words, "you will hear from us again soon."

Had her days perhaps become an unconscious waiting for this promised sign of life?

She did not talk about looking for a new job, even though Mother tried to bring up the subject once. She pointed to an ad in the paper. "If you want another job, Mari, then this one is just for you."

Marion read the ad without much enthusiasm. She shrugged her shoulders. "I don't much feel like it anymore.

If you don't mind, I would like to stay at home for the time being."

Of course that was all right. Having one's own children home was never too much, Mother thought, and yet she did not understand Marion at all. Last year she shook heaven and earth in order to get out the door. Did she find it so bad there in Dintelborg that she had been cured of her pursuit of independence?

Marion rendered no accounting to such comments. She could not even explain it to herself, this reluctance to begin anything new—other children after Inge, another boss after Mr. Van Herewaarden. *No*, she thought, *as long as I don't have to, I will not do it.*

But she found it difficult to make this clear to Mother. She just couldn't.

Then a letter from Borg arrived in a thick envelope. "Pictures," Marion guessed immediately as she grabbed the letter off the mat. She took the letter upstairs and sat on the edge of her bed, looking at them. Inge with a large German shepherd; Inge behind the doll carriage; Inge picking flowers in the large castle garden; Inge with her father high on a dark horse, holding the reins with a triumphant look, he smiling behind her.

The letter that accompanied the pictures was sincere, but short. If it was all right with Marion, they would like to impose on her the following Wednesday. Then they could talk face-to-face and Inge could take part in the conversation.

On Wednesday, they arrived at the front door fairly early. Inge was visibly pleased to see Marion again, and she expressed this in a sweet, childlike way. Marion and Reinier, however, had more difficulty finding their old comfortable air. There was a shyness between them that had never been there before. Only when they were at the playground, on which Inge had set her heart, sitting at a shaky table while

Inge played with total absorption on the swing, did they come around to an actual conversation.

"Can you still remember the church at Borg?" Reinier asked.

Marion nodded. "Of course," she said.

"I hope to make my profession of faith there in the coming year," Reinier continued, playing as he spoke with the bottle caps lying on the table.

Marion felt a quick blush.

"Oh" was all she said, but the happy look in her eyes was enough of an answer for Reinier. So he had imagined her eyes would look as he prepared this announcement.

He also related how it had been with Reverend Gerritsen—of the good conversations he had had with the older man who had for so long now filled the post in Borg.

"My father made his profession of faith with him, and his sisters, Aunt Hortense and Aunt Marguerite, as well. A few years later he married my parents. He baptized Diederick and me. He led the funeral service when Father died. I still remember how much I loved him as a child, the big, friendly man who was already gray back then.

"I had not spoken to him in years. When I married . . ."

He paused for a moment. This seemed so unreal to him. Yes, he had been married. Magda had become like a memory from a former life.

He rubbed his eyes and concentrated on what he was telling her.

Marion spurred him on with a nod, "Yes?"

"When I married, Magda wanted to have a church ceremony. Mama did, too. It was the decent thing to do. It was supposed to be that way. A Van Herewaarden had never before been married outside the church.

"But I did not want a church wedding. I was against it. It ran against my grain—so hypocritical. I had not been in church for years. I no longer was a believer, and I wanted to be consistent. As a result, Inge was never baptized. For years I never regretted it. Then you came . . ."

Again he paused.

Marion's large eyes were riveted to his face.

It's odd, the thought flashed through his mind, *how she can listen so hungrily. Even her eyes listen. Especially her eyes.*

"Then you came."

Was it the way he spoke these words that gave Marion such a warm feeling within that it almost stung behind her eyes?

Reinier gestured with his hand.

"You know the rest. You have reconverted our family, and that is why I am telling you first. You have a right to know."

Marion shrugged slightly. "What did I do? It all just happened. You asked me to read from the Bible that evening in October. I had to, even though I almost did not dare. I was often afraid of you."

Their eyes shared a smile.

Reinier further explained his plans for the upcoming winter. How he had agreed with Reverend Gerritsen to come a couple of hours every week to talk—a sort of private catechization, actually.

"I am attending church every week now," he told her. "I did this summer, when I was out of the country, when it was possible. Now I am taking Inge along, of course."

Both of them looked at the child who was now playing follow the leader with the other children, loudly laughing at every misstep.

Suddenly Marion looked directly at Reinier. "Did you mean what you said back then about guardianship?"

When he nodded affirmatively, she asked, "Is there a preschool in Borg?"

He frowned slightly. "I think so."

"Then I am going to advise you to send Inge there. She

needs so desperately to have contact with other children. At the castle she spends the entire day with adults."

"She has to go to school next year, anyway."

"Yes," said Marion firmly, "but that one year—"

She abruptly broke off her sentence.

"No," he said, intercepting her look. "Go on. Don't just swallow what you were going to say."

And so Marion continued, recklessly. "That one year could ruin her. Inge has a great deal of potential, Mr. Van Herewaarden, both good and bad. During the vacation I saw Magda's fear and hysteria in her, but there is more. She also has the seed of arrogance in her, impulsiveness. But along with that she has a cheerful and playful character. I would love to keep her a child, but I am so afraid that she will become a salon figure at Borg. Against your will, I know, but still . . ."

She fell silent, rather warmed by her excited speech. She had let herself go.

Before Reinier could respond, however, Inge walked up to them, demanding attention. The rest of the day provided them with no more opportunities to discuss this issue.

Two days later, Marion received a long letter from Reinier in which he replied to her spontaneous plea for Inge.

He told her that he had informed the preschool. He let Inge be registered as a student, and she would be going for the first time next week. She was so excited, the little gnome.

He reported nothing, however, of the scene his mother had made over such a possibility.

At the bottom of the letter, hastily written as a P.S., he wrote, "Marion, shouldn't we dispense with that Mr. business? It seems so foolishly formal between friends, don't you think? My name is Reinier."

Marion had to smile. As if she did not know his name!

The P.S. continued to run through her mind the rest of the

day. Reinier, just Reinier. He wanted it that way—they were friends.

There grew a certain resistance in Marion, a certain resentment against him that she could not explain. It was as though this approach of his had brought the distance between them into sharper focus.

That evening she took out the pictures again and looked at them slowly, one by one: Inge in the flowers, Inge with the dog; Inge behind the doll carriage. The most time she dedicated to the last, however: Reinier and Inge together on the horse. It was a beautiful, slender thoroughbred. She stayed there for a long time, her elbows propped in her pillow, looking at the picture.

She laughed a quick, scornful laugh.

So that is how his life is now. Raising thoroughbreds, hunting, playing tennis, bridge, dinners in evening dress. She could see it all so clearly from her position here in the country. It was the life of the "upper crust" of the world, alien and hostile to her because she knew she stood outside it.

And this Reinier, who returned to such a life, esteemed the friendship of Marion Verkerk, a girl like so many thousands of others, a girl who was separated from him by a social gulf of which she was ever more fully aware with each memory of the visit she had paid to the House of Herewaarden.

Her thoughts surprised her.

Was she jealous? Did she begrudge him his friendship with others, with those who circulated in the world of which he was now a part again?

She thought of what she had said to him about Inge. "I would love to keep her a child, simple, the same Inge as always."

You can say something like that about a child, she thought, but deep in her heart she knew she feared the same for him.

The thoroughbreds, the coat of arms, the castle—they were

just so many hostile elements for her, accentuating the gulf between them.

She did not want a gulf. She wanted the friendship of the other Reinier, the Reinier of the Warbler, who sat across from her in the evening with a newspaper or a book, who tucked Inge in, who released his pent-up, helpless frustration at Magda's suffering in a sudden outburst, whom she did not fear, because it was he.

Then they were one, but now—could she address him by his first name now that none of this remained?

Restless in bed, she thought, *I am getting so tired of dissecting my feelings. I must have really been attached to him, to feel this so sharply.*

But I do not want this feeling. I must find a release from it.

One of these days he will become aware of how much his friendship means to me, and then he will feel it to be a burden.

When she awakened the next morning, she had a headache. Slowly her reflections of the previous night returned, and she became angry with herself.

She buried the pictures deep in her dresser, and she was busier and more occupied than usual that day. She wanted to forget her foolish thoughts. But she was only partially successful.

Reiner waited for a reaction to his letter. He waited a week, two weeks, three weeks. In vain.

It made him uneasy, imbalanced, impatient. But he was not aware that this lack of a response was the best thing for him.

Marion was finding her way to the secret of her own heart.

❧ Chapter 22 ❧

It was twilight on an early October evening. Mr. and Mrs. Verkerk had just left for a visit with new acquaintances in the village.

The weather was very mild, almost like summer. Marion sat in front of the garden doors, which were still open. Just a few more moments, then she would close them; although it was lovely, the nights were already cold. But she put it off as long as possible. Back on the neighbors' land, the Boy Scouts had built a campfire, and an older man, his face eerily illuminated under his wide-brimmed hat, was telling a story. Marion could not make out his words, but then the boys sang a song, and it sounded sadly beautiful in the twilight. Now the darkness was closing in.

Marion was getting cold. She reluctantly closed the doors, then grabbed her coat from the coatrack and stepped outside. She went and stood at the property line and managed to hear the last part of the story. Then they sang again. Marion stood and watched them, amused. As the last notes died away, the unbelievable stillness fell again. Then they broke up the meeting, and the magical air burst like a bubble.

As Marion turned around, she noticed that a car stood in front of the house. At the same time she heard the doorbell ring. She was at one side of the house, and so walked around outside to the front door, to see who was calling.

Against the hazy gray of the evening sky, she saw the sharp silhouette of a man, tall and straight, his face turned away from the door. Marion's glance went quickly from the man to his car. Her face darkened. "Reinier," she said softly, almost shocked, and took a step in his direction.

His attention was drawn by the rasping sound of her footsteps in the gravel. He turned a quarter turn toward her and saw her against the background of the holly hedge.

He said nothing for a moment, giving her just enough time to overcome her slight confusion.

"Good evening," she said simply, coming closer.

He extended his hand to her, and she laid hers in his, looking up at his face.

"If Mohammed won't come to the mountain, the mountain must go to Mohammed," he said with unmistakable sarcasm in his voice.

"What?" said Marion, but she knew immediately that he was referring to her unwritten letters.

"You did not answer my last letter," Reinier explained, aggrieved, "and I thought you would be interested in Inge's first days at school."

Marion was somewhat reserved. Suddenly what she had done seemed so ridiculous to her. Two months before she nearly cried at the thought of a separation, and now she seemed to be trying to force one. She shuffled her feet. What should she say? She wanted to be miles away, and yet something inside her was singing because he had come.

"I confess my guilt," she then said, raising her thumb to the corner of her mouth like a child, with a rascally twinkle in her eye. "It won't happen again, sir!"

Only then did he release her hand.

"Would you like to take a little ride?" he asked. "Then I will let you see Inge's first pieces of schoolwork."

Marion agreed. She locked the front door, explaining that her parents were gone. Reinier in turn explained that he had business in Zwolle that day and he thought it too good an opportunity to stop in Garderen to let it slip by.

While he was speaking, his mind was at work. There was something different about her, he discerned. She had lost her openness. She was hiding something, but what?

The question continued to fester in the back of his mind, and suddenly it occurred to him: Could she suspect something of his feelings for her? Is that what changed her disposition? Is that why she did not write?

Apart from these thoughts, in fact rather absently, the conversation babbled rather sluggishly on. It was about Inge, of course.

Poor kid, thought Reinier somewhat guiltily. *You are being used as a foil, today and may other times, if necessary. Forgive me.*

Then he stopped the car and pulled out of his suitcoat pocket some braiding and one of Inge's drawings.

"*Voilà*," he exclaimed, laying them in Marion's lap. "Here are the firstfruits, and I won't even mention the many songs she has learned."

Marion looked at the objects with great interest.

There was a bookmark that was actually very neatly done.

"What deft little fingers she has," she said tenderly.

Reinier leaned toward her a little. "She gave that one to me, but if you like it, you may keep it."

A couple of pieces of paper, he thought to himself. *Not even three cents' worth. Nice gift.*

Who, besides Marion, would he dare offer such a thing with the assurance that she would value it?

Her reaction was precisely as he expected it to be.

"Please," she said spontaneously, and then she laughed, albeit still looking up at him bashfully through her eyelashes. "Thank you, Reinier."

What was it about that name, which now for the first time passed her lips, that made something in him come alive? What impulse suddenly overran his carefully cultivated discipline?

"Mari," he said, more intimately than he had ever spoken to her.

"No," she said sharply. "Don't say that, Reinier. Not you!"

"Mari," he had said, and with it Jaap's face jumped immediately to mind. He had always used this nickname when he wanted her to do something. Jaap could flatter her like no other.

Why should it bother her that Reinier, completely unaware of the history which she alone knew, had used this same name?

There was something decadent in Jaap's manner, she realized, and things which she associated with him were completely out of place with Reinier. He was different. He was decent.

Reinier had recoiled at her reaction, somewhat hurt. He continued with more superficial things, a definite reserve in his voice. The intimacy they had so carefully molded cracked.

Marion knew that she had hurt him, yet it was impossible to explain her reaction to him.

But when in departing he said without emotion, "Well, Marion, all the best. Maybe we will see you again sometime," she answered, in an attempt to make good what she had spoiled, "Yes, I hope so, Reinier. Will you give Inge a kiss for me? And tell her that I think the bookmark is beautiful!"

On the way home, he replayed what he had said. Her reaction was so impulsive. "Don't say that, Reinier." "Mari," he had said. With a sharp stab of jealousy, he immediately knew: This was something from the other one, and she would not tolerate it from his mouth. So she was not yet free of him. It was already a half year since he left—for good, apparently—and she was still not free of him.

Gradually he regained his composure, but other thoughts arose. Words that she had spoken to him that evening, a gesture, her shy laugh when she for the first time called him by his name. Something subtle in her manner, something new to him, which in some imperceptible way made him happy, in spite of the incident that again brought Jaap Dubois into his thoughts.

When he had driven the car into the garage and was walking across the grounds to the castle, the large German shepherd came bounding toward him and jumped exuberantly against him.

He patted the dog on his beautifully colored back. "We are not giving up, Wolf," he said, half out loud. "Did you think we would step aside for a rival that was a thousand miles away? Not for a hundred rivals!"

He laughed softly.

Before he went to bed, he kissed the sleeping Inge good night. *A kiss from her, my little one,* he thought with a slight grin. *You made out better than I did. For now.*

Marion watched the car until it vanished around the bend. Then she went inside and shortly thereafter went to bed. There she lay with her fingers pressed to her temples, deep in thought.

Yes, she had been a fool. She wanted to distance herself

from him, but nothing was more foolish; he wanted no distance. Wasn't he the one who was always looking her up again? It was obvious that he did not want to lose her. And she?

She turned off the light with an irritated flick and threw herself on her side. That night she dreamed that someone was carrying her down a seemingly endless staircase. It was a cold, dark night, but the arms that enclosed her were warm and safe, and the face above her was beloved and trusted.

What was that mouth saying? She could not understand it. There were too many noises. A strange voice shouted, a car engine idled.

Be quiet. I must understand that voice.

With a jump she awakened. She sat up in bed and rubbed her eyes. Was it a dream? It was all so real, as though it had actually happened. She went to the sink and drank a glass of water. She saw her own eyes in the mirror, looking stunned and amazed.

In those eyes there gleamed a secret knowledge, and her warm blood crept up from her neck toward her blond hair.

She lay down again, and in the dark she analyzed piece by piece the dream that once, long ago, was reality.

The staircase, the car, an ambulance . . .

Slowly the subconscious memories returned to her. It was night, a misty spring night. She was in pain, much pain.

But she was being carried by strong arms, and the face over her was the same face that was bent over her for a moment in the car that evening. But the mouth which then said "Mari" had said something else in her dream. She could not understand it.

Nor could she find the words in her memory.

The next morning, as she was dusting her room, she stood still before the painting that Jaap had given her on her birthday.

"Can a person be so wrong, Jaap?" she asked. "Was your father right?" She shook her head, not understanding. "I don't know anymore," she concluded, but never had she been so aware of the fact that her memory of Jaap no longer gave her pain.

It was still inside of her, still as when the sun breaks through in the forest after a snowstorm. An amazed stillness.

Further meetings followed, in which the contact between Marion and Reinier was intensified and deepened. Over Inge's dark head they discussed literature, politics, music, religion.

Reinier made no more attempts to increase their intimacy. His disposition was strictly that of friendship. But a new resilience filled his movements; he felt younger, more vital. He was winning a woman, and each day his desire for success increased.

Buy time, he thought. *Make her forget.* The warm dynamic present had to conquer a past that was shrinking to an unreal shimmer with the passing of the months.

Late in November Marion received a letter from Reinier in which he asked if she would have time to accompany him for an afternoon. He had to buy a Saint Nicholas Day present for Inge, and he would greatly appreciate her advice.

It was an unforgettable day for Marion. It was the first time since that night in October that they were out alone together. Reinier had the whole day planned in his head.

"Shall we see if we can find something in Amsterdam?" he asked Marion when they were underway.

"Amsterdam?"

A glimmer leaped into her eyes. Her birthplace, the most beautiful city in the Netherlands. Did he perhaps know that she missed Amsterdam?

"I know you better than you think," he countered.

And so they went to Amsterdam.

In a large toy store they bought a scooter with inflated wheels, a blue one, from a young woman who pattered from one to the other with animated nods. "What do you think, madame? Oh, of course, sir. Isn't this a lovely little model, madame?"

Reinier enjoyed watching the "madame's" face.

"Not that one," he whispered to her, gesturing toward "the lovely little model," which also had a seat. "Inge calls that a lazy kid's scooter. I wouldn't dare give that to her."

After they had made their choice, they had high tea in a very comfortable place Marion remembered as one of the fashionable places from her high school days, but which, as a result of financial concerns, had always remained off-limits to her.

Marion enjoyed her city. Elated, she showed Reinier the many beautiful places which for her made up the essence of Amsterdam. They rode along the canal on which she had lived for so many years, and she pointed out the old house to him.

"This is where I was born," she said.

Blessed be the hour, thought Reinier, while he drove through the traffic skillfully.

On the return trip, they talked much and without inhibition. About things from the past, about their childhood, about problems from their school years, about the mystery of suffering in the world, and finally about Magda.

During this conversation Marion's eyes remained fixed on Reinier's hands, which held the steering wheel. An amazing tranquility radiated from those hands. They seemed different to her than in the past, but she knew she had to be imagining it.

Only after he had left and she had closed the door behind him did it occur to her what it was that she saw in his hands.

He had taken off his wedding ring.

❧ Chapter 23 ❧

The months passed. Winter brought Mr. Verkerk a heavy attack of rheumatism which laid him up in bed for a long time.

Marion found it harder to get away now, and the little trips with Reinier became more scarce. Their letter writing revived, but they both missed the personal conversations that had brought them so close in the fall.

When nature had finally set aside her gray mask and the first flowers began to butterfly up from the grass, they repeated their trip to Amsterdam, but this time in the evening. There was an art exhibition in which Reinier was very interested, and he wanted Marion to see it.

Many times in the last few months he had been overcome by a strong sense of impatience, but each time something prevented him from investigating whether his love would find answer in Marion. Was it that strange reserve that could so suddenly come over her, which he had most assuredly noticed? He had always had the unpleasant idea that it was Jaap Dubois who came between them. It could not be anything else. But slowly he began to doubt whether his method of patience was indeed the right one.

Months ago Marion had recognized that her feelings for Reinier far surpassed in depth and breadth the love that she had felt for Jaap Dubois.

The hours they had spent together since then had made her happy, but not undividedly happy. The thought of the castle and the whole entourage of Reinier's existence continually gnawed at her. And the longer he endured with his sincere, friendly manner, the larger the small lump of bitterness in her heart grew.

She had the friendship of Baron Van Herewaarden, that could not be denied, but did she have his love, his future? Or would that be reserved for another one from the other camp?

Often she was ashamed of these thoughts. But at the same time, often while they were together, the glimmer of the castle came between them and maintained the distance which Reinier had come to hate.

They were on the return trip from Amsterdam. Marion was relating her experiences of the last few weeks. She had a knack for describing the circumstances and relationships in the village, and Reinier listened, amused, as she related her conversation with the shepherd.

"How did you come across that chap?" he asked, and this gave Marion material for yet another tale.

"We had a visit from a former neighbor boy from Amsterdam," she began. "Otto Van Oord, who has a fascination with folklore. And when Father, in a weak moment, mentioned the old shepherd, we couldn't hold him back anymore. Of course, I had to believe him and act as guide. He had to go and was going to talk to the old man who, by the way, lived somewhere at the back of the bog, more than an hour's walk.

"But, in retrospect, I have no regrets. We laughed, Reinier! Seldom have I ever met such a comical old man as that shepherd. Can you understand how someone who is almost always alone can maintain such a sense of humor?"

Reinier did not respond to her question. "How old was that guy?" he asked, at the same time bringing the car to a stop, since the railroad gates were closed in front of them.

"The shepherd?" wavered Marion. "He must have been in his late seventies."

"No, the neighbor boy," growled Reinier from the back of his throat as he threw a quick look at her.

Marion's intuition sensed something in that look. *Jealous!* she thought with secret pleasure, so she said, without letting on, "Oh, him? One year older than I am. We used to play all the time together in the attic. He was a puny little fellow back then, but he has improved considerably over the last ten years."

A laugh tickled her throat and the corners of her mouth trembled a little, but she continued to look out the window. *Otto. Crazy Otto,* she thought. *The very idea!*

He observed her. She seemed more attractive to him now than ever before. Something in his chest swelled. *Otto Van Oord. What the devil was she doing walking with other men? As if it were not already enough that Jaap Dubois has kissed that lovely red mouth.*

Marion felt him staring at her and grew uneasy. The self-confident feeling of controlling the situation escaped her.

Suddenly she turned her face toward him.

"Why are you looking at me?" she asked him, a little flustered.

"Are you aware that you are a beautiful woman?" he asked, and the fire behind his words chased a blush up into her cheeks.

"No, I'm not," she shyly disagreed. "I'm rather plain. I know that. Edith says that it is because of my eyebrows."

He leaned toward her. "What is the matter with them?"

"They are too blond and too thin," she explained. "They should be dark and long," She drew with her finger an imaginary arc over her left eye. "Edith says I should use an eyebrow pencil. She is a beauty specialist, so she should know."

He impulsively placed his two hands on her cheeks and looked at her closely. Then he lifted one hand and traced the blond eyebrows with his finger. "Beauty specialist," he said with a voice in which resonated both a laugh and a threat. "I assure you that she will never earn a penny from you."

Then he let her go, and with his hands on the steering wheel he said once more with great conviction, "Not a penny."

The railroad gates went up; they drove on.

Marion did not know what to say. Something in her reared up at the thought that he had so much command over her, but at the same time it caused a warm joy to flow through her, a joy that made her tremble.

He had caressed her. For the first time, he had caressed her.

With a slight shiver of happiness she remembered the warm touch of his strong hands around her face and how he had said that she was beautiful.

Her eyes shone.

He looked at her again and again out of the corner of his eye as the car glided along the wide, well-maintained roads.

Marion. Yes, she was beautiful, but in a different way from the other women he knew. Especially her eyes, in which a soft, warm fire burned that could unexpectedly leap into flames.

She was beautiful from the inside out. She was adorable, so pure and unspoiled, but also one to encircle in your arms and never let go, so wonderfully warm-blooded.

A little later they were sitting in a restaurant and talking about Inge, about Dintelborg, about a book that they both had read; but behind their words was beating a mystery.

Suddenly they looked up at the sound of a voice that rang familiarly in the ears of one of them.

The voice belonged to a man who with all the goodwill in the world could not be politely mentioned. He came directly toward them from a group of artists who were sitting on the other side of the restaurant and from which they had several times heard raucous laughter erupt.

"My little Marion!" the voice said, as he extended her a hand. "Fancy meeting you here! Child, child, how odd!"

Marion stood up, and Reinier followed her example. They were standing close to each other, and Reinier sensed more than he saw that Marion was tense. She did not take his extended hand, but said quietly and incisively, "I am sorry for your sake that the satisfaction is not mutual, André Wesseling."

He sized her up with his eyes, then he insinuated, "Come now, love. Don't be so unfriendly! The last time we met, you were much sweeter to me."

That is crazy, thought Marion, with a brief flash of humor as she remembered how she had stood against him like a game-cock that last evening. *Sweeter! That was a laugh!*

She realized he was acting out this comedy for Reinier's sake. *He is suggesting that he and I . . . And Reinier is supposed to believe that. But he wouldn't believe that I would . . . with such a, such a . . .*

The confused thoughts ran through her head while she searched for the appropriate answer.

Reinier did not understand who this person was who had planted himself in front of Marion. He could not remember ever having seen this seedy, half-drunk artist before.

Reinier had not yet said anything, but his dark eyes held

the other in check. He straightened himself, and André felt uneasy under his glare.

Marion regained her balance. She laughed a cold, contemptuous laugh, and Reinier thought that she must have a very basic revulsion toward this man, for he had never heard the sound in her voice as she said, "You don't really expect me to respond to a comment like that, do you?"

André had a thick skin; he went a step further. "Still the same modest young lady. Yet, just like all the others, she has not remained with her first lover, I see."

At this, Reinier intervened. He laid what appeared to be a quiet hand on André's shoulder and forced him to turn around. "I would like to see you stop pestering this lady, sir," he said with so many hidden threats that André willingly returned to his company.

Once more he turned and cast toward Marion a leering yet cowering look, like an animal made subject to a will stronger than its own.

Reinier did not say anything to Marion. He signaled for the waiter, quickly settled the bill, and they left the restaurant.

Now the incident was behind them, blind rage overcame Reinier—rage fueled by suspicion.

In vain, he tried to wrest himself free of that suspicion. The seed André had sown by his insinuating little act was beginning to grow.

Marion looked nervously at his sharp profile. She knew that this expression forecast an outburst that he was keeping under wraps only with the greatest of self-control.

Silently he held the door for her, and a few moments later they were riding with reckless abandon down the highway again, passing one car after another. Marion was not afraid; a certain indifference had come over her.

She did not know how to resolve the situation. On the one hand, she was ashamed that André had done this in front of

Reinier, but on the other hand, she was mad at Reinier for his reaction. She had no intention of giving him an explanation as long as he stared out in front of him with that smug look on his face and flew down the road at a criminal velocity.

Who knew what he was thinking of her?

This thought intrigued her, yet she refused to begin the conversation.

I don't owe him any explanation! she thought stubbornly, but her heart urged her to tell him everything, to explain everything.

When she thought of the delicate air that surrounded them before André made his appearance with his banal talk, the tears welled up in her eyes.

Finally, he brought the car to a halt on a quiet side street. His anger had not been alleviated by his reckless driving. He had, on the contrary, sat there winding himself up.

What slime! To suggest that Marion was any man's girl. Acting as though he himself had a claim to her. Such a slippery, slimy reptile! He lied—that he could hear in Marion's reaction—but she did know him, she called him by name. Jealousy burned within him like a fire, and as soon as the car was stopped, he broke loose. "Nice friends you have! That would have been the last person on earth that I would have suspected . . ."

They looked at each other, and he saw that she was angry.

"You could have at least suspended judgment until you knew what kind of relationship existed between him and myself. That is what you mean, isn't it?" Her look was defiant, and there was deep sarcasm in her voice. That he could think such a thing of her!

The word *relationship* closed the door for him.

"You do not have to explain what you would rather keep to yourself," he answered in a huff, losing sight of all reason.

Marion straightened up, preparing for battle. "But I want you to know," she growled. "What do you think I am? It is ridiculous! Two times I met that creep, both times in the company of Jaap Dubois. There is not a person in the world for whom I hold a greater dislike than him, but for much different reasons from what *you* are thinking!"

I cannot hold back his rage any longer, she thought in fear. *No matter what I say, I cannot hold back his rage.*

She saw the swollen veins on his forehead. He reached his hand out toward her and clamped roughly onto her shoulder.

In his mind he saw the sensual facial features of the man whom she had called André Wesseling. A friend of Jaap Dubois. So that was the direction from which the wind was blowing.

"Is that true?" he said hoarsely, "You mean he never . . . ? Has he ever tried anything with you? Has he ever tried to touch you, Marion?"

"No," she said firmly. "Never." And with a flair of indignation she threw her head back.

But his unrest was not yet quelled, for out of André's words, one had remained hanging from his jealous heart by a poisonous barb: "Lover." He must have meant Jaap.

A memory shot into his head, a story that he had once heard about the adventures of Jaap in France, in Italy. Marion, his little pure Marion—was she really his little pure Marion? Had she given in to that lighthearted, charming, woman-crazy artist?

His blood throbbed through his veins. He forgot himself and went just too far when he spit out, "And the other one, that Jaap?"

Marion tensed up. "How can you ask such a thing?" She reproached him smugly. "That was different. I loved him then!"

She doesn't understand to what I am referring, he thought, somewhat relieved. Jolted by his own words, he could have bitten his tongue off for his ill-considered and shameless question.

His anger was suddenly gone. Of all the words that Marion had spoken to him, only a few continued to resonate: "I loved him then."

So clearly past tense!

Marion, he thought, *liberated, delightfully uninhibited treasure, I have so much to tell you, so much!*

But he was silent, and she as well. A wonderful, articulate silence had fallen, a silence in which they were both occupied with their new thoughts. The rest of the way to Garderen was much too short for Reinier to work through what had so unexpectedly been thrown in his lap like a gift—her honest, reproving words: "I loved him then!"

Past tense, he thought, over and over again. *Past tense.*

Next to him, Marion trembled as she built her house of thoughts, a house into which she almost did not dare to enter.

She wondered how she could explain his intensity, except to say, His heart was at stake. His heart, which he had now so obviously made clear was beating for her.

As his question about Jaap sank in, it suddenly occurred to her what thoughts must have been churning behind it. She turned deep red in the darkness.

Was his fear without foundation? she asked herself, and she knew simultaneously that she had to answer no. She thought of the many times that she had to fight tooth and nail against Jaap's unscrupulous impetuosity. She thought of Octavia, Michelle.

What did Reinier know about Jaap? Did he know what she had only suspected? She remembered that he had always spoken of Jaap with ill-concealed disdain.

She had to speak now. She had to convince him that there had never been anything between Jaap and her—not that.

But she said nothing. Of course, she said nothing. *Another ten minutes,* she thought, *then we must say good-bye.*

She looked up carefully at his face. His expression was completely other than what it had been just a few minutes before. There was something of a subdued happiness, and a smile played about his lips. He felt her glance, and without removing his eyes from the road, he said meekly, "Are you still mad at me, Marion Verkerk?"

"Yes, I am, Reinier Van Herewaarden. Can't you see that in my face?"

Thus she forced him to look at her, but when his eyes found hers, she bashfully lowered hers. A greater excitement shimmered in the air than had ever been there between them before.

In the short, angry argument of that evening they had unwillingly revealed more of their secrets than in all their intimate conversations.

The clock in the car pointed to a late hour. Marion was almost home; her parents would perhaps be waiting up for her.

These thoughts flashed through Reinier's mind, and he hastily formed a plan. He reached for Marion's hand and held it firmly. When she did not pull away, he said, "I am sorry that I forgot myself this evening, Marion. I want to explain it to you, but not now. Tomorrow I have a conference, but Thursday, may I pick you up early? Then we will spend the whole day outdoors. All right?"

When Marion agreed, he slid his arm around her shoulders and pulled her a little closer to himself.

His left hand lay on the steering wheel, a beautiful, powerful hand.

She lay there so relaxed, so composed, that Marion felt the thought arise virtually on its own. *I could never be afraid with him. Not with him.*

But her mouth said, "Isn't this a bit dangerous?"

His eyes scanned the speedometer. Twenty miles per hour, yet they would still be in Garderen in a few minutes. "I am driving slowly," he assured her, and the grip of his right hand grew tighter.

A strange feeling of excitement washed over Marion, but her voice was under control as she said playfully, "Yes, but you are carrying precious cargo."

"That I am," he agreed without hesitation.

Their words were few during the last few minutes. As they said good-bye, Reinier held her hand longer than usual. "Until Thursday, Marion."

"Until Thursday, Reinier."

Was there more than agreement in these words? Promise? Yes, promise!

He watched her until the door closed behind her.

⤺ Chapter 24 ⤻

Thursday dawned, after a Wednesday that appeared to contain more hours than any other day. And Thursday dawned with all the fullness of light and color that a spring day in March can bear.

Reinier got up very early. Humming, he got dressed; humming, he ate breakfast. But when he entered the garage, he discovered that the car had a flat tire. And no spare, of course.

He hurriedly calculated. Bring the car to the garage in Dintelborg. He looked at his watch. Of course, there would not be anyone there at this hour.

Let Marion wait? Today? Never!

He rang the estate manager, Heckert, from his bed, discussed the situation briefly, and ten minutes later rode away in the castle's limousine—a rather dated model, but still in excellent condition.

"If Mama knew about this little escapade," he chuckled, but the laugh died on his lips as he realized that she would have to know about him and Marion, and who knew how soon? Then with a grim gesture he cast these thoughts from him. He was going to Marion. Did he doubt her answer to the question he was planning to ask her today? He marveled at the fact, the entire way from Borg to Garderen, that he was afflicted by no uncertainty whatsoever.

What grounds did he have for feeling so certain about her? Was it because she did not pull away from his first cautious caress? Yes, because of that, but her eyes, which revealed everything, had for the first time in months held no secrets from him. Yes, her eyes had chased away his doubt for good.

Marion heard his horn and leaned out the window. She drew up her eyebrows in surprise for a moment. What a strange car! But Reinier was standing next to it, and he looked up. "Is her ladyship ready?" he asked with a courtly bow.

"Just a moment," she said. "I'll open the front door for you."

"No, I am not coming in," he shook his head. "I have resolved to see no house from within today!"

She disappeared from the window and a few minutes later came toward him over the grass.

Yellow and purple crocuses gathered in large clumps to celebrate the spring. White light snowed from heaven, white and gold.

And all at once they were sitting next to each other, talking about nothing more important than the air that was so crisp and the fields that were already so green, and an early bird that so exuberantly greeted the morning.

Marion asked about the strange car. He told her of his experiences of that morning.

Without noticing, they had already ridden a long way. Marion had not been paying attention. "Where are we, anyway?" she asked.

"Don't you know?" he asked, amused.

"No," she admitted.

"Then I am not going to tell you," he teased. "Besides, what does it matter where we are? It is beautiful, isn't it? But now for something else. How would you like to eat someplace rustic in a few minutes?"

Marion earnestly shook her head. "Thumbs down," she took her turn to tease. "You were the one who did not want to see the inside of a house today. Then you have to be consistent."

He laughed. "What are you thinking?"

"A picnic!" said Marion. "We can buy a few raisin buns somewhere in one of these little towns."

He thought it was a good idea.

In the next village he sent Marion out of the car. He threw his wallet after her. "I have brought you to the doorstep of a store that from all appearances has brought under its roof all possible departments. If you can't find it here, you won't find it anywhere."

Marion walked into the small grocery and bought a few things.

In that way they were able to eat their lunch on the running board of the old car, overlooking a clear narrow canal. Reinier had driven the car down a sandy track that seemed to disappear into a cart path.

Marion borrowed his pocket knife to cut the raisin buns in half and spread them with butter from the stick on her lap. Then Reinier took over the knife to peel an orange. He tucked a slice between her lips.

"Delicious," Marion complimented. They were sitting next to each other. They had to—the running board was not that large. Marion let herself be cuddled by the sun and looked, mesmerized, out over the meadows. Everything was heavy with expectation, including herself.

"Actually I am glad that we had to take this car," Reinier remarked.

"Why?" she asked, not really paying attention.

"Otherwise we would not have had this cozy running board!" He put his arm around her. Marion looked at him and took in his entire face, even though she already knew its every line.

What was it that made her want to stall? She did not know herself. How could one decipher one's own feelings? She picked up the last slice of orange and held it to his lips.

"You may have it," she laughed, "on the condition that you do something for me."

"Anything you want. Just don't send me too far away from you," he said boldly, and his eyes flustered her so that she had to turn hers away.

She pointed to the dogwood tree that spread its blossoming branches on the far side of the canal.

"A branch of flowers," she teased. "I love them so, Reinier, but I do not dare jump over the canal."

She measured the width of the canal with her eyes. He stood up and with a quick movement was easily on the other side. He pointed, "This branch?"

"No," she said. "The one above that—the large branch. You see it, don't you?"

He pretended not to understand her. "You will have to come and show me." He shook his head. "There is no other choice, Marion Verkerk. Just jump over. I will catch you."

He was already extending his arms in invitation.

Marion threw another look at the water. She was no hero where these things were concerned. Then she saw Reinier and how he was waiting for her. A deep hue rose in her neck and then moved up to her cheeks.

Reinier noticed it, and it made him softer. "Come, then," he encouraged. "You don't have to be afraid with me."

Marion jumped and felt herself being absorbed into a pair of strong arms which lifted her off the ground. She felt her mouth smothered by a pair of burning lips which alternately kissed her and whispered so deliciously to her, "Marion, darling!"

When he set her down, she caught her breath. She breathed deeply, and her voice sounded hoarse as she said, softly, "Reinier. I am so happy, so incredibly happy. But I don't dare . . ."

He took her in his arms again. A farmer came down the cart path; they had not noticed him.

"Good afternoon," he lazily saluted with a grin. Marion blushed again.

Reinier grinned back and returned his greeting. "And to you a good afternoon."

It was yet another moment before the flowers were picked. Marion laid them in the back of the car. She combed the hair out of her eyes.

"I still do not understand," she said quietly. Then Reinier pulled her to himself and, as she leaned on his chest, he asked urgently, "Marion, will you have me? I have waited so long for you, Marion. Say yes, if you want to make me happy. Please, darling!"

"I love you," she said, and he knew that this was an answer—yet no answer to his question.

"I don't dare," she had just said, so softly that he had barely registered it. And he knew that she was thinking of the castle, of Mama, of the circle in which she intuitively felt she was not welcome.

He took her face into his hands.

"My child," he said, moved, "never be afraid that anything will come between us. I would deny the whole world for you."

Marion was surprised by his silent perception of her difficulty and loved him all the more for it.

They spoke together for a while, foolish, in-love things that they later would not rightly remember. All of a sudden, Reinier realized that he had a tremendous thirst.

He confided this to Marion, and she said with surprise. "Me, too."

"Come on," Reinier said. "Hearts in love are always thirsty, but they must have a pump on the farm."

Hand in hand, they walked down the cart path and, indeed, at the side of the barn stood a large pump. On a nail a white dipper hung invitingly.

Reinier gripped the handle and pumped. As Marion held the dipper under the flow, a melodious sound filled her ear. She tilted her head and searched the surroundings with her eyes.

On the mossy peak of the thatched farmhouse, a little bird performed—gently in the introduction, but then suddenly full and amorous—the unimaginably beautiful overture of happiness.

Reinier let the pump handle rest. The little bird sang before a very attentive audience.

They looked at each other and Marion said, softly but excitedly, "Is that . . . ?"

She saw the recognition in his eyes.

"Yes, that's it!"

His voice was deep and overjoyed. He embraced her from behind, and for several minutes they stood motionless.

Then they drank by turns the cold water out of the wide dipper.

It had the distinctive taste of iron.

As they walked back along the cart path, the master singer spilled out with abandon his talents in this most beautiful of all songs, his *cantate cantabilé*.

Reinier carefully backed out to the main road, since the sandy track was too narrow for turning the car around. When they had the smooth asphalt under them again, he picked up the tempo.

In a gesture of trust, Marion put her left hand on his knee. "Reinier," she said, "I have so much to ask you."

"Soon," he answered. "First I have to find a place where I can give you my full attention. Marion, I can hardly believe it. The warbler sang for you and me, on this of all days. I'm not dreaming, am I? I am so afraid that I am dreaming!"

"No," she said, "I am quite certain that you are not. But what can I do to convince you of that?"

"Stay by me," he answered. "In the dream there always came a time when you were not there."

He has dreamed of me, Marion thought, tightening the grip of her hand.

They were now in a wooded area. Reinier had apparently been here before, because he found his way down the narrow roads and forest lanes without any effort, until he finally stopped and pointed to a place among the trees. "Here we are out of the wind," he said. "Would you like to, or do you think it will be too cold?"

Marion shook her head. "I'll just sit a little closer to you," she said with an impish laugh.

"That I would also advise," he said with feigned deliberation.

And then the questions came tumbling down from all sides. "How long have you known?" Reinier asked.

"That is a very difficult question," Marion said thoughtfully. "I believe I loved you before I met Jaap." How easy it had become to simply say that name. "Yes, I loved you then, even though you put up so much opposition. Someday I will have to pay you back for all your snarls, Reinier Van Herewaarden."

She tugged a lock of his hair and he put on a penitent face. She went on. "We were comrades, do you remember? We shared so many things: Inge, Magda, grief, secrets, prayers. You had become part of my life, Reinier, and I was counting on you. I trusted you. I thought that it could stay that way between us forever—so simple, such camaraderie. Only after you dismissed me last summer did I slowly wake up. And I think that jealousy played a great role."

"Jealousy? Of whom?" he asked with surprise.

"Of Borg," Marion answered with a vague wave of her hand.

"Well, let me tell you, then, that Borg was a necessary move for me. I had to do something. You understand that now, don't you, darling? Why I could not give you the real reason for dismissing you?"

She nodded. "At first I was angry with you. I thought you thought I was not good enough for Inge. And I could not be without her, Reinier. She had also become my child in that long, difficult year. Later, after that conversation we had in the Warbler, I thought it was for the sake of decorum. I thought maybe people were talking. But now . . ."

She pulled his head toward herself.

"How long have you known, Reinier?" she whispered in his ear. "How long have you known that I was the one?"

"I hardly dare say," he replied. "Can you remember that Saint Nicholas Day party that we celebrated together? Can you remember the following Sunday? It was that long ago, Marion."

Her eyes widened, but she said nothing.

He saw that she was thinking. In a flash, she relived the long months that had passed since then.

Jaap. Magda.

He had loved her all that time, and she had not known it.

She buried her head in his chest and suddenly began to cry. He stroked her hair. "Marion, what is it, my love?"

"Oh, Reinier, it was so difficult for you, and I did not know it! I went to Jaap while you . . ."

She lifted her tear-filled eyes toward him.

"Quiet, child," he comforted. "It had to be that way. It was our salvation. Do you think I would have been able to bear it if Jaap had not been there? And it had to be, because of Magda. Marion, everything happens as it must. Be still, now."

She was calmed by his soothing words, and with his hand, he wiped away her tears with a handkerchief.

"And now, laugh again." He brought the matter to an end. She lifted her hand and followed the lines of his face with her fingers—his mouth, his eyes. She ironed the wrinkle from his forehead and ran her fingers through his stubborn dark hair with the graying temples.

He let her go, but then he said, "Do you know how old I am, Marion?"

"Almost thirty-two," she said without hesitation, and now she laughed radiantly.

"Are you aware that we are nine years apart?" he asked again.

"Eight years and seven months," she confidently corrected him.

He shook her lightly. "You! Do I have to spell it out for you? May I ask you how you feel about marrying an old man with graying hair?"

Marion pulled his head down to her and pointed. "These hairs, Reinier, here by your temples, were already gray when I met you the first time. They belong to you. And these"—her finger followed the light threads of his stiff cowlick—"I think that I have seen all of these come. Sometimes I thought, 'Another one comes every day.' That was during the most difficult weeks. Oh, I have been watching you, Reinier! And did you think even for a moment that I would not love those gray hairs whose origins I knew?"

She looked at him inquisitively. He answered her with a kiss.

The sun was sinking fast; it was beginning to chill outside. They stood up and made their way back to the car.

"Shall we go back home, Marion?" Reinier asked. "May I speak with your father today?"

She hesitated. "But your mother, Reinier," she said softly. "Aren't you afraid that she . . ." She did not finish her sentence.

"That she will throw a wrench in the works, you mean?" Reinier promptly finished.

She nodded.

"Marion," he said proudly, "perhaps there will be difficulties. I don't deny that, but we will withstand them. And you may not, under any circumstances, crawl back into your shell. You are the one I want, and no one else, and in the end, I have the final say at the House of Herewaarden. Never forget that, Marion. And furthermore," his voice lowered, "must I be the one to tell you that love always overcomes?"

Marion surrendered.

⤚§ Chapter 25 ৶

Reinier entered the large salon with Inge in tow. The baroness sat reading by the bay window and warmly returned their greeting.

Reinier had just come home from the factory. It was late, and Inge had it in mind to give him a scolding. "Now we have already eaten, Papa," she said, disapprovingly, "and I almost have to go to bed already, and you have just now come. And yesterday you were also gone all day!"

She certainly is getting wiser, Reinier thought. *Wiser and a little bit catty. She should be growing up in a family. The atmosphere here in the castle does not do her any good.*

He glanced furtively at his mother and decided to open an offensive.

"Do you know where I was yesterday, Inge?" he asked. "With Miss Marion."

The baroness reacted by immediately looking up, but she said nothing because of the child, he knew.

"Oh!" Inge exclaimed, "Why couldn't I go along? Does Grandpa Verkerk already have his chicks?"

"I don't know," her father admitted, "but you can go soon and see for yourself. All right, my little gnome?"

"When?" Inge wanted to know immediately, and he delighted her when he said, "Maybe tomorrow."

With this forecast, she let herself be sent to bed.

As soon as they were alone, Mama said, with a rather pinched mouth, "I would rather that you not permit that child to refer to that man as *Grandpa*. It is absolutely ridiculous."

"Perhaps less ridiculous than you think," her son retorted.

"Do you mean . . . ," her words shot out.

He nodded. "Yes, Mama, that is what I mean. I am going to be married again. Not immediately, but this summer."

"How could you do such a thing to me?" she complained, wringing her white hands.

Reinier was already fighting his indignation, but his voice still sounded composed as he asked, "Tell me, Mama, who of us is the most concerned about the lack of an heir to the House of Herewaarden? Who lured that parade of pretenders to the vacant title of baroness this entire past winter—all very unobtrusively, of course?"

He laughed, somewhat amused.

"Wasn't that you, Mama, who did that? It really did not escape me. And will you then be distressed if I tell you that I am going to remarry?"

"You know very well that that is not it," she burst out. "There are plenty of girls whom I would like to see here, girls who would go to great lengths for you. Amelie Eck van Tellingen you could have had—a lady, the daughter of a very wealthy man. And you let yourself be taken in by your former housekeeper."

She invested infinite denigration into that last word, a denigration that made her son's blood boil.

The dark tone in his voice as he answered served as a warning to the baroness. "Mama, it hurts me to have to defend Marion before you like this. I would rather not, but I will not leave her undefended. You may keep all your ladies and daughters of millionaires who will go to great lengths for me but in reality have their eye on the castle. I have chosen a woman who loves me for what I am, a woman for whom *I* had to go to great lengths. I can prove that no one has been taken in by telling you how much time and trouble it cost me to win her completely. Furthermore, Marion is inwardly refined, Mama. You will never have to be ashamed of her."

The baroness had heard him out, but far from convinced, she immediately took the floor again when he finished.

"She may well be refined," she said impatiently. "I have met her several times, so I know that. And I don't want to say anything about her, Reinier, but she is bourgeois. She is not your type. You forget who you are—the only Baron Van Herewaarden. You forget that the blood of nobles and princes flows through your veins. When a person is born with a silver spoon in his mouth, that brings certain obligations along with it, Reinier."

"You certainly are concerned for my happiness."

He threw his comment into her river of words, and the sarcasm was so deeply imbedded in it that his mother hardly sensed it.

"I am thinking about your future," she said contentiously. "Your son will be a new link in the ancient noble family, and I would not be able to bear it if his mother was without family connections, without a history." She concluded with an articulate wave of her hands.

His frown deepened, but at the same time a slight smile of amazement descended and settled next to his wrath.

Little, pure Marion, he thought, *with your head full of precious quotes and singing verses, with your warm, feminine heart, you would not be good enough to build the family of the House of Herewaarden?*

Reinier rose, and the baroness had to look up at him. Upright and unswerving he stood, imposing in the strength of his youth. Blood, standing, and connections. Must they determine his happiness a second time? The wrath swallowed the smile, and he exploded, "All that wretched allegiance to class and blood holds forth the pretense of extreme refinement, a refinement which reaches to the very fingertips and—I know it all too well—centuries of practice have legitimized these ideas, but when are you going to recognize its poverty? Blood, blood, blood! Doesn't that reduce everything to a primitive biological obsession? Is an heir some kind of animal that you breed? Is it a question of upgrading the herd? Or is it perhaps a question of people, of a heart that longs to be happy?

"I have always honored you, Mama, and I will continue to do so. What I am now going to say I say not as your son, but as a person who has more deeply fathomed the splendor of life: Do not ever consider saying anything to Marion's detriment, or, if God grants, to the detriment of her children. Because I assure you that a heart of gold and a white soul denote a far greater value than blue blood and a silver spoon."

He walked through the open doors and stood on the lawn. It had been a very mild day; the grass was long and damp.

What have I said? he thought despondently. *Did Marion ask to be defended? I said harsh things when I could have put it more gently. I have thrashed a small, lonely woman with my words, when I should have been sharing with her the joy that has blossomed within me.*

When will I ever learn that it is the meek who are blessed?

The baroness watched the broad shoulders of her son, framed by the window. Beyond him was the spring evening sky, deep blue with the twinkle of a single star. Her white hands lay tired and abandoned in her lap, and a tear slowly felt its way down her face, which suddenly appeared years older.

Then, suddenly, two strong arms encircled her and a sorrowful, youthful voice said, "Mama, I am sorry that it had to go this way. Maybe we will still learn. Please, forgive me."

Almost with amazement, she heard her own words, "You are still so young and dynamic, Reinier, and I am old and set in my ways. When you are old, it is not easy to learn. But I will try. More I cannot promise you. You bring that girl here. I will try."

Then she stood up and left the room, a small, aristocratic figure, so lonely, so worn by a life of obligations.

A great compassion grew in the heart of her son.

She must learn the same lesson as Magda, he thought. Of the love that overcomes, and of God. And when it comes right down to it, those two are one and the same.

He turned around, left the room, and sought out his brother, Diederick. He found him in bed; he had had a heavy flare-up of his old condition and his eyes seemed small in his tired, pale face.

"I have come to tell you something, Rick," Reinier said as he grabbed a chair and sat on it backwards, as he used to do as a boy.

"Are you getting married again?" his brother asked.

"Yes," Reinier confirmed, "to Marion Verkerk. Probably in August."

Diederick showed no surprise. "I suspected as much for a long time now, Rein," he said sincerely as he extended his hand. "My congratulations."

This reaction took Reinier somewhat aback. In the back of his mind he had many years ago established the idea that

Mama and Diederick were two of a kind, the same inflexible sort.

"Did you really suspect something, Rick?" he asked curiously.

"Yes," he repeated. "Ever since New Year's Day, when you and Inge had been to see Magda. I was unwillingly witness to your conversation when you came back, and I intuitively felt that you had found someone in Marion who could truly make you happy. And when something like that exists, it is only a matter of time before it breaks its way through the circumstances, if you are willing to wait."

He fell silent, worn out by this long explanation.

"It's amazing that you saw that , Rick," Reinier said. "That you can accept Marion, just like that. Frankly, I did not expect this. Have we gotten to know each other so poorly in all those years?"

Diederick gave no answer to this, other than the slight movement of his shoulders, which looked pointed in his striped pajamas.

"How did Mama react?" he asked, and now Reinier pulled up his shoulders.

"You know her," he said. "She made a scene. And you know me. I was rude to her. It was the same old banal argument about the proper circles. In the end we did move closer to each other, but I am still afraid that we will never completely understand each other. I feel sorry for her, but she, on the contrary, feels proud and impenetrable in her fortress of tradition, connections, ancestors, blue blood, and whatever else there may be. And, because of my plans with Marion, an ugly breach has opened in that fortress, Rick."

"Maybe she needs that breach," Diederick thought aloud. "You know, Reinier, there was also a period in my life in which I thought differently about these things than I do now. But my study of our family history has taught me a great deal. Nobility of blood is not the same as nobility of soul, nor is every sensible marriage a good marriage. There have been many Reiniers in our ancestry who were made unhappy by marrying the wrong woman. And that is why I wish you all the best, Reinier, because I think you have made a good choice."

Again he was silent. He could not say more. Under the covers, he balled his hands into fists.

Everything for him, he thought. *Everything for him.* So it had always been. Even the profound grief that his brother had to undergo was the object of a passionate envy. But in the unvarying years of his life, there was only illness and loneliness and the devoted but never spontaneous love of his mother. No women, no love, no hate, not a single high, crashing wave on his sea of life. Only self-control, acquired through years of training, made it possible for him to say with a laugh, "I am jealous of you, old boy. You've always been the lucky one."

Reinier stood up. When he had shut the door behind him with a sincere good-bye, Diederick turned his face toward the wall and fought the tears that burned his eyes.

Never had he felt as lonely as he did at that moment.

That Saturday, Inge sat next to her father in her most beautiful dress, in the car which had since been repaired. They were on their way to Garderen. *On the way I will tell her,* Reinier had assumed, but he found it difficult to find a way to begin.

He had no doubt of Inge's approval of his plans—she was very attached to Marion—but he was afraid that her little mind would have trouble working through this tremendous change.

"How would you like it if we went to live in a regular house again, you and I, just like before?" he asked.

"Will Miss Marion come back, too, then?" came her immediate eager response, and this reaction moved Reinier.

"Yes," he said unhesitatingly. "Then Miss Marion will come
back, too. And then Papa is going to marry her, and you will
have a mother who loves you, just like Gert and little Marlies
and Pim and the other children that you know."

Inge thought deeply.

"And Mama who is in heaven?" She put the problem which
had risen in her child's mind into words.

Reinier stared at the road. The trees that lined the road in
front of him became one long black stripe, even though he
was not driving very fast.

"Mama loved Miss Marion very much, Inge," he said. "Very
much. I know for certain that there is no one that she would
have rather entrusted you to than her."

Inge seemed put at ease by these words.

"I think it's nice," she said, satisfied, and she gave him a
thankful nod.

"Are we going to live in Dintelborg again, Papa?"

"I don't know yet," he answered her truthfully. "I think we
will build a new house, Inge, but where that will be, we will
have to think yet."

He began to talk to Marion about it as they took their first
walk through the forests of Garderen.

"Where would you like to live when we are married, Marion?"

"Not at the castle," came her immediate response, which
jarred loose his question, "Do you have such an aversion to
the castle?"

She had to think about that for a moment. "No," she said.
"I even think that I could love it. It is a beautiful building,
and I love old things, things with a history. I would also like
to live there, but then . . ."

"Then what?"

"Then we have to be able to set the mood. I would freeze in the atmosphere that prevails there now, Reinier. I cannot be happy in it. Do you understand?"

"You know I do," he answered. "That was the reason I left it for so long, you know. It is actually only Mama that is holding things back, Marion. Diederick would like things to change, but Mama is too old to accept a more democratic way of doing things. Let's leave her to set the tone in the castle in her old age. We'll set the tone in our own Warbler!"

Marion threw a look of surprise at him. "The Warbler? I thought it had been sold?"

"The house has, but not the name! I had that taken down the day after you left."

Sudden joy filled Marion. There would be a new Warbler, made especially for them! When she, for the first time a few days before, had heard the little bird called the warbler sing, she understood better what Reinier was trying to express with that name.

But Reinier was already speaking again. "I would like to have it built, Marion, and you may say where. In Borg, or in Dintelborg—where will it be? If I put my weight behind it a little, the house could easily be done by August, and then when we come back from our honeymoon . . ."

He did not finish his sentence. They looked at each other and at the same time stood still for a kiss.

Even before they were home, Marion gave Reinier her answer. The house must be in Borg.

She saw from the relief in his eyes how happy he was with her choice. Although the atmosphere at the castle may have been just as alien to him as it was to her, yet the surroundings, the village, and especially the people were his own.

"I think that is wonderful, sweetheart," he gratefully accepted. "I did not want to say anything because I thought you had a preference for Dintelborg, but I am at least as attached to Borg as you are to Amsterdam!"

They talked about the new house, how and where it would be, and about Borg. Reinier then spilled out a colorful cornucopia of memories. It was as though the joy of life was spraying out of him like a fountain.

As she listened, Marion mused on how good it was for him that she had chosen Borg, and that he did not know of her childish desire to live out their happiness as far from the baroness as possible. Anywhere but Borg, because she lived there, the woman whom she secretly feared, who even from a distance gave her the feeling she was no more than a mongrel next to a thoroughbred.

She shivered slightly, and Reinier pulled her closer to himself. "Is there something the matter, sweetheart?"

Ah, no, it wasn't anything really. Phantoms that must never taint his happiness.

She tried to laugh off her concerns, but like the shadow of a gigantic bat, the secret fear hung fluttering over the sea of her happiness.

And Reinier did not know.

❧ Chapter 26 ❧

On Easter Sunday, Reinier confessed his faith. The old church of Borg was filled to the last seat.

In the elevated pew of the inhabitants of the castle, Marion sat between Diederick and the baroness.

She thought about Inge, who was with Reinier in the council room. Inge, who would soon be baptized. They had explained to her what this meant, in child's terms, and Inge had nodded. "Yes, I want to belong to the Lord Jesus. But I will still belong to you, too," she had spontaneously added.

A smile played on Marion's lips for a moment. She looked over the congregation and suddenly spotted Ronnie and Laurens Dubois.

Of course. They have lived here almost a year, flitted through her mind. Ronnie picked up her glance and nodded heartily in return, but Marion could read amazement in her expression.

Then the service began, and her attention was completely absorbed.

Reinier was not the only one confessing his faith. He took his place among the others. Next to him stood a hired hand from one of the farms in the area, then the oldest daughter of the principal at the school, a chambermaid from the castle, a couple of farm boys.

He looked up at his family. His eyes first caught those of Marion. "There were stars burning in her eyes," as Inge was wont to express it. He thought of the frightful tension of the previous Easter and how much happiness had fallen to him since that time. A feeling of intense gratitude overwhelmed him, and when he looked at his mother, who had not yet completely worked through her discomfort over the colorful company in which her son found himself, could chuckle at her.

"Look a little further, a little deeper, Mama," that laugh said. "This is the way the Lord wants it. Rich and poor meet each other here. The Lord has made them all and has loved them all with the same infinite love."

The baroness sensed something of the gentleness that went out from him. The lines in her face relaxed. Marion witnessed this, and hope kindled that she might be able to work out her relationship with her future mother-in-law after all. She would do her best, even if only for Reinier's sake.

After the service, there was an opportunity to congratulate the new members in the council room. Inge immediately sought refuge by Marion, who stayed somewhat in the background. The jubilation of the sermon, "The Lord Has Truly Risen!" continued to echo in her mind.

Now to be alone with Reinier, she longed.

The baroness had already left for home when Marion suddenly felt Reinier's hand on her shoulder. "Come along, love. I see a good friend of ours."

Marion followed him, and then they stood eye to eye with Mr. Dubois, somewhat grayer since she had last seen him, but otherwise exactly the same.

He shook her hand with abandon. "You did a good thing, child, coming here on such an important day," he said. And to Reinier, "So you two have carried over your friendship from last year!"

"Actually, more than that, Dubois," Reinier said, with the voice of a conspirator. "Marion and I are going to get married this summer!"

The silence that followed was too short to be painful, but all three understood that they were thinking of Jaap.

She could have been my daughter-in-law, the grounds keeper thought with a flurry of jealousy, but a broad smile spread over his weathered face, "Hearty congratulations, then, children."

The council room emptied. Reinier was latched onto by Reverend Gerritsen, and Marion, suddenly along with Mr. Dubois, shyly asked, in order to break the silence, "Are you staying with Ronnie and Laurens today? You usually go to church in Dintelborg, don't you?"

"I came here especially for Reinier," he answered. "I have always taken an interest in him, and I knew he would appreciate it if I were here today."

"Yes," Marion affirmed, and then she asked with interest, "How are things at home, Mr. Dubois? Is Grandmother still in good health?"

"Mother died last November," Dubois said, and Marion could hear that it was still difficult for him to talk about it.

"Jaap came for the funeral. He was in Normandy at the time. Now he is taking a trip through Egypt. He still asks about you in his letters, Marion."

Marion looked at Reinier, who was holding Inge by the hand. She saw his sharp profile, the sturdy line of his shoulders.

Jaap is only a faded memory now, she thought.

"You write him about Reinier and me." She turned toward

Mr. Dubois and looked him full in the face. "And tell him that I wish him as much happiness as I have found this year."

After Easter, there followed a spring and summer that seemed to pass faster than any ever had. They provided an abundance of sunny days and balmy, scent-laden evenings, on which Reinier and Marion enjoyed each other's company as often as possible.

Marion had without delay introduced her fiancé to the Knol family. For Inge, the old farmhouse seemed a virtual fairy-tale house. Most of the hours she spent in Garderen, she entertained herself there.

Reinier soon felt completely at home in Garderen. He sat in his shirtsleeves on the terrace, helped Marion with the dishes, played chess with Mr. Verkerk, and had endless discussions with him over the most diverse subjects.

Edith, when she was there, he handled with a certain feigned courtliness. From time to time she would attempt to flirt with him, just as she flirted with all men, but he acted as though he did not notice.

To Marion, who could get very upset by the whole thing, he said, "Let her chase her tail, my jealous little kitten. It would be a shame if she had put on all that makeup for nothing. I doubt that the farmers of Garderen have much appreciation for all her effort!" Then he would pull her away along the forest path, and with his arm around her shoulders, he would whisper to her what he thought about her eyes.

Their walks together were innumerable. They could lie for hours at the edge of the forest, their favorite place, overlooking a field of dill in the distance that grew like a yellow flame between the trunks of the trees.

Sometimes they would chat together, but more often there was a peaceful silence between them that was only broken by an occasional intimate word and spontaneous affection, uninhibited and tender.

In the first weeks of the spring, everything was pristine and new between them. The fact that Marion loved him and was willing to share his life with him so occupied Reinier's thoughts and made him so humbly happy that his lack of inhibition was tempered by it. It was enough just to be with her.

Quickly enough, however, the desire grew in both of them to possess each other completely.

It was on an evening in May that Reinier all at once let himself go. They were driving through the Veluwe, somewhere near Garderen.

"Stop for a little while, Reinier," Marion asked him. "We are almost home, and I would really like to be alone with you this evening!"

He immediately assented to her request and drove off onto the shoulder. The sun was almost down. One of the last slanted rays fell into the car and set Marion's hair aglow. Then the red ball sank behind the trees and a gentle light remained behind in the car.

Reinier looked at Marion as though he were seeing her for the first time.

She felt warm, and with her hand she lifted her tickling hair off the back of her neck.

He watched a vein throbbing in her neck. She saw his look and laughed at him. "What are you looking at?"

"What am I looking at?" he asked hoarsely, and he laid both his hands on her neck. Then he laughed.

It was as though the blood in his own veins was getting warmer. "What am I looking at?" he asked again, and his hands slid down until they were around her waist and took her completely into his arms.

His eyes greedily drank in her face, and the vise of his arms turned more tightly. Then he buried his mouth in her neck.

When his grip slacked a little, Marion freed one of her hands and laid it on his pounding heart.

"My sweet savage," she said warmly, and in the glowing face that she had raised to him, the eyes were shining and the mouth was red and moist, like ripe fruit.

He was panting; his searing hot lips engulfed hers. Marion was no longer able to move in his iron grip.

He is going to smother me, she thought for an instant, then she buried her head into his chest.

"Reinier," she said softly, and it sounded like a heavy sigh.

He rubbed above his eyes with his hand. "Did I scare you?"

Marion took his face into her hands. His forehead was warm and moist.

"Scare?" she asked, and her laugh was wonderfully feminine and wise. "I know you are a passionate man, Reinier. I've known your temperament for a long time."

"When . . . ?" he began, but broke off his sentence in sudden realization.

"That evening," Marion said dreamily, "on my birthday. Do you remember? Then you did scare me, Reinier, but I also tried to understand, and so I was not angry with you. Later I really did understand. But I saw the hunger in your eyes that evening, the hunger that you have always controlled."

"I wish it were August," he sighed aloud.

And soon it was August.

A start had been made in the spring on a villa somewhere in Borg, on a country road. A friendly thatched villa between white birches, with a garden which consisted mostly of trees. Immediately around the house there just enough room so that the sun could shine in unhindered. There were cozy rooms with big windows and flower boxes where red geraniums would soon bloom. The new Warbler came closer to completion with every passing week.

"What kind of help around the house would you like, love?" Reinier asked one day.

Marion replied impassively, "Now let's see. To start with, two ladies-in-waiting."

He burst into a hearty guffaw. "Yes, that is just your style, all right! Two strange old maids fiddling with your body all day. It would make you itch all over!"

Marion laughed along with him. "Okay, maybe not," she stoically resigned herself.

"But seriously now," Reinier continued, "a girl for days and one for nights? Any others?"

"Just cleaning help," Marion said. "That is enough, Reinier. I have no desire to sit the whole day with my hands in my lap!"

"Good," Reinier decided. "Shall I take out an ad?"

Marion nodded absently. "I wonder whether Toos Brinkman is working right now?" she asked.

"Would you like her?" Reinier assumed.

"Yes, I would," she found. "She was such a nice girl, Reinier, and she has grown up somewhat in the meantime. She must be seventeen now."

The next meal, Reinier reported on a fully grown Toos, now with round red cheeks and no more wispy braids, but a tight bun and a hair net.

"She is working at the moment for someone just outside Dintelborg," he told her, "but is leaving there in a couple of months because the daughter is returning from school. I asked her if she would come and work for me again."

"And?" Marion anxiously interrupted.

"Oh, she blushed. 'At the castle?' she asked, somewhat leery. Then I told her about the new house in Borg and that I was getting married to you. You should have seen her face, Marion!"

" 'I would love to work for you again, sir,' she said earnestly. 'I cried so hard when I had to leave last year.' "

And so Toos Brinkman was taken on as a live-in maid at the Warbler, and both parties were very satisfied with arrangements.

The baroness, however, did not find the choice to be very suitable.

"How could you do such a thing, child?" she reprimanded Marion. "The girl was your fellow employee. I don't want to offend you, but that is the way it is! I think it is an impossible situation. How will such a girl respect you?"

Reinier looked at her darkly. He was not fond of such meddling. He was at the point of intervening, but fell back when Marion rather sharply retorted, "I am of the opinion that you must win the respect of your personnel through the way you handle them and the way you live. Moreover, Toos is made of good stuff. I know her and am convinced that she would walk through fire for us."

The baroness did not respond. She thought sadly that her good advice was always thrown to the wind. She would never be able to accept the attitude of her future daughter-in-law. Her camaraderie with the personnel set at naught all distance. No, although she had done her best, she had not gotten any closer to Marion.

Reinier thought the same after this little incident. Mama and Marion were not hitting it off very well yet, unfortunately. He had done his utmost to keep the peace over the last few months. Snide remarks about the factory he had let roll off his back, comments about his behavior he had swallowed with an equanimity of which he had not considered himself capable.

It was the small warning "Blessed are the meek" that strengthened him, yet it hurt him that Marion, who normally did not have a rebellious bone in her body, was constantly at odds with his mother.

He was not, however, given much time to worry about such things. The summer was, for the most part, already past, and events were following in quick succession. The last weeks before the wedding went by like a hazy dream.

The house was finished and decorated. Plans were being made for the honeymoon, and Marion had chosen as their destination Lago di Garda in Italy, a place she had never dared dream that she would ever see.

Inge would stay in Garderen with her new grandparents, and when Reinier and Marion returned it would almost be September. Then Inge would go for the first time to the big school, a fact with which she was immensely happy.

The wedding was performed by the old Reverend Gerritsen in the village church in Borg.

Later, Marion could not remember much of the wedding ceremony. Once they were on their way, only the last words spoken by the good, friendly voice of the old minister remained with her: "Go then, bearing the blessing of the Lord."

They did not make a big deal of their wedding day. The circumstances would not permit it, and furthermore, neither of them felt the need. Fairly early in the afternoon they were on their way, after having been momentarily delayed by the tear-streaked face of Inge, who suddenly found the good-bye to be too much for her.

The trip went off with a hitch, partly by plane, partly by train.

All this newness provided Marion, who had seldom left the country, with so many distractions, and soon so much joy, that Reinier enjoyed her beaming face more than all the beauty they passed.

By evening they had reached their destination. The hotel by the lake seemed to be a dream come true. The surroundings smelled of the dark climbing roses which lined the white walls. It was a beautiful evening, and they were silenced by the endless beauty.

They had a cool drink, and sat silently admiring each other, saturated with a happiness which no longer needed words.

"Shall we go upstairs?" Reinier finally interrupted the silence. In the hallway upstairs, however, Reinier was approached by the hotel steward. Marion did not understand much of the fluent French he spoke.

Reinier gave her the key to the room. "You go ahead," he said in Dutch, and Marion took her leave with a polite nod to the impeccable Italian, who smiled at her with a mouth full of pearly white teeth.

A little later she heard Reinier clattering about the bathroom that adjoined their room.

When he came into the room, she was standing in front of the open balcony doors and looking out into the blue night. The air was warm and sweet, saturated with smells. He stood for a moment looking at her, and then he picked her up like a child in his arms.

"Mrs. Van Herewaarden." His dark voice caressed her ear like a warm promise. He drank a kiss from her lips that answered him better than any words ever could.

He set her down and they looked out into the night again. An unbelievably large moon had risen over the lake, and somewhere a nightingale sang.

There was a finely cut charm in this lengthened evening, a contented ache that derived, to be sure, from the certainty that they need only stretch out their hands to pick the fruit that waited, ripe and shimmering, to be plucked.

Marion dreamed, leaning against Reinier's shoulders, and she thought of how strong he was. How could anyone be so strong and so tender? Her husband.

"Are you tired, Marion?" he whispered into her ear.

She turned her head so she could see his eyes—eyes that caressed, eyes that questioned, eyes that desired. With a shiver, she became aware of her longing to share this desire. All the latent femininity of her being blossomed within her.

"No, I am not tired," she whispered back, "but I would like to go to bed."

Was this the timid Marion Verkerk, the youngest and most naive of all her high school classmates?

Was it the Italian air, or the dark roses, or was it life itself that taught her to lift her eyes like that, so that Reinier had to catch his breath?

He buried his mouth in hers, and she felt his muscles tighten.

"Come," he rasped.

When Reinier awoke, the room was filled with a bride-white cloud of light. The sun had already pushed its way through to all corners. He turned to his side and looked at Marion, who was still sleeping.

Propped up on his elbow, he lay there observing her. Her blond hair lay sprayed across her pillow, the long, light lashes touched her cheeks, which were unblemished, slightly flushed. Her pink lips were slightly open, and he had to resist the temptation to press a kiss onto them.

She was sleeping so peacefully.

He sighed. How wonderful it was to awaken thus.

Carefully he slid his arm under her head. She gave a brief moan in her sleep, then crept closer to him and nestled her head against his shoulder.

Very slowly, almost imperceptibly, sleep left her in order to make room for a memory of all the wonderful things of the previous day. The wedding ceremony in the old church, the trip south, the overwhelming beauty of Lago di Garda in the moonlight. And Reinier. Finally nothing other than Reinier. And then?

The wrinkle deepened. Had she dreamed? The castle. The cold, mocking laugh of the baroness. Resentment rose in her. Would that woman always taint her happiness?

She opened her eyes and immediately saw those of Reinier, who looked at her, laughing and wide awake.

The thoughts about her dream dissipated. Only much later, as they lay looking into the blue morning, did she suddenly ask, "Are we rich, Reinier?"

He abruptly lifted his head and, falling back into his pillow, he laughed aloud. "Listen to this little businesswoman! You should have asked that before you signed anything!"

Marion tried to punch him. "What do you think I am? I would have taken you even if you had been walking around in rags!"

"Or in a barrel!" he added, and they laughed together.

But then she pressed on, holding her course. "But you have not answered me!"

"Ah," he said unwillingly, "what is rich? We can get everything that we need and more. I personally am, at this moment, very rich!"

He played with her wedding ring, turning it round and round.

"I am, too. You know that," Marion resumed. "But do you know why I am asking, Reinier? Because of the castle. I have often read that castles are no longer profitable because of the high taxes and everything that goes along with them. And in the House of Herewaarden, such a high standard of living is maintained. How is it possible, Reinier?"

She could feel resistance to this conversation in his whole disposition, and without his saying anything, she suddenly realized how it was possible. She looked at the open curtains that hung motionless. A blooming rose branch, nearly collapsing from its own affluence, was barely visible.

But behind that rocking branch appeared again that face, with the lovely, slightly mocking smile.

The factory, she thought, and now the situation came into sharp focus for her. Yet she did not say anything, but waited motionless for Reinier's reaction.

He will say it, she thought stubbornly. *We are going into everything together, everything. This, too!*

Reinier fought a brief battle with himself. Then he propped himself on his elbow again and said somewhat defiantly, "Do you want to know the truth? Good, then I will tell you. The castle is indeed unprofitable. The income from the farmland and the lumber, leases and rents, and the interest on the capital are indeed insufficient to maintain the House of Herewaarden at its present standard. But never in all these years have any of the lords of the manor considered that a chink might appear, let alone worried about how they might close it, again and again. And you have figured it out, before we have been married even one day, even though you have never been concerned with money matters."

He shook his head in disbelief, and gripped her shoulders. "You little fox, you have already figured it out, haven't you?"

"I thought—the factory," said Marion timidly, rather spooked by the intensity in his voice.

"Exactly, the factory. If I had not had the factory, an end would have had to come to all that display of wealth."

"Are you trying to say that your mother has no idea about all this?" asked Marion, her eyes filled with incredible surprise.

"Only the estate manager knows," Reinier said, still somewhat surly, but then persuasively, "Would you have done differently, sweetheart? I had to, didn't I? I couldn't let it turn into a disaster."

"Of course not," Marion replied sensibly. "But they could have at least cut some corners. Why is it necessary to fill every room with exotic orchids, while there are thousands of flowers strewn about the grounds, just waiting to be picked? Why must there be twenty people on staff when ten would be more than enough? Why . . . ?"

Then Reinier took both her hands into one of his own and with the other hand covered her mouth, so interrupting her argument.

"It is all that she has left, Marion," he said earnestly. "And should we, who are so happy, take away from her the one thing that she cares about?"

Marion turned away and buried her face in her pillow. *He is so good,* she thought turbulently. *He is infinitely better than I am!*

Now she was beginning to understand his sacrifice all those years—not the money, but his silence, the fact that he had not dirtied the hands of his comfortable mother, that she was leading her life of luxury out of the goodness of his heart.

The endless marvel that grew in her at his generosity gave her almost physical pain, for she clearly understood that she would not have been able to make such a sacrifice. Perhaps for others, but not for that woman, who was now her mother-in-law.

The mocking laugh that had awakened her a few minutes before was still pursuing her. She bit her lip. At the moment she felt that she must hate the baroness, who spoke about the factory as though it were an innocent but rather queer obsession of her son, which she permitted by turning a blind eye.

The factory, which was the love of his heart and his young, industrious spirit, meant more to him than a dead money machine, but his mother had never had a good or interested word to say about it.

Again indignation overgrew the rest of Marion's feelings, like a parasite.

Reinier laid his hand over her eyes. "It is a difficult thing for you to suddenly have to work through, love," he said. "I would gladly have spared you, but you wanted to know."

Then she turned her face toward him, tears in her eyes. "I am afraid that I won't be able to bear it, Reinier," she said honestly.

"As long as things go well for the business, we have lots of room to live, darling," he said softly. "Fortunately there is enough money for everyone."

"Bah, money! Just keep quiet about all that money," Marion raged impatiently. "What does money matter to me? But how can she belittle your work like that, Reinier? I've heard enough of her sneers. And then to find out that it is precisely that despised work that finances her exaggerated posturing— oh, it makes me furious just to think about it!"

"Go ahead and be furious," he said tenderly. "With me you can be furious; I can always tame you again. But try to be gentle with her, Marion, and don't play the trump card that you are now holding against her until you are absolutely convinced that you can accomplish something good with it. Do you promise?"

"Of course. I won't give your secret away," she conceded, albeit not with her heart. They did not come back to this conversation again, but Reinier realized more than once how grateful he was that they had a house of their own to go back to, a new Warbler, where only the cheerful, straw-haired Toos Brinkman awaited them—no butlers, no ladies-in-waiting. A house in which Marion could breathe freely without the constriction of the castle, where she could be happy and make him happy. His little democrat, who would never be a real baroness—fortunately.

❦ Chapter 27 ❧

After a delightful vacation, they returned, tanned and happy, to the Netherlands. Then began normal life.

The day after their arrival, they picked Inge up in Garderen, who briefly threw Marion off balance by addressing her as *Mother*. Marion exchanged a brief look with Reinier, but an odd lump in her throat prevented her from saying anything.

On the way in the car, the child forgot and spoke to her once again as *Miss Marion*. But she noticed her own mistake. "No, that's not right," she said, decidedly.

Then Reinier asked her, without taking his eyes from the road, "Aren't you getting a little too grown up to say *Papa* and *Mama*?"

Inge looked to Marion for help. "You say *Mother* to Grandma Verkerk, and Aunt Edith does, too."

Marion pulled her closer to herself. "I know, honey," she conceded. "We understand what you mean. *Mama* is mama, after all, isn't it?"

Inge nodded thankfully.

"But then you must also say *Father* from now on," Reinier decided, and with this Inge was in agreement.

"Okay, Papa—Father," she said, correcting herself, and all three of them laughed the little problem away.

Inge had changed much recently. She had remained a toddler for a long time. When she was four, she was still talking baby talk, and although her intellect was very clear, her way of expressing herself was very childish.

Whether it was the influence of the preschool was hard to say, but over the last few months she had begun to reflect seriously on things. The problem of her mother's death, which she had so easily accepted at the time, had given her a lot of material for questions.

And now a new stage in her life was beginning.

After a long and mild summer, fall suddenly arrived with wild storms and downpours.

On such evenings, it was good to be home. Marion sat listening to the wind and moved a little closer to the fireplace.

She looked at Reinier. He received her glance and they both thought of the sweet secret they had been cherishing for a couple of weeks now. They thought about Inge, who lay sleeping upstairs, and the little being that would make its arrival at the Warbler when the roses were blossoming and summer was in full swing.

A fuller, deeper happiness had been created by their secret, and Reinier's eyes rested on Marion these days with even greater tenderness than before when she bent her blond head over a book or her needlework.

"My little mother," he would sometimes say suddenly, and when she lifted her eyes to him, it was as though sparks of joy were leaping out at him.

Yet it was not an easy winter for Marion. Her pregnancy brought her much discomfort. The mood in the Warbler was no longer golden. Marion had bouts of unease during which it was difficult for her to be cheerful. She often had to fight against irritation, which she herself did not know or understand. Her struggle was not always successful.

Inge sometimes walked away surprised and frightened after an unreasonable rebuke and sought refuge with Toos or her father. That made Marion even less contented, and a shadow of self-reproach was cast over her happiness, which she knew well enough was still there but seemed to disappear at such moments behind a gray veil.

Reinier was very patient with her. When she met him once after a slump of several days, laughing and cheerful, he picked her up in his arms and said, "Hurrah! I have my old Marion back again!"

A glimmer of sadness ebbed into her eyes, "Aren't you mad at me because I so often am unreasonable with you all? I know it, too, Reinier, but sometimes I feel so miserable."

Reinier kissed the words away. "It is not anything serious, sweetheart. That will all soon be over. I just assume that that is the price I have to pay for an heir."

"An heir?" she asked with a comical frown above her eyes. "My goodness. If it is a girl, you will be devastated."

"You know better than that," Reinier replied.

Yes, Reinier had much patience with her, and she knew it, too. And yet her good intentions constantly slipped away from her. One evening, just as they were about to retire, she threw a passionate rebuke at him over some little thing, and when he did not answer, she heard her own voice complaining, "That's right, just let me go ahead and talk. You just don't understand."

She fell silent after these words. Something about them had shocked her. Those words, those familiar words. Where had she heard them before?

Suddenly she knew: Mother. Mother, who had complained

so often in her life, so often that it had finally turned her bitter. Mother, who always thought she was misunderstood. Was this Mother's heritage to her? Would she become like that? Would Reinier have to bear what Father had to bear from Mother all the years they were married?

No, no, no! she thought passionately. She felt a sudden revulsion within herself. She suddenly was able to put her problems in perspective. Egocentrically revolving around her own all-important little "I," worrying about nothing. She, who had happiness thrown at her by the handful.

She turned over quickly to her other side. An impulsive urge grew in her to touch Reinier, who lay silently beside her. Reinier had still not responded to her outburst and silently waited for her to fight this out with herself.

Then he felt a hesitant hand searching for help, reaching for him, and that was enough for him to pull her to himself, a small sad girl who cried it all out against his shoulder and then, in fits and starts, told him what it was that made her so upset.

Long after she had fallen asleep, he lay with wide-open eyes, staring at the moon-illuminated window.

O Lord, he thought with a wordless prayer of thanks. *Lord, what a blessing it is that we need each other so much. Not just me, but her, too—in everything.*

He remembered with a smile his vague worries from the days before the wedding about Marion, who was so strong and so pure, who seemed to know no difficulties, who in his eyes had so wonderfully few faults. Did she really need him as he needed her?

Now she was sleeping, pressed hard against him; his little comrade, who had confessed, whom he loved more than ever because of her faults.

His arm grew tighter around her, and she mumbled something in her sleep.

Outside could be heard the distant bark of a farm dog. Then the silence around the Warbler was complete.

After this evening, everything seemed to go better. A wink or a small gesture from Reinier was able to help Marion through her difficult moments, and gradually she lost her uneasiness.

The most difficult months were now behind her, and as the spring alighted on the Warbler like a dragonfly, a young woman could be found there who entered each new day like a celebration.

Everything seemed to contribute to making the scene extraordinarily festive. In the fall, hundreds of bulbs had been planted in the ground between the birch trees, and now groups of graceful yellow daffodils elegantly nodded their heads in the breeze. The red and white tulips stood like small bright lamps illuminating the border of the gently curved path. The birds competed with one another to see who could unleash the highest and loudest trills, and the sun was present almost every morning to touch all these beautiful things with its golden finger and prod them on to even more abundant expression.

It was during this time that Marion learned to distinguish the song of the warblers who had built their nests there from all the other songbirds. Sometimes she stood before the open bedroom window for quite some time listening, and let the folded sheets or the dust cloth in her hand fall limp. Only seldom did the humble creatures allow themselves to be seen, but their song was everywhere.

One dissonant chord had continued to resound in the harmony of this happy life, and it continued to irritate Marion with thousands of tiny pricks. It was the knowledge that there was still a snag in her relationship with her mother-in-law and that she was partially at fault.

When Reinier told his mother months before that there

was a child on the way, the baroness, in a tenderness which surpassed her, set her grievances against Marion to one side and met her halfway, with more sincerity than she had up to that time, with an intimacy that must have cost her a great deal of self-control.

Marion, on the other hand, was not able to let go of the grudge against her mother-in-law that she had nurtured for so many months. The older woman sensed this and withdrew again, offended, hurt, and sad.

Would she ever try again?

Marion had a great deal to think about, now that the day on which the child was due was drawing near, and the subconscious feeling that every sour note had to be brought into line before that day arrived grew into a decision in the warmth of these spring days.

On an afternoon in May, she undertook the walk to the castle on her own. The doors of the servants' quarters stood wide open on this warm day, and Marion found her own way in. She stood in the hallway and heard the soft tinkling of piano music coming from the salon.

Probably Diederick, she thought, but when the door noiselessly fanned open under her slight pressure, it was not her brother-in-law whom she saw at the piano. It was the baroness, seeming more fragile than ever in her silver-gray gown, her white hair like a diadem around her small, pale face, in which the eyes were very dark and absently staring off into nothing.

She was not playing from music, Marion noticed as she stood motionless in the doorway, not thinking that she should make her presence known.

There was something in the small figure behind the piano that moved her. Something very lonely, which was only accentuated by the melancholy music, in which every note sounded like a tear. She recognized the melody of the "Volga Boatman."

When the hands finally fell silent on the keys, Marion took a couple of quick steps into the room.

What were the words she had composed on the way? Where were the carefully prepared sentences she had brought?

She could not remember. But suddenly it dawned on her, more clearly than ever before, that it did not really matter whether she was within her rights in her conflict with this small, lonely woman. More important was the fact that she was old and alone, that she needed love—that it had to come from her children: Reinier, Diederick, Inge, and the new baby, and herself. Above all, herself.

She laid a warm, bare arm around the cool gray shoulders and said warmly, "Hello, Mama. Are you here all by yourself? Why don't you come and spend the rest of the day with us?"

The baroness had an acute ear. Had she perhaps tested the sincerity of Marion's warm tone? Whatever the case may have been, no carefully prepared sentences could have produced a better effect.

The baroness accompanied her daughter-in-law down to the Warbler in the car, which was hastily driven around front by the correctly uniformed Albert.

Marion reminded herself that Rome was not built in a day and that she should get accustomed to the idea that not only her mother-in-law would have to compromise her principles in order to bridge the gulf. She would have to, as well, and Reinier.

"Sometimes compassion comes before rights," he had once said to her. She had not understood it then, but now the meaning of his words was clear to her.

And that is what she told him after the fact, when he, in a hastily arranged tête-à-tête in the kitchen, asked her with amazement and joy to explain the fact that his mother, who so seldom came without first announcing her visit, now sat laughing and babbling with Inge on the sun porch.

"I went and got her," she laughed. "And she is staying for supper, too."

"So." Reinier understood, taking her face in his hands, and his voice sounded very gentle. "So my wife has finally bent her stiff neck?"

"She is so alone," Marion said without edge, "and we are so happy, Reinier."

He did not make it easy for her, however.

"You're right," he said. "She is alone, and we are rich. Rich enough to share our happiness with her. But did it occur to you, Marion, that older people do not change easily? That she will undoubtedly still say things that irritate you, and rightly so, and that she will continue to do things that will offend your sense of justice?"

Something quivered about her mouth, a mixed emotion that resolved into a smile.

"Compassion comes before rights," she said by way of explanation, removing his hands. Shyly turning his wedding ring, she added, almost in a whisper, "That is also how we live, Reinier Van Herewaarden."

Then he knew that this was not just a whim, and that she had passed the darkest moment of her struggle.

"Shall we go inside?" he invited, taking her by the hand.

Spring flowed imperceptibly into summer. When Marion's time came, the calendar was open to the last week of June. These days it barely became dark at night.

When Reinier called the doctor, the moon hung like an anxious observer just above the trees, but within a few hours the sun would be making its triumphal entry once again.

It was a wonderful, exciting night in the Warbler. All

attention was focused on the petite figure on the large bed. Several people moved about the room—the doctor, the nurse—but she did not notice them. Her mind was concentrating on the new life that was about to emerge and on the father of the child, who was holding her tensed hands in his own.

For a moment between contractions, she thought of the world outside, silent and sleeping—a strange silence, broken only here by their wide-awake excitement.

Yes, it was still quiet outside. But soon the flowers, whose dew-brushed leaves were still folded to the night air, would incline their little brilliant heads toward one another and whisper, "Have you heard? Ingeborg Louise has a little brother!" and the elderberry tree would send out its aroma with such intensity that passersby would turn their heads to see. The rabbits sat motionless at the edge of the forest, their ears perked. The birds ironed their glistening feathers with their beaks. All that lived on the Warbler estate prepared for the great and wonderful celebration of birth.

Then young Reinier Van Herewaarden blazed his trail to life.

As Marion held her son in her arms, she overflowed with happiness that was a subtle mixture of pride and gratitude, and in these first few moments, she experienced motherhood down to the very fiber of her being.

Behind the back of the nurse, who was telling her that she must sleep, she secretly shook her head at Reinier, and he answered with a wink. They laughed like conspirators when he was finally able, with tact and wit, to arrange for them to be alone with their child and their happiness.

"Sleep?" said Marion, and she stretched out her arms in a gesture of ecstasy. "I can always sleep! Oh, darling, I am so happy!"

He understood what she meant, for he himself was filled with a happiness nearly too great to contain.

They clasped each other's hands and looked toward the white cradle, where their son reveled in his first sleep.

"Do you know what I would really like now, before I go to sleep?" Marion asked.

He looked into her damp, shining eyes, "I think I know, Mama," he said as he kissed her eyes and felt the warmth of his joy in his chest because their knowledge and understanding of each other had become so complete. So fragile and firm are the bands which bind a man and a woman together.

"Psalm 103," Marion whispered, and he answered: "I know."

He read the psalm for her. Sometimes his voice wavered, sometimes it sank so low it could hardly be heard, but that did not matter; Marion knew the words within.

> Praise the Lord, O my soul;
> All my inmost being, praise His holy name.
> Praise the Lord, O my soul,
> and forget not all His benefits.
> He forgives all my sins
> and heals all my diseases.

How many injustices had there been, Reinier thought. How many times had he been impure or cold or selfish, and how perfectly it had all been forgiven. How many sicknesses had there been: pain, sadness, fear, and how gloriously they had been healed!

Yes indeed:

> The Lord is compassionate and gracious,
> slow to anger, abounding in love.
> He will not always accuse,

nor will He harbor His anger forever;
He does not treat us as our sins deserve
or repay us according to our iniquities.
For as high as the heavens are above the earth,
so great is His love for those who fear Him;
as far as the east is from the west,
so far has He removed our transgressions from us.
As a father has compassion on his children,
so the Lord has compassion on those who fear Him.

Never before have I understood how deep and beautiful this image is, thought Marion. As a father has compassion on his children—Reinier and Inge, two and yet one. Reinier, as he stood bent over the cradle of his heir; as a father has compassion on his children, so the Lord has had compassion on us.

Marion was crying, but even these tears were understood by Reinier. He read on.

His deep voice, which had been subdued, swelled with the closing words, which expressed everything that lived in both of them: more than just a song of thanks—a jubilation! "Praise the Lord, O my soul."

After this last, majestic chord, a tangible stillness hung in the room, but the stillness was sung away. A note pressed its way through the slightly open window, and then another, and then another: high, piercing shouts of joy, full and sweet.

Marion tilted her head to listen, Reinier stood up slowly and threw the casement open wide. "Listen, the warbler sings!"

He went to the cradle and took his son in his arms. Then he walked to the window and looked out over the world.

The day awakened, a gilded summer's day. The sounds multiplied. Roosters crowed, a farmer's wagon clattered on its way. The sun ascended the birches and in the midst of their golden branches stood Reinier Van Herewaarden, his son in his arms.

Sought by Christ, blessed by God.

The sunshine poured down from heaven.

And the warbler sang.